Secrets
of
Foxglove
Cottage

BOOKS BY REBECCA ALEXANDER

Rebecca Alexander

Secrets
of
Foxglove
Cottage

bookouture

Published by Bookouture in 2025

An imprint of Storyfire Ltd.
Carmelite House
50 Victoria Embankment
London EC4Y 0DZ

www.bookouture.com

The authorised representative in the EEA is Hachette Ireland
8 Castlecourt Centre
Dublin 15 D15 XTP3
Ireland
(email: info@hbgi.ie)

ISBN: 978-1-83525-908-5
eBook ISBN: 978-1-83525-907-8

To our youngest son, Isaac and his love, Penny.

1

PRESENT DAY, FEBRUARY

This has to work, we are running out of time. Zosia paused before she rang the doorbell and looked over at the view. The taxi had brought her down narrow lanes topped with hedges, over cattle grids and through farm gates onto Dartmoor. To Zosia it was alien, although she had camped many times on the expansive heathlands of Poland. This was different, the bare rock of the moor breaking through its veil of grass and heather, scattering boulders even among the grazing cattle and sheep. It felt like a place where nature was in charge and humans had to tread lightly.

'Mrs Armitage?' Zosia hadn't noticed the door opening. A tall older woman was looking down at her from the porch. 'You must be here for the interview. I'm glad you found it all right, we're on the edge of the village.'

The interview was for the position of cleaner, gardener and general assistant at Foxglove Cottage. Miss Wojcik owned the cottage, a former B & B and garden café. It was a rundown cottage with granite walls covered with a climber, just coming into leaf. It looked maybe a hundred years old, with an over-grown front garden curving down to a low wall against the road, and a gravel drive full of weeds with room for half a dozen cars. Zosia took a deep breath before following her into the house.

Walking with a crutch, Miss Wojcik led the way through a shabby oversized hall and past several doors to an old-fashioned kitchen at the back of the house, which at least was warm after the chill outside. Miss Wojcik patted a chair for Zosia and sat down opposite, before looking up from the reference Zosia had sent with her application. 'Come and sit down,' she said, reading on. 'How long have you been in England?' She sounded absolutely English, not Polish at all.

'I came to the UK eight years ago,' Zosia said, trying to look nonchalant. But she desperately needed this job, even if she didn't warm immediately to this reserved older woman. 'But I studied English for many years, as child, and at university.'

'And you married Mr Armitage?'

'I am divorced,' Zosia said firmly. She moved to touch the pink scar on her forehead, stopped herself, caught her hands together in her lap. No need to remember that terrible day. 'Eight months ago. I am seeking a job where I can live in. Accommodation is so expensive in town, and I don't have a car at the moment.'

Miss Wojcik turned over her CV. 'But you do drive?'

'Yes. I have a clean driving licence,' she added.

'I've recently had surgery,' Miss Wojcik said, not looking up. 'I have a car but it would be useful if someone could drive it. Just until I get fully back on my feet. I had a hip replaced a few weeks ago.'

Oh. Zosia's heart sank. 'But the job is for longer, yes? All year round?'

'Yes. I need help all year round if I'm going to get the café back up and running. Obviously, the wages take into account the accommodation.'

Yes, the accommodation accounts for half the wages, Zosia thought but didn't mention. She still had to drop the bombshell.

'I can do cleaning, simple fixing things, cook, serve—'

'How much DIY can you do? Fixing things?'

Zosia shrugged. 'Woodwork, I can do simple repairs on appliances, hang a door and put up shelves, that sort of thing. Decorating, I'm good at that. I can use most power tools. My husband and I renovated our own house.' *His house, now.*

'Well, that's certainly good news. The old house needs a bit of care. My father always did it, but as he got older...' Her voice faded away and grief flashed across her face. 'My father was Polish,' she added. 'Thus the name, Wojcik.'

'My name was Nowakowska, before I married,' Zosia said. 'The English called it Novak.'

'Of course they did! The locals used to bodge my father's name terribly. Mostly they just called him Casimir or Cas.' Miss Wojcik smiled and wiped away a little dampness from under each eye. She looked quite different when she smiled, her silver and gold hair curled around her blue-rimmed glasses. She didn't look Polish, Zosia decided, except her chin – that reminded her of the women of her own family. A proper Slavic chin, her *babcia* would have said. 'How do you pronounce your name?'

'It's *Zo-sha.*' She held her breath for a moment.

'I'm Hazel,' she answered.

'I was wondering when you would let me know?' Zosia said, trying to be polite but her voice was shaky. 'About job. About *the* job.'

'Well, I have to be honest. You are the only applicant I wanted to interview.' Hazel hesitated. 'I asked you to come because I see you are a translator.'

'Polish is my first language, but I've been speaking English every day for more than ten years. Also, I speak German, French and a bit of Italian,' Zosia said.

'It was Polish I was wondering about. I learned to speak it many years ago – I'm rusty now. But I never really mastered reading it. My father left some papers, and I'd love to be able to read them. I'd pay extra for the time.'

'I would love to,' Zosia said, trying not to sound too enthusiastic, too desperate.

'Great. Perhaps you would like to have a look around at the house, at the accommodation, and see if you like it? Then I can explain what else I need help with.'

'That would be – wonderful,' Zosia admitted, holding the idea close. She bit her lip to avoid mentioning Krys. *Not yet.* The thought of what was at stake was almost suffocating her, and she took a couple of deep, slow breaths to steady herself.

She followed Hazel back into the hall, past a dining room covered with dust, to a living room overlooking the front garden.

The bay window was dirty but the house was a little elevated and looked over the moor and the granite stacks of Combestone Tor. A hedged lane opposite ran down to the patchwork roofs of a village, at the edge of which stood a small church. It almost took Zosia's breath for a moment, and she put her hand over her jumpy heart. 'Oh. So beautiful,' she whispered in Polish.

'Isn't it? I grew up here, and missed it terribly when I was away. But now I love it all over again. My mother's family, the Dukes, owned a farm on the moor.' She walked over to the large fireplace. Alongside an imposing wood burner sat a bowl of something that looked like grain and dried fruit.

'Do you – have a rodent problem?' Zosia asked, wondering if it was a trap.

'Oh, no!' she said, and laughed awkwardly. 'It's an old family tradition of my father's,' she answered. 'Come upstairs, I'll show you the bedrooms then we can look at the study and conservatory at the back, on our way to the garden.'

Broad stairs with two turns rose up to a long landing. 'We used to have four guest rooms with their own bathrooms, and two smaller rooms for the family,' she said. 'I thought you could choose one of the en suite ones. I can't have guests any more, it's too much work to get the rooms up to standard. People want so much more now from a bed and breakfast. But the café, that I think I can handle with some help.'

As Zosia looked in each room, she could see their potential. 'It would be a good project to create one or two letting rooms,' she said, walking into one spectacular room above the living room, with a higher view of the tumbled rocks, windblown hedges and spots of early yellow flowers. 'If you wanted to. I could help. This is magnificent, isn't it? Is that the right word? *Wspaniały.*'

'It's the right word,' Hazel said, looking around the dilapidated room. Paper was curling off the walls in the corner, black mould speckled the edges of the ceiling. 'Well, maybe we could look into it,' she said, uncertainly. 'But I think the most important thing is resurrecting the café in the garden. This room next door is mine...'

Several antiques furnished Hazel's room, including a large bed with leaves and fruits carved into the headboard and frame. 'Oh, I love the bed!'

'Dad always said it reminded him of home. If you look carefully, you're supposed to be able to see fairies peeping out from the branches.'

Zosia leaned forward and started laughing. 'I think I can! My grandfather was always talking about fairies and elves. And *domowik.* I'm sorry, I don't know what they are in English.'

'Brownies,' Hazel said, smiling. 'That's why we put raisins and oats out by the hearth. In case we had one. Just for luck. It gave him the idea for the fairy theme of the café, many years ago.'

Zosia continued down the hall and peered into one of the back rooms. 'That's the garden?' she asked. A lush, green expanse stretched out before her, the extensive patio overgrown with grass and plants. An old pergola surrounded much of the patio, some of it filled in with glass panels to provide shelter. Old wooden furniture was scattered about, mostly fallen over. 'It's so big.' The lawn looked boggy, covered with spikes of sedges, the heather encroaching like a green mist at the back, the remnants of snow under the edge.

'A quarter of an acre. This is where my parents used to run the café, and there were extra tables in the conservatory,' Hazel said, leaning close to look over her shoulder. 'We could put out sixteen tables in its heyday, and they kept all the hedges and plants trimmed. It's a bit of a mess now. It seems appropriate that a young Polish woman should come and revive what a young Polish man created.'

'You need me to rescue the garden?'

'Rescue? Goodness, yes, that's exactly the word.'

Zosia took a deep breath, but still couldn't say the words. She wanted to live here, she wanted to bring this faded place back to life. She was beginning to feel drawn to this strong, kind woman, too. She couldn't bear for Hazel to find out about the guilt she carried.

'You are obviously trying to say something,' Hazel said. 'What is it? You seem worried.'

Zosia managed a smile. 'There's just something I didn't mention on my application. I have a six-year-old son, Krystof. He lives with me. Krys. He's the only good thing that came out of my marriage.'

Hazel stared into Zosia's eyes, as if she couldn't look away. 'Goodness, your eyes are amber,' she said finally. 'Does Krys look like you?'

'His hair is darker brown than mine,' Zosia managed to say after catching her breath. 'I dyed mine, it's normally what my hairdresser calls mouse. But his eyes are the same.'

'I'm not sure I can cope with a child around the house. And I don't know about the rooms—'

'We live in one room now,' Zosia said quickly. 'He is a good boy. You will hardly know he is here. And he'll be at school all day.'

Hazel winced an awkward smile. 'I suppose the school would be grateful for another child, they're struggling to keep it open.' She looked around the room, then pulled the door to as they stepped back into the hall. 'Won't he be bored out here? The village is so small, there are very few children here.'

'He will be happy wherever I am,' Zosia said, realising her hands were clasped in front of her like she was praying. 'He's such a good little boy, so quiet.'

'I don't think children should be quiet,' Hazel said. 'I think they should be laughing and singing and kicking a ball around in the garden.' She seemed to come to a conclusion. 'I feel like you're meant to be here. My dad would have loved a little boy growing up here, he always wanted more children. Let me show you the rest of the house.'

The biggest job was going to be the garden, Zosia realised. The pergola which looked lovely from upstairs was so insecure she wouldn't be able to let Krys out there until it was taken down. The old furniture was mostly just fit for a bonfire, but she could save a few tables and a couple of benches. But the atmosphere outside, rain starting to spatter foot-long grasses and dripping from seedheads, was magical. As they stood talking, a vole made a dash across the patio slabs in front of them, and a patch of shrubs covered in berries was being attacked by a blackbird almost hanging upside down to tear off the fruits one by one.

'I love it,' Zosia said, spontaneously. 'It's enchanting. I'm sure we can do something amazing. We'll have to be careful with nests, though.'

'Of course,' Hazel said. They stepped into the conservatory, which ran the width of the house, giving onto the kitchen door first then a window onto a study, with a beautifully carved desk.

Leaning in, Zosia could see an old-fashioned typewriter on the desk, with a sheet of paper still in it. The letters were familiar but unfamiliar, too. 'Is that a Polish typewriter?' she said, almost disbelieving.

'It has Polish characters, yes,' Hazel said, staring at her. Her own eyes were light blue, almost turquoise, and they were wide now. 'I don't go in there much. Dad left hundreds of pages of memoir...' Her eyes were bright with tears. 'He had an extraordinary life. He fled Poland during the war and came here. But he hardly ever talked about it.'

'So he wrote about it instead?' Zosia said, looking back into the room, locked in the past. 'He must have wanted it to be read.'

'Not in my mother's lifetime,' she said. 'Maybe not in mine either. Perhaps he had memories of the terrible things he saw during the war, and he found it hard to share them with us.'

Zosia nodded, following Miss Wojcik back into the conservatory. 'We can focus on his memoir on rainy days. There are plenty of good chairs in here for the café,' she said, looking around. There were several square tables, too, as well as a long bench. 'On sunny days we could always take a few of these outside.'

'It would be nice to have a few guests for the café again, the locals loved it as much as tourists. I'd like to put some of my dad's fairy houses and doors up as well.' Miss Wojcik took a deep breath. 'Of course, that would be more work for you.'

'Which is why you called it a job,' Zosia said, laughing, and after a moment, Miss Wojcik joined in. 'Let me bring Krys here, please meet him. Let him interview for the position of a lovely little boy who will be no trouble.' She held her breath until Miss Wojcik started to smile.

'In that case, I hope you'll both be very happy here.'

2

MARCH 1940

In mid August 1939, I earned my silver eagle insignia. I had completed three months of combat training, followed by a month on an old biplane learning basic manoeuvres and skills. We then transferred to the precious P.11s to complete the testing required to be a pilot of the Polish Air Force. We all knew the threat from Nazi Germany was real. We had no doubt that we could hold them off, and I was proud as I stood with my closest friends, Karol and Bronisław from Poznań base. We were joined by Tomáš Masaryk, a Czech who had escaped to join the Poles. We felt invincible with our silver insignias; we were going to defend our homelands. I was twenty-one years old.

— *EXTRACT FROM THE MEMOIR OF
CASIMIR WOJCIK*

Rosemary wandered towards Combestone Tor, a granite outcrop that looked, in her seventeen-year-old mind, like piles of library books. Old stories said you could see your future husband there at sunset, although she didn't dare stay out that long. Dad would be after her if she didn't help Mother with the lambs. She brought her light brown curls forward over each shoulder, and sat with her back to a flattish bit of stone on the springy grass, peppered with primroses. It prickled the backs of her legs through her woollen tights, but at least there were no gnats yet. It had been a mild February, but she knew a sprinkling of snow this high up was possible in March or even April. The war, hundreds of miles away in London, couldn't stop that. Nothing big had happened yet, not in Britain anyway, but the news from Europe was just awful.

Nevertheless, there was a sound that could be a gnat... no, maybe a hornet. A few seconds later, she recognised it as the drone of a motor, high in the air, and jumped up to look for it. A sleek plane with a long nose was silhouetted against the thin shreds of cloud. She thought of the view from up there, the whole moor from Postbridge to Princetown with Hartford village somewhere in the middle. The pilot might even be able to see her red coat as a tiny blur, like a poppy.

The plane was approaching, slowly getting bigger and lower, and she could just make out a head, light glinting off goggles that looked like insects' eyes. There was no RAF insignia, and she wasn't familiar with the painted shape on the fuselage.

German. Her heart sped up, thundering in her ears. She had heard of planes shooting people and she was the only person in sight. As it dropped closer, circling slowly around her as if looking for somewhere to land, she couldn't see a swastika. She started racing along the road towards home.

It seemed to be aiming for her, which made no sense. The tor reared up over her as she dropped off the path hoping to reach the shelter by the great rocks. No, she could see he was veering off too, closer, he would pass her in a minute or two and he was awfully low. Now she could hear the engine, it had an odd break in the sound, like it wasn't working all the time, and it was getting worse. A trail of black smoke wound around the pilot, light as a scarf, getting longer and longer behind the plane.

No matter how perfect and green the moor looked from high up, like a carpet, there wasn't a flat place to land and the ground was littered with granite rocks. As she jogged up the hill she could see the man in the cockpit now, battling with something, leaning out to see the ground below. He must be trying to find the Holne road, the flattest thing for miles but hardly wide enough for a horse and cart. She stumbled over hollows treacherously filled with icy water, running between boulders bigger than her head.

The plane was close now, sputtering then roaring, smoke blowing into the pilot's face. Then the engine stopped, and the hillside fell quiet, save for the rush of air whistling over the wings as it raced past her towards the road.

'He'll miss it,' she panted to herself, her chest tight both from running and knowing what was about happen. Suddenly she really didn't want to see him die in a fiery crash, even if he was German.

The sound of the crash as he smashed down was deafening. The plane had put down on the grass by the side of the road, bounced up and landed again, still as fast as a racing car. One wheel slammed into the carved granite mile marker by the side of the road, and the plane cartwheeled onto one wing. It folded in half, twisted and crumpled, consumed by black smoke. She didn't stop to think; she flew into the cloud, the stink catching in the back of her throat. The pilot had fallen back in the cockpit, which was skewed towards her, the plane making a straining, tearing metallic creak.

His mouth was open, his head tipped back, and she wondered if his neck was broken, if he was already dead. She battled through the foul smoke and grabbed the arm that was hanging out. When she pulled, he didn't move, but he gurgled a moan. She found a brass handle, and twisted it. As a door gave way, his body slumped to the side and she clutched his jacket and pulled.

He didn't help, just groaned some more. 'It's on fire!' she screamed in his face, as his eyes, cornflower blue, opened. 'Get out!'

'*Ogyen?*' he mumbled, or something like it. This time he wriggled into her arms as she yanked at him. He unfolded his legs and fell out of the twisted plane onto her, both of them collapsing onto the grass.

For a moment, Rosemary lay there, ribs and shoulder hurting from all the pulling, her other shoulder compressed by the body of the pilot. 'Go,' she struggled to say. 'Go, now!'

'Now,' he repeated, pushing himself up on his arms over her and staggering to his feet. He reached down as if to help her but she had scrambled up, away from the stink of the fire, terrified the plane would blow up at any moment. He took a step before falling again, and this time she forced him up and draped one of his arms around her neck.

He was slim but heavy, and he managed to limp with her to the grass on the other side of the road, a safe distance away. The smoke was billowing now, a column reaching into the air, twisting like a dancer, before being blown lightly towards the village. She lay down next to him, trying to get her breath, coughing up the oily, rubbery fumes.

He turned his head, his leather cap half off, his bug-eyed goggles blackened and pushed back on his forehead. He was young, not much older than her, with wheat-coloured hair that stuck out like a scarecrow's. She couldn't see how badly hurt he was, it was hard to believe he had survived at all. He could have internal injuries, fractures. He could still die.

'We live,' he said, still staring into her eyes intently. '*Dziękuję*. Thank you.'

'I was afraid the plane would catch fire,' she stammered.

'Me, also,' he said, lifting his head to see the crumpled wreckage. 'But engine – oh, there.'

She followed his finger and saw the smoke – and flames – that were billowing from his broken-off engine, many yards from the plane. 'Are you hurt anywhere?' she said, sitting up and looking down his body, searching for blood or funny angles, like the lamb who had broken a leg on one of the stone walls and had to be put down.

He moved his arms carefully, bending his elbows and wrists. 'All *zdrowy*,' then added, 'good.' Lifting his knees up brought more grunts of pain and he ran his hands down them. 'Good,' he said again, although his ankle seemed very painful. There was blood trickling down from his hairline. Rosemary wadded her handkerchief up and pressed it to a two-inch cut in his scalp, wondering if that was what had knocked him out.

'What happened?' she said, sitting up and covering her knees with her dress.

'Engine,' he explained, unnecessarily. 'No fuel.'

'I mean, what were you doing flying over the moor?'

He looked puzzled at that, as if he had to rearrange some words. 'Pilot,' he managed. 'Go England.'

'You're a pilot?'

He nodded, winced, and put his hand over the fingers she was still pressing to his scalp.

'What are you called?' she asked.

'Called?'

'Yes,' she explained, pulling her fingers out from under his cold ones. 'Your name. *I*,' she said, patting her chest, 'am *Rosemary*.'

'Rose-marna?' he hazarded.

'Rosemary,' she answered. He tried a couple of times, struggling. 'Call me Rosie,' she said, although she had been trying to get people to call her Rosemary for years.

'Ah!' He patted his own chest with his free hand. 'I *Casimir.*'

'Casimir,' she repeated staring into his smiling blue eyes.

'Casimir Wojcik,' he said, and passed out.

3

PRESENT DAY, MARCH

Zosia had four days left on her rented room in the shared house in Exeter. She ran around town picking up things she couldn't buy in the village shop. Colouring pens for Krystof, some warm socks from a pound store and extra credit for her phone. She barely made it back in time to pick Krys up from school, where he looked small and vulnerable being jostled by a bunch of older kids.

'*Chodź tu,*' she said, waving him over and giving him such a hug, his feet left the ground. 'Come here.'

He giggled. 'Put me down, Mama, I'm too big.'

'I bought some cakes from the Polish shop,' she said, knowing that he loved Polish *paczki*, doughnuts glazed with icing. 'We won't be able to get them from the place we are going to live, a little village called Hartford. It's on a big wild moor with ponies and sheep.' She held his hand to cross the road.

She missed having a car so much. It was another thing that Declan had kept in the divorce. He had the house, every stick of furniture and a three-year-old Volkswagen, but she had kept her son. That was all she wanted, but sometimes money was so short, too short. At least with Hazel she would have somewhere safe to live. She couldn't bear to go back to Poland, penniless and divorced, to hear her father say 'I told you about him,' with sadness in his eyes. He had read Declan like an unpleasant book the first day he met him.

'What's it like, Mama?' he said, walking alongside her.

'It's a big house in a garden full of fairies,' she said. 'The lady says you can just feel them. They will bring good luck.'

He dragged the toe of one his shoes over the pavement. 'Are fairies *real*?' he said. 'Are they real like rabbits and horses?'

'Maybe like rainbows,' she said. 'You can see them but not touch them. Don't scuff your shoes, baby, I can't afford to buy new ones. But we will have a lovely room overlooking the garden so you can watch out for them. Who knows? Maybe they are real, and I bet there are rabbits. I saw a tiny vole, like a mouse, already.'

'Can I have my own room?'

She was silent for a few more moments, remembering the nursery she and Declan had created for Krys as a baby. 'I don't know. We have to be super good and helpful and then the lady that lives there will be nice to us. I will be working for her, for money.'

'I'd like my own room,' he said. 'Then I could get my cars out. The ones Daddy gave me, with the ramps.'

'Miss Wojcik has already said you can have your own bed, and it has toy drawers underneath it. And there's a bookcase for our books, and a chair for watching the television.'

'OK.' He didn't sound very enthusiastic.

'And we'll have our own bathroom, with a big tub and a shower over the top so I can wash my hair.'

His face lightened a little as he looked up at her. 'I'd like that. Can I keep my boats in there?'

'I'm sure you can. And you'll have a new school. Smaller, with nice children.'

He smiled distractedly at that and slowed down as they

walked past the bus stop. He often ran out of steam on the way home. It was only three more stops through the town centre, and she sometimes caught the bus. But she didn't have any money to spare; they would spend the last of her benefit money getting to the village.

Her heart was skipping beats at the idea that Hazel wouldn't like Krys being in the house, that she would have to leave. If Declan ever fought to get a solicitor to get her son back, she would need to have a good home and a regular income.

Krys was dragging his feet by the time they reached the large house, divided into flatlets. Technically they weren't suitable for children, but the council had nowhere else to put them. The shared bathroom facilities were frequently dirty; last week a fellow tenant had got drunk and thrown up all over the only bathroom on their floor. It had taken most of an hour, a pair of gloves and half a bottle of detergent to clean it up so they could use it. He didn't even apologise when they met on the stairs, and she'd wondered if he had forgotten.

When she gave her notice, the house manager had offered to store some of her belongings for a few weeks. He'd been more than friendly, in fact, uncomfortably so. Now he wasn't making it easy to get away.

'Where you off to, then?' he said, leaning on the hall wall so she would have to slide past him. 'I need to know where to forward your post.'

'Onto Dartmoor. I'm working for an old lady.'

'Oh. Carer, then?'

She wasn't willing to explain further. 'If you could put any post with my stuff, I'll pick it up soon.' Apart from her benefits, which she could deal with online, no one ever wrote to her anyway, and it was better if Declan couldn't find her.

'I suppose you need a lift,' he said, staring at her. She was tall enough not to have to look up very far. He smelled of stale weed. It reeked like he had peed himself.

'I'm all sorted, thank you,' she said, wishing she could take up the offer. At least Krys, like most six-year-olds, loved public transport. 'I'll see you when I come back for my stuff.' She forced a smile. 'I've liked staying here, it's a good room.'

'Yeah, it's OK,' he said. 'The landlord's going to hike the price when you go. But if you need to come back, I can probably help you do a deal on the rent.'

I am never coming back. She tried to smile at him. 'Thank you. Now, my son is hungry, I must go.'

She slipped around him, heard him mutter something disappointed and fumbled with her key as she unlocked the door. He had a master key for every room, but a chair wedged loudly under the handle made her feel better.

Zosia and Krys looked up at the stone house, wrapped in leafless creepers, on its mound of grass above the road. The bus had dropped them in the village and they had walked up the hill. It hadn't looked so far before, but now she was juggling two cases and three boxes it felt further than quarter of a mile. She hadn't noticed before how long the drive was – a hundred metres or more, and steep. No wonder the view was so good, but it was hard going carrying their luggage, even if Krys was carrying his favourite toys and a rucksack.

Hazel came out to meet her before she'd got halfway to the door, leaning on a stick. 'Oh, let me help!' she said, reaching for the toy box and looking at Krys, who was half hiding behind Zosia. 'Hello, there,' she said. 'You must be Krys.'

Krys hid his face against Zosia's leg. 'He's a bit shy,' she said apologetically. 'We met a lot of people on the buses. Come, Krys, this lady is Miss Wojcik, our new landlady.'

An emotion Zosia couldn't pinpoint crossed her face. 'He's such a handsome little boy,' she said softly. 'He looks a lot like you. Would you like to come inside for some food, Krys?'

Krys ventured a quick glance at Hazel then up at his mother. 'Food?'

'And I think you can call me Auntie Hazel,' she said. She held out one imperious hand, and to Zosia's surprise, he took it. 'Whatever's in this box?' Hazel asked, shifting it under her arm.

'My toys,' he said, in a little voice. 'My best cars and my books. And a boat for the bath.'

'Oh, I used to love playing in the bath!' Hazel said, and led the way into the hall, through to the back and into the warm kitchen. 'I had special-coloured soaps so I could draw in the bath. And bubbles, do you like bubbles?'

Zosia put down the bags, resting them all together as he nodded. Hazel was quite different today, warm, welcoming. The kitchen smelled lovely, savoury meat scents coming from a large pot. There was something of her childhood memories in the steam, as if from a pot roast.

'I made dumplings,' Hazel said. 'From my grandmother's recipe. Let's have a drink then I'll take you upstairs. I hope you don't mind, but I made a few changes once you told me about Krys. My friend Leon moved some furniture for us.'

Zosia sank into a chair at the table. 'I'm sure it will be lovely,' she said. 'I'm sorry, it was such a long journey. The train was late, so we missed the first connecting bus.'

'Well, why don't you both go and wash your hands – the cloakroom is just off the hall – and I'll dish up some dinner. It was my father's favourite.'

Zosia could feel her eyes filling with hot tears. 'This is so kind,' she managed to say. 'Thank you.'

'Well, I've been thinking,' Hazel said. 'Let's just work on getting the house and café back on its feet and then we can decide when to tackle Dad's papers. Go, I'll get some plates out. Is it all right to eat in the kitchen?'

Zosia could just nod, her throat was crowded with tears, and guided Krys into the downstairs bathroom.

'I like it here,' Krys whispered.

'Me too,' she managed back.

Hazel had made one important change. The front bedroom, next to Hazel's, had an adjoining room through a door beside the wardrobe into what had probably been a dressing room. She had put the single bed in there, and a tiny chest of drawers and two small shelves, one with a dozen old books. The only window looked out over the house next door, but it was a private little space for Krystof. He raced around, exploring.

'Leon helped me move the bed in. He's a nice chap, he was the one who found me when I broke my leg after I'd slipped on the patio. I had a number of hours to think about resurrecting the old café. You'll meet him soon. You'll meet the whole village, they are a nosy lot but very friendly.' Hazel reached for a blue book embossed with a gold design and handed it to Zosia. 'This was from my childhood.'

'My grandfather had a copy of this!' Zosia leafed through the first few pages. 'Not with these gorgeous illustrations, though, and not in English. Look, Krys. Polish fairy tales!'

Hazel smiled at her. 'It's from 1920. My dad spent ages tracking a copy down for me.'

'Thank you so much,' Zosia said, overwhelmed. 'I look forward to reading these to Krys. You said you had a hip replaced?'

'That's what they do when you break your leg at my age.' She smiled at Krys, who was sitting on the bed exploring the drawers. There was a small box of building bricks and a colouring book about robots. 'They give you new metal bones.'

'Like a robot?' he said, awed.

'I suppose so. It's very shiny, and called titanium. When Leon moved the furniture, he offered to help in the garden with the heavy lifting,' Hazel said. 'He also dropped in to warn me –

us – about the new neighbours. I think we should keep the net curtains closed on this side, Krys. Those men seem cross all the time.'

As Krys started unpacking his toys and arranging them on the shelves, Hazel beckoned Zosia into the larger room and sat on the bed. Zosia sat next to her. 'What's the matter?'

'I don't know if there is anything the matter, really. We're right out on the edge of the village, and the people who own the house next door got too old to get to the shops and moved into sheltered housing. They rented the house out several times, but the new tenants seem a bit odd. You know, rowdy.'

Zosia couldn't see much around the large camper van obscuring the old bungalow next door. 'What do you mean by odd?'

'Leon says they are trouble,' she said, reddening a little. 'My dad would have gone mad if he heard me say that, he thought we should always give new people a chance. But they aren't very friendly and they have a lot of visitors at all hours of the day and night. There are several men about your age there, but they make vulgar gestures if I go out there.'

Zosia started to feel uneasy. 'Just men?'

'I think there are two women, like you, in their twenties, but they don't speak. There are two children, too, two boys about eight or nine. They go to the school, but they haven't been here long.'

'I'm sure I'll meet the mums at the school gate,' Zosia said. She wondered if she would fit in. 'I'm sorry they aren't friendly, I know what that's like after living at my last place. Some of the tenants were fresh out of prison. I never found out what they had done.'

'Well, apart from a few swear words and a few flying fingers, they've never done anything bad. But I keep an eye on them.'

Every instinct in Zosia made her want to persuade Hazel to

completely ignore them, to not get involved, to even use the little door at the other side of the house to avoid annoying them.

I've let myself get scared. Declan did that to me, and living at the hostel with strangers. 'We'll be polite but observant,' she said.

'Exactly,' Hazel said, squeezing her hand. 'And if Krys makes friends with their children, perhaps they will become more sociable, become part of the village.'

4

MARCH 1940

All I could see against the sky was a halo of hair and her eyes. Oh, my, her eyes, bright like headlights, looking down at me. I thought I was dead, that an angel had reached down from heaven, sent by Najświętsza Maryja Panna, mother of Jesus. Then she said something, shouted, pointed at the smoke darkening the sky and the stink of oil and burning rubber. I had been robbed in Romania, arrested in Hungary, interrogated by Italian fascists, escaped to fight for France, only to flee to England and to this angel's arms. Not an angel. A girl, a beautiful girl staring down at me, trying to move me away from the plane. I would have followed her anywhere.

— EXTRACT FROM THE MEMOIR OF
CASIMIR WOJCIK

'Get away from him, girl!' one of the men shouted, pointing a shotgun at Casimir. She recognised him as the farmer, Mr Cawsey, who lived in a neighbouring village and often outbid her father on ewes.

'No!' she shouted back. 'He's hurt!'

'He's a bloody Hun, that's what he is,' he answered, now close enough to point the gun straight at the pilot's head, resting in her lap. She put a hand up to protect him from the shot.

'No,' she said, firmly. 'Look at the plane. He's not German – he's from somewhere else. His name is Casimir. And his plane crashed.'

The gun barely wavered. 'Wake him up, maid.'

Rosemary looked at the white face of the boy in her arms, his head lolling against her arm. 'He's badly hurt,' she said firmly. 'He needs a doctor.'

The other man was carrying his pitchfork upright now. 'He spoke to you, maid?'

'He did,' she said. 'He said he was trying to get to England.'

'Leastwise, he managed that all right,' he said. 'Let's just search him, maid, then we'll take him up to town in the truck. Likely the doctor will be able to help him.'

Finally, Mr Cawsey put the gun down and they stretched Casimir out on the ground. In one pocket was a revolver, mercifully unloaded, and a box of ammunition in the other pocket.

'Don't look German,' Mr Cawsey said. 'I reckon he's one of those Polish pilots that keep turning up on the coast. Running away from the Nazis to fight for us.'

With a bit of work, they managed to lift him into the back of the truck, Rosemary climbing in after him and making him as comfortable as she could with broken bales of hay. She knew how bumpy the track would be. 'I just hope he's not dying,' she said, settling his head on her knees. His eyes opened but he didn't say anything, just stared up at her, his gaze wavering.

'I don't know your dad would like you up there,' Mr Cawsey said, then shrugged and put up the back. 'Don't fall out.'

As the old truck screeched into gear, Casimir shuddered. 'Rosie,' he murmured.

'We're going to get help,' she said. 'For your head.'

He put a hand up to it, looking blank when it came away sticky with blood.

'Are you – German?' she asked, getting a blank stare in return. 'German?'

The word seemed to hurt him. 'No! No – *Germański, Polski! Jestem Polakiem!*'

He propped himself up on his elbows, his face angry but his eyes overflowing with tears.

'Good, good!' she said, pulling him back down. 'Be careful, we don't know how badly hurt you are. Polski, yes. Polish, good.'

After a moment, he relaxed into her arms. 'Where?' he asked, closing his eyes as the truck bounced over the ruts in the road.

She tried to cushion him from the worst. 'Where are we going, Mr Cawsey?' she shouted.

'We'll go up to Princetown,' he shouted back over the sound of the engine. 'They have a phone there, at the pub. And police and the doctor.'

They rattled up to the road across the moor. When the truck paused, Casimir turned towards her. 'Stay,' he said. 'Stay.'

'I will stay with you,' she said, a warm energy she had never felt before rushing through her. 'I'll look after you.'

The truck had stopped to let a fire engine past, its siren blaring. Rosie caught snatches of their conversation.

'... pilot, maybe he's a Jerry...'

'Better get him...'

'Is that girl...?'

The fire engine turned down towards the column of smoke, and the truck took off again. Rosie settled against a bale of hay that had broken free of its strings. It was far too cold and windy to do much more than hunker down and try to keep them both warm. They pulled up alongside the tiny police station, a thatched house at the edge of the small town. Rosie had only been there a few times. Except for the huge granite prison dominating the skyline, Princetown was a small, humble place.

Two men in uniform came out to greet the truck, and one of them climbed into the back.

'He dun't look like much of a threat, Cawsey,' the sergeant she recognised from the village said, pushing his hat back a little and leaning over. 'There you go, lad. You look like you need a doctor. *Parlez-vous Français? Sprechen sie Deutsch?*'

Casimir looked panicked. '*Polski,*' he said, and Rosie interrupted.

'He's Polish. He's flown here to England. I think he's come to help.'

'Polski, huh?' said the policeman. 'Well, whatever you are, we should get you to the prison infirmary.'

Rosie jumped. 'Prison?'

'They've got a doctor there. If they patch him up, we can get the authorities to interrogate him – talk to him.'

'Oh.' She looked down at Casimir. 'We're going to take you to a doctor.'

Casimir put his hand over the wound on his forehead, matted with blood and hair. 'No doctor!'

'It will be fine,' she soothed. 'They will make you better.' He still looked alarmed and she smiled down at him, her arms cramping from holding him. 'Good.'

The other policeman, a boy she recognised from the class above hers at school, came forward with a big blanket. 'Come away, Rosie,' he said, and wrapped Casimir up as well as he could. Two of the pilot's fingers were going purple, deformed and swollen. 'Looks like he broke his hand.' The blanket stank of sheep, and Rosie thought it must have been used to rescue animals.

Rosie sat down next to him again. 'He'll fall out if someone isn't with him,' she said defiantly.

'Your daddy won't like that,' he drawled. 'If he's a Jerry.'

She shrugged. 'And you can get rid of the gun,' she said, sniffing. 'He won't hurt anyone.'

He nodded, patted Casimir's foot under the blanket and said very slowly and loudly: 'Let's get you to hospital, my lad.' He turned to Rosie. 'Better stay under that blanket, too, you look frozen. It won't take long, we'll get him looked at properly by the doctor.'

Casimir touched his broken hand to his face. '*Lekarz?*'

She looked down at him. 'If that means doctor, then yes. Make you well. Good.'

The sergeant climbed up after her, carrying a cardboard first aid kit. 'Better get a dressing on that cut, young man.' He glanced at Rosie while he dabbed some disinfectant over Casimir's forehead. 'What's his name?'

'Casimir – Voychick? Something like that.'

'*Wojcik,*' Casimir said, smiling up at her.

Unable to help herself, she beamed back.

5

PRESENT DAY, MARCH

For a graduate with a degree from Nicolaus Copernicus University in Toruń, in French and English, Zosia found the manual work of cleaning the house satisfying. Hazel was embarrassed when Zosia moved a piece of furniture or pulled up a rug, because there were layers of dust everywhere. But beating the dirty rugs out in the garden or deep-cleaning the old carpets brought fresh colour to the rooms. Zosia found herself singing the songs her grandmother had taught her as they cleaned the big property three generations now shared.

Part of moving in was spring cleaning the main rooms. Now Krys was playing with his cars in the kitchen, and Zosia was trying to get her head around what they could do with the café as she cleaned downstairs. She suspected the recovery from the fall had been difficult, and that it had been harder to keep on top of the house than she would have liked.

'I never liked all these knick-knacks,' Hazel said, after they had all been polished and replaced on clean shelves.

'I like them. Did they belong to your parents?'

Hazel picked up a shepherdess simpering at a plough boy. 'I

have a feeling some of them belonged to my grandparents, from the farm.'

'They lived on a farm? I mean, I don't know how many English people are farmers, it all seems to be cities and towns. And moorland, of course. And so much coast!'

'Does Poland have a coast?' Hazel asked.

'Some after the war, when Poland was granted East Prussia,' Zosia replied, 'on the Baltic Sea. It's very cold in the winter, but it's good in the summer. We used to go there on holiday.'

Hazel folded a throw that had been covering a sagging sofa with stained cushions. 'Mum and Dad always had a dog,' she explained, waving at the marks. 'As they got older, they didn't worry about in here.'

'Did they have many people staying?'

'Later on, they concentrated on the Fairy Café. But when I was a little girl, they would rent out the four large rooms, with anything up to a dozen people, including children. My dad was forever running about, putting up cots on changeover day. If we had extra kids staying I had to give up my bed sometimes.' She smiled. 'Dad always paid me a shilling a night for renting my bed.'

Zosia smiled at that as she lifted a little china figure of a child hugging a lamb. 'These are probably worth something now. You could put them in an – oh, I forget what they call them! – an online marketplace.'

'You mean an auction?' Hazel looked at them. There were about a dozen on the mantelpiece alone.

Zosia nodded. 'Would you like me to box up some of these ornaments if you want the room less cluttered? I rather like them.'

'You do?' Hazel laughed out loud.

'Yes, I do,' Zosia defended herself. 'They are so – English.'

Hazel looked around while Zosia got on with polishing a

side table. 'Do you know,' she said slowly, 'I think we can do better than this. Follow me.'

Putting down her duster and spray, Zosia followed her into the long, dirty dining room. It had a dark wood table that would seat a dozen easily, and matching dresser, heavily ornamented with carvings of fruit and leaves, like the bed. 'It's beautiful,' Zosia said, running her hands over the carved wood, leaving tracks in the dust.

'It's two hundred years old. My father bought it in an auction many years ago, when I was little. I think it's walnut and the carvings are pearwood. For some reason, he stained it all to look like mahogany.' She smiled over her shoulder at Zosia. 'It must have been in fashion. Dad always wanted our house to look like English people's, he really wanted to fit in.'

'You can get the wood stripped back and re-finished,' Zosia said. 'I've done it with paint, I'm sure it's the same process.'

'I don't want to send it away,' Hazel said, running her hands over some grapes and an apple peeping out from the wood. 'Look, the varnish ran here.' Her eyes welled up with tears. 'I remember him doing this. I remember him complaining how runny the stain was.'

'I'm sure we could get it back to the wood.'

'I think my dad would say "Get rid of those drips".' She started pulling at the drawers. 'This is where I keep batteries, and there's a couple of torches, too. Oh, a box of matches. Perhaps I'll put those things right on the top of the dresser, out of Krys's reach.'

'Thank you,' Zosia said, looking in the next drawer. 'Are these knives and forks silver?'

'I expect so. Dad loved buying old bits and pieces. He said, back in Poland, it was like having a bank account.' She looked up. 'Sorry, I'm sure it's all different now. He meant, from before the war.'

'My grandmother would have said the same,' Zosia said, and

their eyes met and both smiled. 'What do you want to do with the table? It's enormous.'

'It was always too big,' Hazel said. 'It's more than four foot wide, it's hard to reach across if you want some marmalade. And the tablecloths were huge, too. My mother used to overlap two or three to cover the whole thing.' She crossed her arms. 'It should be sold.'

'Are you sure?'

'Well, think about it. If we put modern tables in here, we could use it when the weather is too bad in the garden. It's off the kitchen, just like the conservatory – we could keep an eye on both.'

Zosia looked back to the kitchen. She could imagine it working, trays carried from the kitchen to the rooms either side. She sat down on the faded window seat looking over the property next door. The camper van was parked at a different angle, suggesting it had been moved.

'What exactly would you like to achieve here?' she asked, catching her breath. 'I don't think we can run a café on our own.'

'I know that,' Hazel said. 'But my parents and I always ran it from the beginning of the season around Easter, just half a dozen tables, teas and coffees and a few cakes. That put enough money in the bank to employ a local teenager or two, and a pot washer for the summer holidays.'

'You don't have much parking,' she said, peering out at the curving driveway. 'Four or five cars?'

'People used to walk around from the big car park along the road. But now they have to go past that eyesore next door. I've written to the landlord, but I don't think they can do anything about the camper or all the rubbish they leave outside.' She tapped the side of her head. 'The landlord's wife's got dementia, poor soul.'

'I mean, the people who live there haven't actually done

anything yet. They seem to stay out of sight if I go out there.' Zosia had seen a woman's face at the window a couple of times, but that was all. 'I might meet them at the school.'

'Oh, that's another thing,' Hazel said. 'The garage are bringing my car back on Monday, first thing. It's had a proper service. If you would like to take it for a test drive, maybe take little Krys to school?'

'That would be great. He does not have to be there until nine thirty,' Zosia said. 'To get enrolled properly Monday morning.'

'Can you drive gears?'

'Of course,' Zosia said. 'What is it?'

'A battered old Golf, but I love it,' Hazel said. 'It's been so long since I drove it, and now I'm worried, with my leg...'

'Maybe we can get you some lessons to get your confidence back,' Zosia suggested. 'Then, if they think you're OK to drive, I can take you out to practise.'

'I might need an automatic,' Hazel said, as she wandered into the kitchen.

Zosia heard her put the kettle on. She got off the window seat, noticing the bleached and fragile fabric on the cushion. *It's all fixable, if we have time. If we don't have to move on.*

Zosia sat in the head teacher's sunny office, Krystof clinging to her side. Mrs Bartlett was tall, with a wide smile and kind eyes, dark skin and short, grey hair. She had shaken Zosia's hand, then Krys's.

'Krys is a native English speaker?'

Zosia nodded. 'He was born here, his father is English.'

'And who else lives at home?' The head teacher looked up from the form she was filling in, one eyebrow raised.

'We are living in Foxglove Cottage bed and breakfast,' Zosia said. 'I'm staff, Krys has his own room. It's very nice.'

'Oh, the cottage with the Fairy Café! It was such a shame when Hazel had to shut it down a couple of years ago.' She smiled. 'They made a believer in pixies out of me as a child. You know Cas, Hazel's father, used to run a bakery in the village, too? It's where the pottery is now. They used to make the scones and cakes for the café.'

'You grew up here?'

'My dad was born here. If you didn't inherit a house here you probably couldn't afford to buy one now. Several houses in the village are second homes or holiday lets.' She hesitated. 'Like your neighbours.'

'I was wondering if their children go to school here?' Zosia said. 'Hazel said there are two boys.'

There was a long pause. 'They attend from time to time,' Mrs Bartlett said, finally. 'They haven't assimilated very well. They've moved around a lot.'

Zosia looked down at Krys. 'We were hoping they would be friends for Krys.'

'No,' she said, smartly. 'Those boys are too old, but we have several others around Krystof's age. We have a combined reception and year one class, a group of really lovely children.' She turned to Krys. 'I hope you like football? The boys like to kick a ball around at lunchtime.'

Krys shrugged one shoulder, looking up at Zosia.

'He's a little shy at first,' she explained. 'But he soon makes friends.'

'We have a separate classroom for the younger ones. And reception and year one do forest school two afternoons a week. Would you like to see?'

Krystof didn't look enthusiastic, but Zosia rapidly spoke to him in Polish, and then added, 'Come, on, *kochanie*. Let's go and meet the children. It will all be fine.'

Mrs Bartlett raised both eyebrows and smiled, waiting.

Zosia stood and held out her hand again. 'Come,' she said

calmly. He reluctantly went with her as Mrs Bartlett led them through a small extension to a large, light classroom overlooking a cluster of trees and a covered area of benches around a firepit. Over the hedge, a small church stood, in front of the moorland rising up to the tor.

'Look,' Zosia said to Krys. 'That looks like fun.'

'We make fires and sometimes toast marshmallows out there,' Mrs Bartlett said, with a big smile. 'Ah, this is Miss London. She will be your teacher. This is Krystof Armitage, he prefers to be called Krys.'

Miss London crouched down to his height. She was about Zosia's age with very short blonde hair and a friendly smile. 'Perfect. We were just about to get some blocks out to work out some number puzzles. Do you like puzzles?' she asked him.

Krys didn't answer but he nodded. Miss London took his hand and settled him next to a little boy who looked about the same age.

Zosia turned to Mrs Bartlett. 'Thank you,' she said in a low voice. 'The divorce was hard on him and he didn't like the school back in the city.'

'Divorces always are difficult for children,' she answered, and pressed Zosia's forearm for a moment. 'Unhappy marriages do more damage, though, don't they? He couldn't be in a kinder home now, and I think you'll see how well he does with Miss London.' She paused for a moment. 'Do watch Krys with the boys next door.'

6

MARCH 1940

I do not like hospitals. Since I was a little child, I was afraid of doctors after I broke my arm at school. But with every smile, Rosie gave me confidence that everything would be all right. They took us to a huge grey building that I know now is a prison, a terrible place, but it had a doctor. For a while I thought I was going to be imprisoned for stealing a plane from the French, or for crashing on the countryside. Or even for what I had done in Hungary. An officer came and spoke to me. I understood very little but I looked at his smart clothes, his officer's moustache and military bearing and was reminded of my own officers, back in Poland. I could only pray that more had got away, to stand against the enemy, fight for Britain and then back to liberation.

— EXTRACT FROM THE MEMOIR OF CASIMIR WOJCIK

Rosie was escorted into the infirmary half an hour after they arrived, after sitting uncomfortably in a waiting room by the draughty door. There were dark blood smears on her coat, and her skirt was covered with grass. Casimir sat in a wooden chair in a treatment room, looking as if he would rather be anywhere else but here. She could see how bloodstained his fair hair was, matted against his head.

She hesitated before walking over, but he spotted her and beckoned. His flying suit looked more like a farmer's overalls now, his shoes old and scuffed, but he smiled.

'Are you feeling better?' she asked, as she took the empty chair next to him. Now she felt awkward, very young. 'Good?'

'Good,' he said, taking her hand and squeezing for a moment. It was an intoxicating feeling; she looked down at her hands as if he had branded her, and the awkwardness was gone. 'No doctor.'

'You *need* a doctor,' she said firmly, feeling more like her mother as she added, 'it will only hurt for a little while.' It was strange, feeling protective and fluttery at the same time.

Shoes clicked on the linoleum of the waiting room and a smart man in some kind of uniform walked towards them. She involuntarily stood, and with a groan, Casimir tried to as well, clinging to the back of her chair.

'At ease, Mr Wojcik.' When Casimir didn't sit, he pulled up another chair and sat. 'Are you the young lady who came to his assistance?'

She nodded as she sat down. 'Yes, sir. I saw the plane crash.'

'My name is Major Drake. I am from the army training camp at Okehampton. We are training men from all over Europe. They tell me Mr Wojcik is Polish?'

His voice was light, but there was a sharp look in his eyes, as if he didn't trust Casimir yet.

'*Polski*, yes.' Casimir nodded, wincing as he sat down. He seemed to understand more English than he could speak.

'Can *you* tell me what happened? I doubt Mr Wojcik can put it into words for me as well as you can.'

'There was a funny noise, like the engine was coughing and

spluttering,' she explained. 'There was black smoke coming out of the front, he was struggling to see but he lined up with the road.'

'It would have been better if he'd actually landed on it,' the man said drily.

'Well, he really couldn't,' she said. 'The road was all potholes and cart tracks. But the grass verge was smooth and I suppose he thought it was safer. He couldn't see the mile marker.'

'It's not easy making these decisions in a moment,' he agreed, looking back at Casimir.

'It was completely covered in grass and moss,' she explained.

'Well, not much harm done.' He looked closely at Casimir's forehead. 'Nasty bump, though. It will need stitches.'

'No doctor,' Casimir repeated.

'You will get stitched up and report to us tomorrow,' Drake said. 'Then we'll talk about the plane.'

'Plane,' Casimir repeated. 'Crash.'

'Yes, well. I don't think your English is quite up to a debriefing, but the air force will salvage the engine. The body of the plane will just be spare parts, I'm afraid.' He turned to Rosie. 'Honestly, the biggest problem with these young men is their English. If he learns to understand instructions, we might be able to use him.'

Her heart lurched in her chest. 'I could teach him,' she said. 'I'll help him with his English.'

'Well, young man,' he said, looking at Casimir. 'If we offer you a place in the British military, will you promise to study just as hard on your English – your words?'

'Yes, sir,' Casimir said, smartly. 'RAF.'

'Maybe they will be able to use you. Not if you smash up *our* planes, though.' He smiled. 'It looked like an old French Caudron.'

'Caudron, yes,' Casimir said, followed by a flurry of Polish.

Drake laughed. 'We call them flying coffins,' he said to Rosemary. 'Terrible planes. He must be a good pilot to have got all this way.' He turned back to Casimir. 'I'll get the doctor to fix that nasty wound then we'll take you to Okehampton and recruit you properly.'

'Yes, sir,' Casimir repeated. She wondered if it was almost the only English he had learned.

'Well, he may have crashed his plane,' Drake said, standing up again, 'but if he flew it across enemy lines from France and survived to tell the tale, he deserves a chance to fight back.' He leaned forward and spoke more loudly. 'Well done,' he said, leaving Casimir looking baffled, and walked away.

'Well – done?' Casimir replicated.

'Good,' she explained, using her hand to look like a plane coming into land.

'Crash,' he repeated. 'No good.'

She smiled at him as a nurse came through. 'Mr... oh, my. Is that Voychik?'

'Wojcik,' he said, although Rosie couldn't hear much difference.

'Come through, the doctor is ready now.'

He looked at Rosie, eyes huge and intense. 'No doctor,' he repeated, as he stood up.

'Yes. *Doctor*,' she said, then looked up at the nurse. 'I'm afraid his English isn't very good yet.' She looked back at Casimir. 'I'm going to teach him.' She took his arm.

'Well, you'd better come and make him feel safe,' the nurse said, laughing kindly. 'Because he's going to need a few stitches. I think the word "ow" translates into several languages.'

Rosie stood in the telephone booth just outside the prison and called her neighbour.

'Mrs French? Hello, this is Rosie – Rosemary from Duke's farm. Yes, Marion's girl, yes, thank you. Could you let my parents know I'll be late? I've been helping someone, so I'll catch the bus back.' She listened to the confused conversation at the other end of the phone. Mrs French had the only telephone besides the ones at the doctor's house and the vicarage. She didn't like asking her but this felt like an emergency. She was shaking inside so much she wondered if she was in shock herself.

Mr French came on the phone just before the money ran out. He promised to tell her mother she would be home by seven just as the pips went. 'Thank you!' she half shouted down the phone. She felt like skipping, but had no idea why. It could have been the worst day of her life, a young man had almost been killed in front of her, but instead – it had turned into something wonderful. Because he came back from the dead, she told herself sternly. There were still butterflies in her stomach when he smiled.

She waited by the door until Casimir walked out of the building, squinting into the last of the day's sunshine, a bandage around his head. 'Where you go?' he asked.

'I have to catch the bus home.'

He looked as if he wanted to say something, but couldn't find the words.

'Ah, Wojcik. All mended?' Major Drake walked up to them, smiling at Casimir who looked dazed.

'He was very brave,' Rosie said. 'Didn't even jump at the stitches. Twelve of them.'

'Good. Well, I'll get him back to our barracks. The team have already examined the plane, and it's definitely not German. How will you get home, miss?'

She couldn't stop looking at Casimir, who looked terribly pale, like he had in the cockpit. 'I think he's going to faint—' she said, before darting forward to grab his arm.

Drake caught his other side and they shuffled to a bench outside the prison clinic.

'Do you live near Holne?' he asked.

'Not far,' she said, patting Casimir's hand. 'He looks a bit sick.'

'Here, lad,' Drake said, offering a small silver flask. 'Have a nip of this.'

It smelled like her grandmother's disinfectant, the one she swilled out the chicken coop with, but he took a cautious sip, then a bigger one. At least it put a little pink in his cheeks.

'Yes, sir,' he said.

'I think you'd better sit in the back with our young casualty here,' Drake said, turning to Rosie. 'I'll drop you home on the way.'

Rosie sat in the back of his car with Casimir, marvelling at the most extraordinary day, shy of the way his shoulder brushed hers when they went around a corner.

'My house is just east of Holne,' she said. 'Duke's Farm. Thank you for the ride.' It was only the fourth time she had even been in a car. The scent of warm leather and some sort of brilliantine in Drake's hair made it seem exotic. She became aware that Casimir had turned to her, in the darkness of the dusk.

'Duke's Farm,' he murmured to her. 'Duke's Farm.'

'Yes,' she breathed back. 'Remember it.'

7

PRESENT DAY, MARCH

Zosia, Krys and Hazel had begun to form a family. Zosia enjoyed talking to Hazel as they made breakfast and packed Krys's lunchbox, then Zosia would drop Krys at school. Sometimes Hazel came along, though she didn't want to drive yet, and they would stop for a coffee in the village. They picked up any shopping that was needed, then returned to clean the house. Hazel wanted to help more, but her mobility was limited and she still tired easily and needed her stick for balance.

By Friday, Zosia had persuaded her to potter about in the downstairs rooms while Zosia worked on one bedroom at a time. The rooms were all clean but the carpet in Hazel's room was declared unsalvageable so Zosia started to roll it up. The bed was too heavy to lift so they regrouped for coffee downstairs.

'I've asked Leon to come over to take the carpet to the dump,' Hazel said as Zosia brewed the coffee the way her parents had always made it: Polish-style, just grounds infused straight in the cup with boiling water and allowed to settle.

'I prefer it filtered, but my father always liked his coffee like this,' Hazel said, pouring it out. 'And so strong. *Kawa czarna*, always black.'

'My father, too,' Zosia said, opening the biscuit tin. It always had cookies or cakes in it. The smell of Hazel's baking warmed the house every other evening, and there was usually something fresh for Krys's lunch, too. Today, there were delicate Viennese whirls flavoured with lemon and dipped in white chocolate at one end. She waved one at Hazel. 'Delicious,' she mumbled through the crumbs.

'Krys likes white chocolate,' Hazel said. 'He's such a lovely boy.'

The doorbell chimed, and Zosia jumped up. 'Stay there, I'll get it.'

A large man wearing a black shirt and blue jeans stood in the doorway, blocking out the light. He was tall and broad, older than her, with a string of brightly coloured beads around his neck. Over his priest's collar. She stared up at the man, not able to connect the beads to the dog collar or the thick dark hair tumbling over his smart black shirt. His size made her hands feel clammy, it reminded her a little of Declan.

'Hi.' He smiled at her. 'Is Hazel around? I've come to move a carpet.'

She broke out of her shock. 'Oh! Sorry, I w-wasn't...' She stopped stammering before she said anything stupid. 'I'm Zosia, I'm helping Hazel.' She stepped back, letting him in. He towered over her as he walked past her into the kitchen, and she followed in his wake.

'Leon!' Hazel stood up to greet him, leaning heavily on her stick. She was taller than Zosia but she seemed to disappear into his bear hug. 'This is the Reverend Leon McArthur, the vicar of St Mark's,' she said as he let her go. 'This is my new assistant, Zosia Armitage.'

He reached out a huge hand to shake hers, her fingers swamped by his warm clasp. 'Good to meet you.'

'I don't think... I wasn't expecting a vicar to move rubbish,' she admitted.

'We do all sorts of useful things. Well, I'm not completely disinterested,' he said, sitting on the biggest chair, next to the stove. 'There are sometimes cakes.' He smiled at Hazel as she sat down and poured him the last of the coffee. 'You're walking well. Just one stick now?'

'I'm getting better all the time,' she said. 'But Zosia's been a godsend, she's blitzed most of the rooms already and I can't wait to get decorating down here.' She put a plate with four biscuits in front of him. He took one and demolished it whole.

He *was* big, Zosia decided, but there was something bear-like and comforting about him.

'*Zo-sha*. That's a pretty name. Polish?'

'Yes,' she said, putting the kettle back on.

He washed another biscuit down with some coffee. 'How are you settling in?' His deep-set eyes were dark, and she was aware of being scanned and assessed.

'Good. Fine,' she managed to say, taking a few breaths to calm her racing heart. He was nothing like her ex-husband, but there was something a little intimidating about his sheer size. *Not all men are violent. Not all men are Declan.* But she was still reacting nervously to him. She cleared her throat and fixed a smile on her face. 'I hope you have a big car. It's a big wool carpet.'

'I already have a taker for it,' he said, looking at her again, his eyes narrowing in a smile.

'It's no good for indoors, it's eaten away with moths,' she protested.

'It's destined to mulch half a dozen trees on the village green, fruit saplings we put in a year ago. It should stop the grass stealing food from the roots. And it will kill the weeds,' he said, putting his plate out for another few biscuits.

'I'm saving a few for little Krys, Zosia's boy,' Hazel said, putting the lid on the tin.

'She's really saying I'm fat enough already,' he said to Zosia.

She couldn't think of anything appropriate to say in response to a vicar, or such a physically imposing man, that wouldn't be rude. He must have seen something of her confusion in her face. 'You can agree if you like. My doctor says I need to lose a couple of stone, but people like Hazel spoil me.'

She shook her head. 'If you're ready, I can help you with the carpet, Father.'

She led him upstairs and he stopped on the landing. 'You can just call me Leon, if you like. Or Vicar. I answer to "hey, you" as well.'

Her face grew hot, and she looked away. All the priests in her childhood were automatically called Father, she couldn't imagine speaking so casually to one. 'It's just in here. I managed to roll it up halfway but it's stuck under the end of the bed. It was too heavy to move.'

'If I lift the bed frame, can you roll it a couple more feet?'

She nodded, kneeling down to get a good grip. He grunted as he lifted the end of the solid bed, and she hauled the carpet towards her. He looked at the floor. 'There are nice boards under here.'

'Hazel prefers carpet, but she could buy a lovely rug to go by the bed.'

'So this is her room?' he asked, looking back at the carved bed. 'That's a grand bed. A museum piece, even.'

'It is.' She ran her hand over a sprig of leaves carved deeply into the wood, a tiny face grinning out of a forked branch. 'I like all the little faces and animals,' she said.

He bent down close to her to look, brushing her shoulder. She started, not sure why she was having such a reaction.

'I'm one of the good guys,' he said softly, as he stood up. 'I'm guessing you've met one of the other type?'

She shook her head. 'It is just ...' She ran out of words. 'You're so big,' she blurted out. 'I mean, so tall.'

He laughed, a deep booming chuckle that made her hot with embarrassment but smile as well.

'Perfect for moving carpets and lifting furniture,' he admitted. 'Sometimes people are confused about the collar.'

'And the beads,' she said.

'The collar comes on and off but the beads were a birthday present so they have to stay,' he said, his smile warming her. 'My niece gave them to me for my fortieth a couple of weeks ago.' He seemed younger than forty to her, but she could see the silver at his temples and more in his stubble as he bent over to lift the carpet. 'Good grief,' he said. 'Are you sure you haven't got a body rolled up in here? It weighs a ton.'

She laughed then, as she caught one end to help. 'That is what we do with the not-nice guys.'

He pushed the door open and they carried it out to the hall. 'Well, that's all right then.'

It bumped down each stair but they finally got it onto the gravel drive. He was driving a battered old Land Rover, which had once been white.

'It's not mine,' he said, out of breath as he folded the rug into the back. 'I borrowed it from the local farmer at Duke's Farm. You should meet them, they're good people, Hazel's cousins.' He rolled his eyes. 'Of course, Mrs Duke is Catholic and I expect you are, too.'

'I am. I was,' she said, snapped back to memories of the beautiful church back home in Chocz, parts of it six hundred years old.

'Well,' he said, hefting the last of the dusty, smelly carpet into the back of the car and trying to close the door on it. 'You are always welcome to worship with us. We have all sorts of worshippers at the church, everyone makes themselves at home and joins in.' He managed to wedge the door shut. 'We pride ourselves on our Easter egg hunt.'

She couldn't imagine the serious, perfectly robed priests of the Church of the Assumption hiding eggs for children. The idea made her laugh.

'Thank you,' she said, formally, as her smile faded. 'You've been very helpful.'

'I like being helpful,' he answered, still looking at her intensely, as if he was trying to work something out.

She nodded, turning back to the house where Hazel was standing, braced against the doorway.

She had no idea why she was suddenly tearful.

8

MARCH 1940

The first week at the training camp was exhausting. I was drilled along with the new recruits, just boys, as eager to play their part as I had been when the Germans invaded. I had joined the Polish Air Force in April 1939, as I had my glider pilot licence. My aim was to fly our premier planes, the PLZ P.11s, as an aviator of the Poznań Army. There was another pilot there, a Czech called Josef who had flown for the Łódź Army, he knew a little Polish. I had done three months of hard training in Poznań camp, much more than these young boys, but I was much more injured than I thought. Bruises hid cracked ribs, my head was very sore, but they all helped me on long runs. I ate the English food, dull but filling, and slept well. I dreamed of that moment the girl, Rosie Duke, had leaned over me next to my burning plane, and dragged me away. But my nightmares were filled with memories of my journey across Europe, and the destruction of Poland.

— EXTRACT FROM THE MEMOIR OF
CASIMIR WOJCIK

It was hard for Rosie to settle down to normal life after the adventure of seeing the plane come down and, of course, meeting Casimir. A working week dragged on, milking to do twice a day, sterilising everything and straining and chilling the milk for collection in the old dairy, the oldest part of the farm. Its whitewashed stone walls and limestone floor kept the dairy even colder. By the time she had weighed and set out the filled churns and put leftover milk aside for the farm on the Friday, she was worn out and smelled of bleach. She looked over the pasture and wiped sweat off her forehead as she noticed someone standing at the farm gate.

'Casimir!' This was not how she wanted him to see her, in her dairy apron and cap.

'I remember – Duke Farm,' he said, pointing at the sign. 'Friend give me...' his English failed him, 'truck.'

'He gave you a lift?' she hazarded. 'How's your head?' She tapped her own crown.

'Good. Good,' he said, his grin even wider. 'I come – English lesson.'

Her stomach dropped in a painful lurch. 'My father's expecting me back in a minute,' she explained. 'I have to go.'

'No, no,' he said his smile vanishing. He touched her arm. 'When? Lesson?'

She thought rapidly. 'Sunday afternoon,' she said, looking down the path to where a truck was parked. She started walking towards it and he followed, with a slight lurch as he favoured one leg. 'Oh, did you hurt your leg in the crash?'

He stopped, looked down to where she was pointing. 'Crash, no,' he said. 'Francja.' He pointed a finger and fired a pretend bullet. '*Niemiecki żołnierz.*' He shouted something to the driver of the truck, who was smoking out of the open window.

'German shot him,' he translated. 'In France. Come on, Cas, you'll be late.'

'Your friend can teach you more English than I can,' she said primly.

'But *you* teach,' he insisted. 'You save me.'

'Maybe I will,' she said. 'I can meet you outside the church, on Sunday, two o'clock. Will you be able to get there?'

'I'll bring him over,' the man said. 'Come on, Romeo. It will give you something to live for until Sunday.'

Casimir walked around and climbed into the vehicle, leaning out of the open door as she followed him, feeling helpless. She didn't know what she wanted.

'Bye,' he said, softly, and shut the door.

By the time she lifted her hand to wave them goodbye, she knew exactly what she wanted. She wanted him to kiss her.

Her father was scrubbing his hands in the pantry sink. 'Your ma made us a bacon pie,' he said, looking sideways at her. 'You all right, maid? You look a bit bozzam.'

'I'm fine.' She put her hands to her hot cheeks. 'I ran up from the dairy.'

'I thought it might be something to do with that pilot. He din't die, did he?'

'No, Dad. He just got a bang on the head.'

As they walked through to the kitchen, he dropped his voice. 'You an't been the same, that's all. It must have been a shock.'

'What was a shock?' her mother asked, lifting out an egg and bacon pie, the smells filling the kitchen. 'Not that old plane?'

'No, Ma, it's fine,' Rosie said, changing her dairy clothes for an apron and walking over to the deep sink and the scrubbed wooden drainer. 'Let me help with the greens.'

She drained the vegetables and put them in a warm bowl, as both the farmhands stamped mud off their boots outside and washed their hands in the scullery. Hopefully the steam would explain her pink cheeks, but she couldn't stop thinking about Sunday.

'I stewed some apples,' Ma said, catching Rosie's eye and pressing her lips together for a moment. She lifted a heavy pan from the shelf over the stove. 'With a couple of those cloves. I'll get you to make the custard, you've a light hand with it.'

'Rosie's custard's the best,' blurted out Charlie, up until now the most exciting person Rosie had ever known. At nineteen, and broad and tall as her father, she knew her parents liked him. Since they only had Rosie to leave the farm to, they were starting to look for likely husbands and he was hard-working and honest. Now, though, she thought his eyes were a bit close together and she didn't like the way he swallowed every time he looked at her, his Adam's apple jumping up and down.

Rosie turned to the egg basket and cracked a couple into an enamel bowl.

'I saw an army lorry, out on the lane,' Old Adam said, a former worker who had come out of retirement to help – and to criticise everything Charlie did.

'Yes, they were kind enough to tell me that Mr Wojcik was on the road to recovery.'

'Is he staying nearby?' her mother asked in a disinterested voice.

'Okehampton camp, I think. Not near.'

Her father sat at the head of the table with a big sigh. 'Those piglets aren't getting any less flighty. Or heavy. Time was, you could let them out all day and call them back in for their dinner with a bucket of food. It took me and Charlie half an hour to catch them.'

Rosie warmed the milk, added a spoonful of sugar and a dribble of precious vanilla extract into the eggs. It could be left on the edge of the hotplate to thicken, so she sat down next to her father. 'Why can't you leave the sty gate open? They'd probably still come home by dark.'

'The Yeos had a pig stolen a month ago near Tavistock,' he said, trimming the lamp hanging from a beam over the table. 'People are keen for meat. Lambs have been taken off the Postbridge road, slaughtered at the roadside.'

Her mother sat down and began to say grace. Rosie closed her eyes and tried to concentrate on the words.

'Be present at our table, Lord. We thank Him for this food, by His hand, we all are fed. Thank you for our daily bread. Amen.' Ma had grown up a Bible Christian and her father went along with whatever she did.

The food was lovely, as always, and when she stirred the custard over the heat, it didn't get lumpy. The talk was about the bullocks grazing out on the moor and coming up to slaughter weight. For once her eyes didn't fill with tears at the thought of the calf she had bottle raised that was to be sold at market. She realised as she started to clear the first course and put out a jug of cider that her mother had been very quiet. She set Charlie to stir the custard.

She took the leftover bread, wrapped in waxed paper, to the larder in the scullery, and her mother followed.

'That boy?' her mother said in a low voice. 'The pilot.'

'Yes,' she said, avoiding her mother's gaze by looking across the dim room with its shelves of preserves and metal canisters of sugar and flour.

'You must have got friendly. Since he nearly died and you saved him.'

Rosie couldn't answer. She looked at her mother, her eyes watering.

'Oh, maid.' Her mother caught her up in an embrace that smelled of baking and cloves. 'You've got a tender heart, chick. And him a furriner.'

'He came to help us, to be a pilot here,' she said, muffled in her mother's arms. 'To save Poland.'

'Well, maybe he'll go back home when we wins the war,' she suggested, stroking Rosie's hair. 'To his family. Maybe he has a sweetheart. Or a wife.'

The thought was horrible. 'Maybe,' Rosie mumbled. 'I know, Ma. I just want to be his friend.'

Her mother held her by the shoulders and pulled her back to look into her eyes. 'Well, I won't tell you not to let your heart fall, because it looks like it's too late. But you're a good girl. You just *stay* a good girl and let it run its course. Understood?'

Rosie nodded. 'I know, Ma.'

'Because I know, affection is a powerful force for a young maid.'

'I'm meeting him on Sunday,' Rosie blurted out. 'To teach him some English. So he can join the RAF. I'll probably never see him again after that.'

'Will they even let him?' her mother said, gathering up a bowl that needed washing.

'They said, in the papers, that pilots from all over are joining.' She had spent hours in the last week reading the news in the library. 'From Canada and even Australia.'

'Well, they are our cousins. But them countries near Russia, Rumany and Hungary – we don't have anything in common with them.'

'He's Polish. And soon he'll be going away, because he's really a good pilot to fly all this way.'

'He crashed on the moor.'

'He just ran out of fuel coming from France. He's been shot by the Germans,' she finished, with a pleading note in her voice.

Her mother seemed to decide something. 'You're not a child, I won't stop you going. But I expect you to behave proper, you hear me? Like a good Christian maid.'

9

PRESENT DAY, MARCH

Leon was right, the floorboards under the bed were great. Zosia vacuumed then washed them with a damp cloth and they came up honey coloured, with a dark grain.

'What do you think?' she asked Hazel, suddenly excited. 'They would look lovely with just a few coats of varnish. We won't need to aggressively sand, just take the top layer off.'

'Could you do that?' Hazel looked doubtful. 'You'd be on your hands and knees most of the time.'

'I don't mind,' she answered, running her hand over the floor. 'Look, it's so smooth, it just needs a tidy up. Do you have a sander?'

'Dad had some tools. It will be in one of the sheds, if he had one.'

'Can we have a look?'

Hazel laughed at her as she led the way down the stairs to the conservatory. 'I love that you're so enthusiastic about a few floorboards! Maybe we should paint the walls and skirting. I know a decorator, he could do the floor as well.'

'I'd like to do it all,' Zosia said, suddenly shy. 'I could do it while Krys is at school, and catch up with the cleaning in the evening.'

'You need time off in the evenings. Anyway, I can help. We could make up a bed for me in one of the other rooms.' Hazel pushed her feet into her wellington boots and shrugged on a scruffy fleece. She pushed the door open and stepped into the garden, leaning lightly on her stick.

Zosia paused to look at the door, touching the cracked paint by a rusted lock. 'Hazel, the door was unlocked. Was it open all night?'

'Oh, I never lock this outside door. The one into the kitchen is done every night. Unless I forget.' She smiled. 'Honestly, no one worries about all that out here. We know everyone.'

'Except your new neighbours,' Zosia reminded her. A heavy bassline was echoing from the bungalow next door, and a man's voice shouting as if to a dog.

'Well, yes. You're right. Perhaps you could check each night before you go to bed. If we both do, we'll be sure it's locked.'

Hazel pushed her way through the long grass to three dilap-idated wooden buildings, one just an open store full of plant pots and buckets and one a summer house jammed up to the roof with what looked like mouldy cushions and ornaments leaning against the glass, beaded with condensation. The third was a shed, secured with huge bolt.

'The tools are in here,' Hazel said, pulling on the bolt. 'Oh, it's rusted.'

Between the two of them, they managed to twist it loose.

It creaked open as if it was haunted. Inside was an orderly workbench, above it a rack on the wall was filled with hand tools, and a chainsaw was leaning against a metal cupboard. Metal shelves held a range of power tools, including a circular saw she wouldn't trust herself to use, and a couple of sanders. Zosia took the smaller one, which was bundled with a withered rubber band full of sandpapers cut to the right size. 'This will be perfect,' she said, a little sad. Here was a glimpse into the mind of the man who had lived here, who had labelled jars of screws and nails in faded pen, who had painted the wooden walls to match the bench.

'I feel my dad close, in here,' Hazel said, her eyes glistening with unshed tears. 'It's been twenty-one years since he died. I used to help him, when I was a child. Fifty, sixty years ago.'

Zosia stepped towards the door. 'I'm sure he would love to know you were still looking after his house,' she suggested, her voice a little rough. Her own father was just the same, always fixing something, always planting pots.

Hazel cleared her throat and bolted the shed. 'I ought to lock this up,' she said. 'In case Krys comes up here – there's some dangerous tools in there.'

'And there's a locker behind it that looks like it could have other tools in, only there's a padlock.' Zosia was suddenly aware of the people next door. 'Perhaps we should be discreet about the tools,' she whispered.

'Oh. Yes. I'll ask Leon to find anything dangerous a better home.' She walked back through the garden, avoiding the sagging beams of the pergola. 'Perhaps he could use the chainsaw to take this down before we let Krys play out here, if it still works.'

Zosia tried to ignore the way her heart lurched when she heard his name. 'Is he – Leon – from around here?'

'No, not at all. He used to be a policeman, in Kent. But he got the call – he tells it like that – and retrained as a vicar. He doesn't like to talk about it too much. I think it was quite a painful time.'

'Oh.'

They walked back into the house, and as an afterthought, Hazel leaned back and turned the key in the door to the garden. 'When they first got here, I popped a card through the neighbours' door, just welcoming them. They never called round to introduce themselves. I'm sure they're harmless but they aren't friendly.'

Zosia walked through to the kitchen and put the kettle on. 'Let me make another coffee and I will try to get this sander started.'

'Well, if it gets too much, we'll pay someone to do it for us.'

Us. The word brought a lump to Zosia's throat. She was really beginning to feel like she was part of an *us*.

She had lightly smoothed a quarter of the floor, punching in nails that stood proud as she went, before it was time for her to get Krys. It wasn't until she looked in a mirror that she realised how messy a job it was. Her dark curls had gone creamy with dust, even her eyebrows and lashes were dusted.

'You're leaving it a bit late,' Hazel called out.

'I know,' Zosia said, leaning out of the bathroom. 'But I ought to get some of this mess off before I go in the car.'

'It's less than half a mile,' Hazel said. 'I think I can drive my own car for one half-mile. I've been cleared to drive by the doctor, I just lost my confidence.'

'But—' Zosia coughed as some of the sawdust caught in her throat.

'You shower, I'll pick Krys up.'

Zosia rinsed her mouth out with water from the sink. 'I'll call the school,' she said. 'To let them know you're picking him up. I'll walk down if you get stuck, just phone me. I'll just be a few minutes.'

'Have a good shower,' Hazel said, and Zosia could hear the clink of keys from the hall table. 'We won't be long.'

They weren't, but Zosia spent most of the time imagining Hazel running off the road into a ditch or crashing into another car. Since she wouldn't be out of the village and traffic mostly moved at walking speed, she knew they would be fine, but it was still a very long fifteen minutes.

'Mummy! Auntie Hazel drove the car and she let me honk the horn!' Krys raced upstairs for a hug.

'What did you do today?' she asked, sitting on the side of his bed while Krys slipped his school uniform off and got into his jeans.

'Number snakes,' he said, obscurely, pulling his jumper over his head. He never explained much they did at school. 'And we went for a nature walk and I found a teeny-tiny woodlouse, only they call them chickypigs here,' he mumbled.

His head popped out of the top of the jumper and he grinned at her. Then his smile faded.

'What's wrong, *kochanie*?'

He shrugged, and glanced towards the side window overlooking the neighbouring house. 'Two new boys came to the school today,' he said.

'Are they in your class? Are they nice?'

He shrugged one shoulder. 'They're in with the big children. But they made someone cry, and one of them spat at me when we came out after school.' He sounded properly indignant. 'Auntie Hazel said to ignore them, that they were just rude.'

'Well, it sounds like they were.'

Then he grinned at her. 'And I have a wobbly tooth!'

'Well, I'm sure the tooth fairy knows where the Fairy Café is!' she said, laughing. 'This deserves a celebration.'

Hazel made an earthenware jug full of her thick hot chocolate and brought out the last of the biscuits she had baked. As Zosia looked around her new family, she felt warm inside, and the future looked softer, kinder. The memory of Leon's smile crept into the corner of her mind, only to be banished.

He's a priest.

10

APRIL 1940

The training camp shipped me and Josef off to an airbase, a civilian one I think before the war. It had a few de Havilland Tiger Moths, little biplanes that looked outdated but performed well. The first time I took the controls I felt like a complete beginner, the plane was so responsive to my movements. By the end of the flight, I was at home in a way I had never been in France in the Caudron. When I landed, all I wanted to do was talk to Rosie about it. But I had our first date to look forward to, and I had to beg or borrow a decent set of civilian clothes to impress her with.

— *EXTRACT FROM THE MEMOIR OF*
CASIMIR WOJCIK

Rosie kept her Sunday best on after church, to meet Casimir, although she changed her shoes to a pair with a small heel – her only pair of grown-up shoes. She was cursing them by the time she reached the churchyard lychgate, a stone structure with a slated roof. Ma had insisted she take Tig with her, the farm's sheepdog, as a chaperone, perhaps. The stones were decorated with the curliest writing and some terrible spellings. Her teacher had taken them to make notes in the churchyard once, then they learned all about the evolution of the dictionary and how it had improved spelling. She turned to her favourite one, reading to Tig.

'*Here lyeth the bones of Henery son of Adam Wreford, buried 15 January 1686, also his wife Jane and two of his childeren, Adam aged 2 and Henery aged 2 weeks. A plague dealt the mortall blowe.*'

The sadness of the story always surprised her, four people dead for so long, yet tragically young. Today, the war was killing people of all ages, yet somehow the old tragedy seemed worse because they were from the village. The newspapers were full of the stories of refugees fleeing the Nazis in Poland, but it didn't seem real, the numbers were incomprehensible. One of her teachers had been a German lady who left to get married. Rosie wondered what had happened to her. Had she gone back to Germany? Or was she being locked up, as they had foreigners in the first war?

Tig barked and she jumped and spun round.

'Rosie?' She hadn't heard a truck, or footsteps. She had rehearsed how she would be dignified but friendly, but all her plans evaporated when she saw him. His eyes were so bright, his face so excited to see her. She flew forward, almost tripping in the stupid heels as he caught her in his arms. She didn't hesitate, she kissed him. It was the most exciting thing she had ever done, and her whole body felt more alive. Tig pressed up against her and whined, and Casimir laughed as he patted the dog.

He pulled away first. '*Ktoś nas zobaczy,*' he said, looking around. He tucked her hand into the crook of his arm.

'Someone might see us?' she hazarded. He indicated his eyes, mimed looking around. 'Come over here, by my favourite tombs.'

There was an area filled with the tombs of previous vicars,

going back hundreds of years. A wooden seat dedicated only to *Susie, 1913* sat between stone angels and wordy memorials. 'Come,' she said, sitting at one end, Tig leaning against her leg, staring up at Casimir.

He sat at the other end, his gaze roaming all over her face. He took her hand and kissed it, leaving her fingers tingling, then patted the dog.

'How can we talk?' she wondered alone, watching him frown, trying to work it out.

'Speak English,' he said, pointing at her.

She was stuck for a minute. Then she lifted her hand. 'Hand,' she said.

'Hand,' he echoed in his funny accent. '*Ręka.*' Then he kissed her palm, leaving her breathless.

'And fingers,' she said, wiggling them once he released her hand.

'Fingers,' he said. 'Fingers.' He took her hand again and kissed each one. 'Fingers.'

She reclaimed her hand and wagged a finger at him. 'No,' she said, smiling to soften the words. 'No.'

He slid a little closer. 'No?'

She had to lean back. 'No. Be good.'

'*Kocham cię,*' he said, his voice dropping. Whatever it meant, he really believed it. Her heart skipped as she somehow understood. He liked her.

She beckoned to him to move back. 'I'm not one of those girls,' she said weakly. *Oh, but I am*, she discovered. She pointed to herself. 'I'm a good girl.'

He nodded. 'Good man,' he countered, pressing his finger against his chest.

'Friends,' she said, trying to convince herself as much as him. Maybe he did have a sweetheart back in Poland, maybe he was engaged. He was far too handsome to be single, she reasoned, even if he did have a big square face and one eyebrow higher than the other, and sandy hair.

He spoke for a couple of minutes in impassioned Polish. She wasn't sure he had understood her but he seemed to be trying to tell her he wanted much more from her. Tig wagged her tail; perhaps she understood him.

She pulled on the chain around her neck and pulled out her crucifix, a gift from her parents when she was little. She had got embarrassed recently about it, worried that she would seem to be one of those religious girls, but she didn't know how to tell him she wasn't like the other kind of girls she had been at school with. They were always walking out with farmhands and writing to young men who had joined up.

'I'm a good girl.' Her face warmed up.

'Good,' he said slowly. 'Yes, good. But this good, too?' He leaned so close that her lashes brushed his, and they kissed.

'Yes,' she said, catching her breath. 'Kissing is good.'

He touched his lips to hers again. 'There,' he said, unexpectedly. 'Kiss like *kościół*.' He took her hand and pulled her to her feet. 'Come,' he said.

'We can't kiss inside the church,' she said, but he was pulling her along the grass path, faster because his legs were so long, and she hung onto his hand to keep her balance on her best shoes, dragging Tig by the lead.

'Here, *kościół*,' he said, pulling her into the doorway, pointing at its weathered mediaeval saints on either side. She knew them well.

'Church?' she guessed. Out of the light wind, the world grew breathlessly quiet.

He held her hand between both of his.

Her heart lurched, and she almost pulled away. She certainly gasped. He circled her ring finger with one of his, crooked into a C. 'Good man,' he said, earnestly. 'Come.'

She almost fell, she felt so dizzy. She tied Tig up at the entrance and let Casimir lead her forward, into the church.

It was still warm inside from the morning service, and she imagined the singing still filled the high ceiling with echoes. It was three hundred years old – not ancient by local standards. The dark pews were uncomfortable and designed for longer legs than hers, forcing her to perch forward. The aisle was soaked in colour from the afternoon sun slanting through the stained-glass windows. He let her go and knelt, bowing his head, crossing himself. With his limited English, she couldn't explain that this wasn't a Catholic church. This was how he spoke to God.

'Ah,' said the vicar, who appeared carrying an armful of hymn books. 'A Romish visitor.' He smiled, his white hair flopping over his face. 'This, I suppose, is our young pilot?'

'Casimir Wojcik,' she answered. 'He's from the Polish Air Force.'

'I hear they are all being moved to training grounds. They performed heroically in defence of their homeland.' He put his hand out to Casimir, who took it. 'Welcome, sir.'

'I saw his plane crash,' she said, out of breath.

'He does seem close to you, on very short acquaintance,' the vicar said softly. 'I suppose that would make you feel responsible for him.'

'He's trying to explain something,' she said, her words tumbling out. 'I'm not sure what he's trying to say, but he said he's a good man.'

'I suggest you don't rush into anything reckless,' the vicar said, looking from one to the other. 'We've had a lot of that with young farmhands dashing off to join up. War makes romantics out of all of us, my dear.'

'I can't bear the thought that I won't ever see him again,' Rosie blurted out.

'Well, what I suggest is you write down your address. Once

he can read and write a little English, he can tell you his address, and you can correspond.'

Rosie beamed at him, and a bemused Casimir smiled, too.

'Home,' Casimir said, tapping his watch.

'Yes. I'd better get home, I promised my mother I wouldn't be long.'

As they turned to leave, Rosie tucked her hand into Casimir's arm.

'Home,' he asserted, as he had no other words. He slid his finger around hers again as warmth spread through her body.

11

PRESENT DAY, MARCH

Zosia saw Leon again sooner than she had expected. Hazel had asked him to take the heavy bed to pieces, and he whistled at the expanse of beautifully sanded floorboards.

'Are you going to paint or varnish?' he asked Zosia, bending down and running a hand over the floor. 'It makes the room look so much bigger than that busy carpet.'

'Hazel's chosen a light oak varnish, just a hint of colour,' she said, watching him get up. He was heavy, but not wobbly like her dad. Like a rugby player, she decided. She gave herself a mental slap for being distracted again.

'I'm going into Exeter tomorrow. I could get your varnish if you want.' He made a face. 'A diocese planning meeting. They're very important, but I struggle to sit still for that long.'

She thought fast. 'Are you driving to Exeter?'

'Yes, I'm borrowing a neighbour's car, I don't have one of my own. I cycle most of the time. But my neighbours are happy to help out when I need four wheels,' he explained. 'But I can get to most places OK. Why do you ask?'

She bit her lip. 'It's nothing. It was just an idea. I have to pick up some stuff from my old place. I was thinking of borrowing Hazel's car but...'

Hazel couldn't walk the distance down a steep hill and up again. Zosia's phone was full of increasingly manipulative messages from the building manager at her old place, and she needed to collect her things.

He moved closer and looked down at her, holding her gaze for a moment before she looked out of the window. 'Can I help? It looks like something's bothering you.'

She shrugged. 'It's just a few boxes and bags,' she said, her accent stronger, her voice hoarse with tears. She really didn't want to lose what was left of her belongings.

'Things that you need brought back here?'

'It's being held by the building manager,' she said. 'If he hasn't sold it already. I thought I should get it back, when I get the chance. But I don't want to trouble you.' She glanced back up at that intense stare.

'You won't be troubling me,' he said, scanning her face again. 'We'll have to leave early. I'll be a couple of hours in the meeting but' – he pulled his beard, starting to smile – 'I'll go to my favourite Turkish barber's first. I need a haircut and a shave before I confront the bishop's commission. We'll have lots of time to pick up one carful of stuff. Unless there's furniture?'

'No, just boxes.' She thought rapidly. 'I don't know, what about Krys?'

'Hazel will sort him out and take him to school.'

'But I work for Hazel, I should ask her...'

'You do many more hours than she expects or asks you to do.' He smiled at her, and she involuntarily smiled back. 'Take a day off. You can get your belongings and draw a line under living in the city.'

When they ran the idea past Hazel in the kitchen, she was enthusiastic. 'I'd like you to pick up some wood primer as well as the varnish,' she said, jotting down a list. 'And some brushes. You'll be away over lunch, can you find somewhere nice in the city?'

'There's a Polish restaurant,' Zosia blurted out. She used to visit it when she could afford it, and the owner always gave her a bag of doughnuts to take home. 'It would be nice to say goodbye.'

Leon raised his eyebrows. 'Sounds good,' he said, looking out of the kitchen window through the conservatory. 'I'll come and take that pergola down on Saturday, too. I'll call in a favour to get rid of it.' He glanced at Zosia. 'One of my parishioners loves a good bonfire.'

Hazel handed him a mug, steaming with fragrant coffee. 'If we could make it safe, Krys could go out there to play,' she said. 'There's a chainsaw in the shed.'

He sipped his drink. 'I'll bring my own. I can get rid of the old one, in case the boy goes in there. Which reminds me. I would love you both to come to the family service at Easter.'

'I'm atheist!' Hazel said, indignantly.

'I'm still Catholic,' Zosia said. *And my faith was no help when life was difficult with Declan.*

'It's a non-denominational community gathering of celebration and chocolate,' he said.

'With God,' Zosia added drily.

'Well, it would be rude not to invite him, or even mention him on the day we celebrate his sacrifice for us.' His eyes were wide and he looked as guileless as a child. He suddenly laughed with a deep chuckle. 'Look, it's a new thing for the parish. We're trying a family, kid-friendly format I used to use in my old parish. The thing is, my regulars are a bit stuck in their ways. It would help to have you there. And I'd like to meet Krys.'

'We would only be there to make up the numbers?' Zosia said slowly. But she knew Krys would love to go. 'And to say thank you for helping me get my stuff.'

He shook his head. 'No, I'll still do that anyway. But,' he added with a smile, 'I might make you pay for your own lunch if you weren't attending.'

Hazel tutted. 'We'll come, strictly to make you look good.'

'And try not to bring a book this time,' he added.

'And *I* will pay for lunch, since you're bringing back the varnish,' Hazel said. 'And Zosia can bring me back some *pierogi*.'

Zosia wasn't sure how she felt about Leon. He was very friendly, but he was kind to Hazel, too. She didn't trust her own instincts. The last time she had, it had been with Declan and that had turned out disastrously. Besides, there was something guarded about Leon, as well as the matter of him being a priest. A Church of England vicar, sure, not a celibate Polish priest, but in her head the two were related. *Can I be friends with a priest?*

She was still thinking about him as she waited at the school gate with three other women and an older man. The school was surrounded by a hedge, looking over the gate the Victorian building looked hardly bigger than a house. The parents smiled but were a little reserved. Apart from coming to the school, she hadn't been seen around the village much. Maybe attending the church service – to make up the numbers – would help her meet people. She was a little nervous that she wouldn't know what to do. She had no idea what the church service would be like. Another part of her leaned towards the comfort she had always taken from regular attendance and confession, and being part of the church community. As a teenager she'd sung in the choir, and she missed that, too.

Krys hung back, waiting until the older boys from next door had left together. They walked past her, climbed into a car and were driven off. Too fast, she noted. Krys looked different, shy and sad. He walked out with another boy, who looked like he'd been crying.

'What's wrong?' she asked Krys urgently.

'One of the big boys pushed Michael into a hedge,' he said indignantly. But he looked frightened, too.

The older man, tall and grey-haired, stepped forward and bent down to hug Michael, who burst into tears.

'Did you hear what happened?' she asked him. 'Those bullies.'

The man looked at Krys and then back up at her. 'You don't know them?'

'No. They are our neighbours but I've never spoken to them.'

He hesitated before he spoke, watching Krys put his head on one side and murmur something to Michael. 'We thought you might be something to do with them,' he said. 'There seem to be new people there all the time. Most of them look lost, and they don't speak much English.'

'I've recently started working for Hazel Wojcik, we're staying there. The neighbours are nothing to do with us.'

He straightened up. 'They're up to something,' he said. 'You need to be careful, living outside the village.'

Zosia moved away a little so the children didn't hear her. 'Up to *what*, do you think?'

He leaned in. 'My wife thinks drugs – they often drive past our lane at three, four in the morning and far too fast. But I've seen a lot of young women, too, different girls.'

'Have you contacted the police?'

He looked away. 'I don't want to stir up a hornet's nest. There are three or four men in charge, they look like thugs.'

'Who picks up the boys from school?'

He shrugged. 'One of the men, usually. I bring Mikey to school because my daughter works night shifts at the hospital. I did see a woman, dark, short hair, who looked too young to be their mother, a few times. She didn't talk, maybe she doesn't speak English. Or she's too scared.'

Zosia shivered inside. She didn't want Krys being frightened, especially after everything he had gone through with Declan.

12

MAY 1940

A month later, the RAF accepted my application as a pilot officer trainee and sent me to the aerodrome at Northolt, outside London. I had barely a day to organise one of the ladies in the canteen to write a letter to Rosie, and I was taken in an open lorry with a dozen other recruits, including my Czech friend Josef. We had both excelled in the Tiger Moths, but that was hardly surprising as we had seen active combat in more advanced planes in the defence of Poland. I never felt alone in the air – we always used to say the ghosts of birds flew with us – but the British pilots complained of gremlins that played games with the engines. My gremlins kept me company, and I never feared them.

A big surprise was a long letter back from Rosie, which I could read a little of. The full letter was wonderful and alarming in the same measure. My love, my Rosie was now eighteen. I used to imagine her safe in her family's farm, but now she was coming to work at a factory near London. To be close to me. I read the words so many times they were almost worn away.

Rosie glanced into her handbag one more time, the scuffed and tattered letters from Cas held in a packet with baling string from the farm. She looked again at her notebook, enclosing her ticket first to Paddington station, the furthest she had ever travelled by train in her life, and then to Waltham Abbey Gunpowder Mills.

The train was slowing, the view out of the window growing dim as the station's canopy blocked the view of the cloudy sky. *I'm here. He's nearby.*

At first, he had got one of the canteen girls to write his letters for him, just a few lines. But the girl, Bessie, had always added a line or two. *He's looking well... He misses you terribly... He's looking forward to flying.*

They hadn't let them fly much yet, just training flights in biplanes. Now his English had improved, he was scribbling his own notes, and sending at least one a day. Her parents hadn't commented, but exchanged worried looks when the post boy brought the letters to the farm. She usually had one to post back. Some included little watercolour sketches of things she thought he would like: the view from the tor, the flowers on the ridge of the hill where he had crash-landed, a sketch of the farmhouse. Every one of his letters was filled with his passion. *I love you* was the first thing he wrote to her. *I kiss your hands* was another one.

Hers were more restrained. *I look forward to seeing you soon... I hope you are well... I miss you.*

What she actually wanted to say was how she longed for him to kiss her again, but she didn't want that read out by Bessie.

Leaving the farm had been difficult. She was exempted

from war work as farming and especially dairying was an essential skill. But she had gone into Exeter on the bus and spoken to the recruiting office for an interview, the day after her birthday. Thousands of women had already signed up to work in factories, and she'd found one less than an hour from where Casimir was training. Even if their relationship was just a fairy-tale bubble that would burst when she saw him again, as her mother had said, she wanted to do something for the war. To her, it felt like a storm was truly coming, even though many people in Devon seemed to think it would pass them by. She could almost feel it as she caught the London train in Exeter; the newspapers were full of Germany's advances in Europe, the blackout regulations were observed, and she never saw someone without a gas mask.

From the train, the countryside looked as it always had, but the towns were adapted for war. People in uniforms crammed on at most stations, jostling with gas-mask cases and luggage, squeezing onto the seats, perching on the armrests in the aisle, standing for hours by the doors. She had never seen so many people smoking in such a tight space, the windows mostly shut against the rushing wind and the air turning blue and foul. She was grateful when someone opened a couple of windows, just to throw the cigarette butts out.

At Paddington station, sandbags protected the entrance. The two Tube journeys on the underground towards Waltham were quite alien, the stale air rushing ahead of the train, throwing dust everywhere. She'd never been on a moving staircase either, one of which clattered between two levels at King's Cross. On the overland train, she scanned the passing landscape for fields or woodland, but mostly there were just parks and gardens and innumerable houses in brick ranks.

She hugged her bag. Ma, crying all the time, had embraced her for ages, then pressed a biscuit tin on her as if she could feed her forever. 'There won't be proper food up there,' she'd said, her voice hoarse. 'You make sure you eat proper, that ration isn't enough. There's scones and cake in there, and a bottle of tea.'

'I'll be all right,' she had said, her own voice wobbling as she faced the terror of being away from home for the first time. 'We'll be well looked after.'

Then Dad had driven her all the way to the station, hardly saying a word beyond commenting on the weather, but she knew he was upset. He hugged her at Exeter station. 'You look after yourself,' he said, then pressed something into her hand. It was two folded pound notes. 'Now, maid, this isn't to spend. That's enough money to get you all the way back, if you need to come home. You hear me? You remember.'

'I will,' she said, standing on tiptoes to kiss his cheek. 'That makes me feel very safe.' She smiled through a mist of tears. 'And I'll write, all the time. I'll let Ma know my new address.'

The train had been so full that people almost fell out when someone opened a door. Most were young men and women, some in uniforms and overalls. Rosie disembarked and spotted a tall man holding a sign that said Waltham Abbey, the factory she had been assigned to.

A few young women, clutching bags, were already assembling. The man, in a grey suit, seemed to have a clipboard and a list. 'Name?' he barked at every new arrival.

When it was her turn she found her mouth was dry, her voice squeaky. 'Rosemary Duke,' she stammered.

'Duke,' he mused, looking down the typed list and ticking her name off with a pencil. 'Join the line for the bus.'

He had already moved on to the woman behind who was jostling Rosie with her heavy suitcase. 'Audrey Dreyfus,' she called out clearly, in a cultured voice, like a radio announcer. 'Come on, man, it's starting to rain.'

As Rosie walked away, she turned around to watch the loud

woman – Audrey – and the man barked something back at her. Unabashed, Audrey walked over to Rosie. 'Honestly, give a man a clipboard and he thinks he's in charge.' Her dark hair was styled in even waves, her wide smile painted in scarlet lipstick. She was fashionably slim, and half a head taller than Rosie.

'Isn't he?' Rosie blurted out.

'He just looks like the bus driver. He could at least leave the door open, it's going to pour down in a minute.'

His list completed, the man unlocked the door to the luggage compartment then opened the door to let the women in. They kept on coming, two then three squeezed onto the cracked leather seats, handbags crammed into overhead wire baskets. Audrey had pushed Rosie onto a seat by the window and sat beside her, making room for a third woman to perch on the end of the seat.

'I hope it's not far,' joked Rosie, her shoulder pressed against the window.

'It's only a couple of miles, I looked it up,' Audrey said, pulling a compact mirror from her pocket and checking her face. She smiled at Rosie. 'Come far?'

'From Devon. You?' Rosie looked around at the row of women standing in the aisle as the driver got in, pushed his way to his seat and started the engine. It spluttered but caught, growling in a cloud of foul-smelling smoke drifting in the front few windows.

'Just the middle of London,' she answered. Her voice was deep and she drew out the end of the words like a film star. 'Chelsea.'

'Hold tight,' he ordered, starting the bus.

The passengers started chattering like a flock of birds, the sound cheering Rosie's spirits. She was fascinated by the view out of the window: the area was crammed with terraces of brick houses with front gardens in tree-lined streets, which soon gave way to woodland and the odd glimpse of grassland.

'I'm Audrey,' the loud young woman said, holding out a cramped hand.

'Rosie Duke. Have you ever been here before?' Rosie asked Audrey.

'I've been to Waltham Abbey, but when I was just a kid. Do you think they let us smoke on the bus?'

There was a chorus of 'no!' from the standing women. 'You'd better wait until you get there,' Rosie said. None of the women in her family had smoked, and it seemed racy and exotic to her.

'You won't be lighting up at the factory, either,' one of the other women said. 'Strictly no matches or lighters in the place. It is full of gunpowder.'

Rosie hadn't thought of that. 'Goodness, I suppose not,' she said.

The bus pulled up and two guards opened double gates for it. They drove across the grassy campus, several buildings looming up ahead. Trucks were being filled with boxes, a small group of young soldiers were marching up and down, and a group of young women in heavy brown overalls and bright headscarves were drinking from mugs outside one of the buildings.

'That will be us, soon,' Rosie said, hardly able to believe how much things had changed in one short day. A magpie cackled overhead and it almost felt like a connection to the moor. She looked around for its mate but it was alone. *One for sorrow...*

'You're not in Kansas any more, Dorothy,' Audrey said, preparing to stand up.

Rosie had at least seen the film in Exeter last year, and she recognised the quote from *The Wizard of Oz*. 'Definitely not,' she said, grabbing her bag and following Audrey off the bus.

'Line up,' a woman shouted, and they did, as the driver

started throwing the bags out of his bus. Rosie wondered if she should be standing at attention.

The woman stepped forward. Tall and well built, she had improbably black hair and wrinkles around her pale blue eyes. 'I am Miss Consett, your manager. I will be doing your training over the next few days, and will help you all settle in. We'll start with a cup of tea, as I'm sure some of you have travelled a long way today.' She glanced down at the list. 'Goodness, one from Edinburgh and one from Devon!' Her scarlet lips curved into a smile. 'Well, ladies, welcome to your new home and thank you for volunteering for this essential war work. Our boys' lives literally depend on this work.' Her smile faded. 'I cannot say strongly enough, this is a place of danger. The rules seem draconian but they save lives. This place is literally the biggest firework in the world. So I say now, if any of you have lighters or matches, this is the last time you will ever bring them to this place. You will wear rubber shoes, you will tie your hair back at all times, you will wear your work uniforms – no turn-ups, no pockets.'

Audrey spoke into Rosie's ear. 'I wonder what they think we'll do. Steal some gunpowder?'

Miss Consett seemed to have heard. 'One of our girls once took home a pair of trousers to wash, then dried them in front of her fire. The powder in her turn-ups caught fire. Fortunately, the blaze was contained to her room. It was lucky the whole place didn't blow up.' Her expression was kind again. 'I know you're a long way from home, and some of you have loved ones at war. We'll do what we can to make your work easier and your accommodation comfortable. But you are here to work and you will work hard. My colleague Theresa is about to come out with a tea trolley, then we can talk to each of you about your lodgings.'

Over a hot mug of tea, Rosie learned that she would be lodging with a family living just a few miles from the factory, in a room with another girl. Audrey was in a hostel half a mile the other way, on the base.

'I wonder if that's far enough to be safe, if the Jerries hit the factory,' Audrey quipped, reaching for one of the biscuits handed around by Theresa.

'It depends where they hit,' Theresa replied. 'Cordite is a gunpowder compound, it burns and explodes. You'll learn all about it in your training tomorrow.' She looked at Rosie and her eyes narrowed. 'You're not a conscript, are you?'

'No. I volunteered.' She could feel her face warming. 'I wanted to help.'

Theresa smiled, not unkindly. 'Oh, my. Your accent is lovely, like a summer holiday I had back in thirty-three. You from Cornwall, love?'

'Devon,' Rosie said, and bit into the biscuit. 'Is there anyone here from the west country?'

'There's girls from all over,' Theresa said, turning away to serve some older women.

Rosie could see she was one of the youngest. Some of the women looked more like her mother's age. 'What about you?' she asked Audrey. 'Did you volunteer?'

'I was volunteered *by* my mother,' Audrey said, and finished her tea. 'She thought I was getting too friendly with my chap.' She grinned over the chipped white cup. 'I was, of course. But I was sick at living at home.'

Rosie smiled back. 'I wonder what we have to do next?'

'I would guess there'll be some sort of welcome speech then a whole load of regulations,' Audrey said, sighing. 'I was training in a uniform factory a few weeks ago before they moved me here.' She winked. 'They thought I was a bad influence.'

She was right about the speech. They were shown to a large canteen building, and another busload of chattering women joined them before the chief engineer came to talk to them. The speech was quite shocking to Rosie – she had no idea that workers had been killed making bullets, let alone missiles and bombs. But it all needed doing and the speech ended with a rousing story about how our fighting men would be helpless without the millions of rounds the filling stations made, and for that they needed explosive powders. The shifts were around the clock, and they would be allocated them when they started. Then they were shown pictures, black and white photographs of injured and dead workers who had broken the rules and nearly blown up whole factories. One girl was sick and another fainted, and both were taken aside to be revived. Rosie felt like she might do both, but steeled herself to breathe deep and look at her shoes.

'That's a horrible trick,' Audrey whispered in her ear.

'I understand, though,' Rosie answered.

They were served a hot meal, and Rosie could barely eat it. Some sort of stew made with what she suspected was offal or, worse, whale meat.

As they filed towards the door twenty minutes later, the chief engineer called out to them. 'And don't forget, what you are doing is secret. You cannot talk about it to anyone. Any post sent from the base must be left unsealed, for our censors to look at. To the world, you are making fastenings for soldier's uniforms. Understood? The last thing we want is German bombers targeting factories full of explosive. Any questions?'

Audrey shot her hand up. 'How much of a bang would there be if they did?'

He smiled as if he wanted to be asked the question. 'Enough to destroy the site, Waltham village, the train line and the church.'

13

PRESENT DAY, MARCH

Zosia leaned against the headrest of the car Leon had borrowed from his neighbour. It was comfortable with leather seats and a good heater against the slight frost in the air. They had set off early, before Hazel and Krys had got up, and the sky was still red with a spring dawn, making the high moorland seem darker. It was a relief to get away from the presence of the house next door, the shouts and slamming doors, the frequent visitors. So many people drove up and away again in just a few minutes, she couldn't ignore the possibility that they were selling *something* illegal.

'Will we be able to get all your stuff in the back?' Leon asked. 'The seats fold down, it's quite big.'

'We will. Or I'll get rid of something,' she said. There was little she could have comfortably lost. Krystof's baby pictures and her books were in bags. She might not need a clothes airer or some of her other domestic items, but she missed her air fryer and coffee machine. 'It's personal things.'

'I'd need a pantechnicon to move just my sport stuff and my vinyl collection,' he said, slowing down behind a dairy tanker with pictures of happy cows on the side.

She wasn't familiar with the word. 'Pantech— what?'

'It's an old word for a removal lorry,' he explained, glancing sideways at her and smiling. 'And that doesn't include my favourite gaming chair and console set-up.'

She smiled at what she thought of as a typical bachelor lifestyle.

She looked forward as they trundled over cattle grids, past intricately stacked stone walls. Something long and thin darted across the road, disappearing into high banks dotted with primroses. 'Is that a rat?'

'Stoat.' He glanced at her and smiled as they slowed down at a corner. 'They eat rats.'

'How far is it to Exeter?'

'About forty-five, fifty minutes into the city centre,' he said.

Zosia thought back to how they had arrived. 'It took more than four hours to get here by three buses,' she said. 'Carrying bags and boxes.'

'Well, hopefully you won't need to go back again.' His expression changed as he negotiated a pothole, and she stared at him. 'Your landlord, is he going to be a problem?'

'The landlord is in London,' she said, her voice tight and strained in her throat. She tried a smile. 'The man I have to deal with is just the building manager. He has a tough job – the building houses people who would otherwise be homeless. There are people awaiting trial, people fresh out of prison, men who've been made homeless. It's sad, really.'

'Not the right place for a woman with a child, I would have thought.' His hands tightened on the steering wheel for a moment. She liked him for that.

'We had nowhere else. The council were trying to find us somewhere better but then I saw the advert for the job.'

'Hazel had other applications for the job, you know,' he said, 'but she ruled them out straight away. She didn't think most young people would want to settle in the middle of nowhere.' He shrugged. 'Maybe it was the fact you came from Poland.'

She thought about the interview. 'She wants me to translate some notes for her. But she hasn't given them to me yet.'

'Casimir's old pages? She told me about that. I think she's a bit worried about what she'll find.'

Zosia had wondered the same thing.

The hedges thinned out to reveal the massive greenness of the moor, punctuated by tiny stone walls everywhere, hardly tall enough to contain a rabbit let alone a sheep. One adventurous lamb stood on top of one, watching them pass.

'Why are there so many walls?' she asked.

'Some are from thousands of years ago, from the Bronze Age, or the Stone Age – or even ten years ago. They don't weather away, they just sit there. You can see little round enclosures. There's one over the next hill.'

As they rattled over the highpoint, it seemed the whole moor was revealed before them. In the distance, bigger tors sat on top of other hills, the shadows of clouds drifting over the greens of the grass and darker shrubs. Leon drove slowly past sheep grazing on the verge and sometimes ambling across the road. He pulled off into a small layby and pointed to the curved stone walls, circles barely a few metres across. 'Were those houses?' she asked incredulously.

'Many centuries ago, I think so,' he said, indicating a rounded valley between them and the peak ahead, topped with stone tors, dotted with the circles. 'They were thatched, with a fire in the middle. They must have been very smoky. You can see some deer, too, in front of that bit of woodland.' They watched the majestic animals stare back for a few moments, then walk into the trees, disappearing between the trunks. He started the car and drove back onto the road. It was empty of other vehicles this early. Shreds of mist veiled the grass alongside them, and rabbits hopped across the highway ahead, unafraid.

'It's so beautiful here,' she murmured to herself.

'Maybe one day, a Saturday maybe, I could take you and Krys to the visitors' centre. People come here for the nature and the prehistoric history. You'd enjoy it more if you knew what you were looking at.'

'Do you go there regularly?' she asked.

'I've been a few times. It could be a fun outing. I think Krys would enjoy it, there's a lot of interactive stuff there and an exhibition on the legends of the moors. *The Hound of the Baskervilles*, Kitty Jay, the hairy hands legend, all of that.' He laughed. 'Some of that might be a bit scary to a six-year-old. But there are stories of giants and fairies and magical animals, too.'

She thought about it. *An outing.*

'It wouldn't be like... a date,' she said, uncertainly.

He glanced at her for a moment. 'I thought you and Krys might enjoy it, that's all.' Before she felt too stupid, before the heat in her chest rose into her cheeks, he added, 'I have a feeling you aren't looking for a date.'

'I'm not,' she said, glancing at him. She really didn't want to upset him. 'I don't even know how long I'm staying.' She managed a small smile. 'But he does love fairies and giants. Hazel's reading him stories from an old book of Polish tales.'

'I'm not quite ready for a date either,' he said, his voice deepening. 'I left a long-term relationship two years ago and ran away to the other end of the country. It's complicated.'

'Me too,' she whispered. She cleared her throat. 'It's a great place to run away to though, isn't it?'

He nodded and drove on for several moments, slowing to rattle over the cattle grid to drive off the moor. 'About twenty minutes to town, now,' he said. 'But just to clarify. If I *was* asking someone on a date, a long way down the line when we knew each other better, it might be you.'

That made her smile, and a different warm feeling spread. 'A long way down the line?' It was an unfamiliar term.

'A long time in the future,' he clarified. 'Your English is amazing, by the way.'

'I trained as a translator. I used to work at the university in Newcastle, where we lived.'

She was jerked back into the past for a second, and it felt like a thump to the chest, filling her with greyness.

'That must have been rewarding.'

'The work was,' she explained. She tried to force a smile at the sight of the trees, still leafless, joining overhead to make a tunnel. 'We used to translate a lot of leaflets, legal and medical information for people. Sometimes we translated for the police or for patients at the hospital.'

She could still remember every word of the information flyer about abusive relationships, and how she could escape the hell that had built up at home.

They reached some traffic lights at the edge of the city. 'What would you like to do first? I have to get my hair cut so I don't look too scruffy. My barber is by the cathedral – I thought you could get a coffee? Then we can go to your old place on the way back.'

'I'll just check the manager can meet me,' she said, bringing her phone out. 'He doesn't normally get up until late anyway.'

The tranquil green space in front of the Norman church dropped a veil of calm over Zosia. She got herself a hot, milky coffee and sat on a bench looking up at the ancient building. It had once been a Catholic cathedral, as all churches had been in England long ago, and it called to her. She had loved going to mass as a child, the solemn drama of it all, the smells and sounds. She had sung in the choir, a competitive environment but which gave a poor girl from the country some status, and it came with a scholarship. There, she had stood among stone saints and sung the beautiful words of praise and love. The priests were universally kind but distant. They acted as if they were not quite human, not quite real.

She couldn't quite see how Leon – friendly, jokey Leon – could dig deep inside to find that solemn faith she had seen and felt as a child. Sometimes, on her own in church in Chocz, she could almost feel Jesus behind her, invisible and loving and overwhelming, his arms reaching behind the choir. She missed that.

Most of the trees were still in bud but two yews stood dark and wide, like they had welcoming arms, too.

When Leon came out of the barber, she almost didn't recognise him. He was dressed in smart black clothes, a jacket, and a shiny white dog collar under his now smooth face. His hair was trimmed short, and even his beads were tucked inside his shirt, just a couple showing at his neck. He smiled broadly at her.

'Ready for the bishop!' he announced, carrying the sports bag he had brought with him.

'Would he mind if you turned up in your normal clothes?'

'He might mind today,' he said. 'I helped Margaret with her chickens this morning when I picked up the car. I seem to have picked up some chicken poo on my trainers and I have wood stain on my jeans.' He smiled again. 'Seriously, he probably wouldn't mind but his colleagues might. They feel that clergy should have some sort of gravitas and standing as leaders in the community.'

'Probably so,' she said, in a small voice.

'My meeting is in the diocese offices. Can you find something to do? I'll be about two hours.'

'I'd like to go into the cathedral,' she said, not sure why it made her feel self-conscious. 'If it's open.'

'I'll text you when I get out, then we can pick up your stuff on the way back.'

'Thank you,' she said, holding his gaze for a long moment. He had really long eyelashes, she noticed. 'And we'll have some lunch.'

His smile broadened. 'Something to look forward to.'

14

MAY 1940

When we were ordered to leave our base in Poznań in 1939, we had marched to the Romanian border, catching lifts off lorries, cars, even carts pulled by horses. The border was open but we were soon herded in groups to a barracks and stripped to our underwear. They stole everything, they were a ragged police force brandishing swords. They changed into our smart uniforms, and gave us their rags. At least, we joked, the Nazis couldn't tell us from the Romanian peasants now. I had been forewarned that we might be searched for valuables, and tucked my Polish Air Force wings, so recently earned, in my shorts. They took my money, my sidearm and argued over the crucifix my mother had given me. In the end, they crossed themselves many times and let me keep it. I bear them no ill will, we knew their own country would be overrun in weeks. These things were my only remaining possessions.

— EXTRACT FROM THE MEMOIR OF
CASIMIR WOJCIK

The first week at the factory was different to anything Rosie had known. She barely had time to do more than work, eat and sleep. The bed was hard, the food dreadful and the work required so much concentration she got headaches. Or maybe that was the chemical smell that followed her home, sat in her hair and nose and made everything taste metallic and sharp.

The solvent that was used to turn wood pulp into nitrocellulose was acidic, and Rosie was warned not to get too close to it. Stirring the mixture was a highly skilled job, several women stirring so smoothly they didn't generate bubbles or agitate it, but Rosie's job was limited to delivering the wood pulp, breathing shallowly through a cloth mask as she unloaded it, then gulping down the fresh air outside as she left. She spent a lot of time trying to remember the smell of heather on the moor, the flash of brilliant yellow lichens on exposed rocks, the taste of the peaty brook that ran down to the valley.

The respite was short; the work was relentless. Even a bathroom break had to be timed between deliveries, and lunchtime was just thirty minutes, with hot food and several mugs of tea or fruit squash to dilute the effect of the chemicals on her system.

Between shifts she travelled by bus, trying not to fall asleep, then back to her room in the Parkers' house. She found talking to her roommate fascinating. Connie worked in an aircraft factory that didn't sound much safer than working at the gunpowder mill. She was so short and petite Rosie couldn't imagine her carrying engine parts, but that was her job. A woman working next to Connie had put a rivet right through her hand, shattering the bones. The paint department had once caught fire, and Connie had been sent home with a bad cough from the smoke.

For the few minutes between chores, shifts and sleep, Rosie wrote letters to Casimir. Now he knew she was in London, his own notes took on an urgency that made her feel sick with longing. *Two training missions, got back quick time. Engine failed, is good I am glider pilot.*

Rosie found it hard to write to him, not knowing how much he could understand and not wanting some other girl to read it to him. *I hope to see you soon* peppered all of her letters. Finally, she sent him a list of her days off. He sent a quick note in reply arranging the meeting. 'Meet Waltham Abbey church, noon, Friday.'

Reading his letters with his limited English was like looking at him through a pinhole; she could barely recall his face, his voice – had she imagined how musical it was? But when he had looped his finger around hers, she had been electrified with feelings and sensations she had never experienced before. She could remember the touch of his skin, the warmth of standing next to him, the blaze of colour in his eyes as he looked at her. The kiss she remembered in her dreams, waking with the soft imprint of his lips on hers.

She couldn't hide her excitement from Audrey at work, nor Connie at home. Living in London, she had soon realised that her home-sewn dresses and best blouse were outdated. Audrey lent her a smart navy dress with polka dots – she had to tack up the hem a couple of inches but the dress suited her. The night before, Connie tied her hair in rags after she washed it in the sink in cold water. 'My mother always says cold water makes your hair shiny,' she said pragmatically, pulling Rosie's natural curls through a comb and curling them more. 'Hopefully, this way it will be curly, not frizzy,' she added, with a scrap of cloth in her teeth.

'I'd like to get a picture taken,' Rosie said impulsively. 'For him to keep. Maybe he could get one, too.' Inside, between the waves of excitement, there was a glowing coal of doubt. Suppose he was disappointed when he saw her? Maybe she would look too young, now he'd met lots of women in England.

Everyone knew the Polish pilots had girlfriends all over north London.

'Stop fidgeting,' Connie said, pulling her hair a little.

'I've only spent a few hours with him. We met one time, for a date.'

'And now you're having another one. Who knows? That might be enough. My parents married after their first few weeks together.'

Rosie swivelled around to look at her, making Connie drop the comb. 'Really?'

'Well, my grandmother realised I was on the way, so they had to get married,' Connie said. 'Turn back to the mirror.' She smiled at Rosie's reflection. 'They are still happily married.'

Rosie managed a weak smile. 'Oh. Good. That's not going to happen, though.'

'Don't overestimate the power of feelings,' Connie said, her hands stalling for a moment. Rosie met her gaze in the glass.

'Connie?'

'It happened to me, too,' she said softly, so no one in the next bedroom would hear them. 'I was seventeen when my son was born.'

'No!' Rosie's hand went to her mouth. 'What happened?'

'Well, feelings happened, that's why I'm telling you,' she said, slowly drawing another curl around her fingers and tying it up. 'I thought I loved him. He was a bit older and exciting, no one had ever liked me that much before. I'm not pretty like you.'

'But you are,' Rosie said, studying her round, pink cheeks and mass of wavy, dark hair. 'Of course he liked you.'

'Well, we did talk about getting married for a little while, but then I noticed how he was always late. And he swore a lot, smoked those horrible French cigarettes. I broke it off, but then I found out...'

'And told your mother?'

Connie shook her head. 'Not at first. She just thought I was getting fatter. Now they're looking after little Freddie, and I'm here.'

Rosie couldn't hide her astonishment; she'd never met someone who'd had a baby out of wedlock, let alone talk about him so matter-of-factly. She wondered how her own mother would deal with a baby. 'Do you see him?'

'Of course! All the time. He's six now, he's started school. My parents let me keep him, no matter what the neighbours thought. They adore him.' She put a hairnet over Rosie's head. 'There. You'll look lovely for Casimir.'

Rosie could only hope. She couldn't get to sleep for excitement, doubts creeping into her head at midnight. Then sheer exhaustion took her off until Connie woke her at seven.

'I've got to go home to see Mum and Freddie,' she said. 'I'll get your rags out.'

At first the curls looked artificial, but they softened over the morning. Rosie did her laundry, as Mrs Parker worked Fridays, so she could hang things on the line that was strung across the garden. It was a patch not much bigger than a room, with grass a foot high. The neighbours had a few chickens. Rosie usually pulled some grass and weeds for them, sorry that they were scratching around on soiled mud.

While her clothes dried, she wrote her weekly letter to her mother, with lots of details about how important (but safe) the work was, and how she had made some nice friends. She didn't mention the many things that had shocked her, such as injuries sustained in the factory, girls flirting with the male workers and young women who got drunk and kissed men in the street.

By the time Rosie had styled her hair again, put on her borrowed dress and her best shoes, it was past eleven. She bought an apple from the corner shop to eat on the bus out to the abbey.

She knew the timetable as it was also the route to her work, and knew it got in before twelve. She was impatient to see him, to get that first moment over with. She had imagined it a hundred, maybe a thousand times. He would look at her as he had at the church, or as he had at the prison infirmary, like she was a rare flower.

The bus was a few minutes late and it terminated less than half a mile from the abbey, at an old church surrounded on one side by factory, and on the other by woodland. She walked past the entrance to the factory campus, one of the guards giving her a wave, and alongside the fence.

As she walked around a bend in the road, lined with houses and shops, the magnificent church rose up ahead of her. A man, seated on the low wall of the churchyard, stood up.

She hardly recognised him at first glance. His hair was longer, bleached by the sun, his eyes like cornflowers. He was smiling, holding out his hands. The buzzing in her ears grew louder and she almost stumbled into him.

He must have been encouraged because he kissed her, and she flung her arms around his neck until a tutting from a passing woman made them draw apart. Her face was so hot she knew she was blushing. He put his arm around her waist and led her to the row of shops.

'Cas, I'm so happy to see you,' she said, brushing a tear from her cheek.

'No cry.' He stopped and pulled a handkerchief from the pocket of his blue uniform. He dabbed her face carefully as she stared up at him. He seemed taller, or maybe he was just standing taller now he wasn't injured. A pink line running into his hairline was all that remained of the crash.

'You're really here.' She still felt dizzy, and took a deep breath. 'How are you?'

'Good. Good, tired,' he said, staring at her face, into her eyes, looking at her mouth...

When the kiss ended she let him lead her by the hand towards a tea shop.

'Have cake,' he said, opening the door for her.

A girl smiled at him as she flicked her fringe out of her eyes. 'Hello, Casimir.' She was pretty, auburn pigtails around her face.

'Hello, Daisy,' he said, grinning at her. 'This is my Rosie.'

'I saved the best table for you,' she said, smiling at Rosie but without the enthusiasm she had given Cas.

'This good café,' he said. 'Friends brought me one time. Good tea here,' he said, taking Rosie's coat off her shoulders and passing it to Daisy without glancing at her. Daisy had a bit of a flounce in her step as she hung the coat on a stand by the door.

'It looks nice but...' she leaned forward to whisper, 'I think the cafés in Devon are nicer. Friendlier.'

He still hadn't taken his eyes off her. He lifted one of her hands to his lips. 'Beautiful Rosie.'

'Cas,' she whispered, pressing her other hand to a hot cheek. 'Not here.'

He turned her hand over, pressed a burning kiss into her palm that made her heart falter, then smiled and let it go. 'Cake here, very good,' he said, shaking out a napkin.

It was a pretty place, it had flowery wallpaper and real linen napkins, and looked expensive. She looked at a chalkboard on the wall. Cake was sixpence a slice with a cup of tea. 'It's very expensive,' she whispered. 'Too much money.'

He patted his uniform breast pocket. 'I pay, English money,' he said.

She put her napkin in her lap and folded her hands on top of it. 'Well, maybe you should save up,' she said, a little primly.

His brow wrinkled as he tried to work out what she was saying. 'Save?'

'Keep money for your future,' she said. 'You know, for after the war.' The moment she heard herself she gulped back a lump in her chest. What was he saving for? He could be dead in a few weeks.

'Save… for wedding?' he said, his eyes sparkling. '*Dom*.' He struggled to explain the word, then outlined a roof and walls with his hands. 'You, me, *dom*.'

House? Her breath had caught in her throat. 'Maybe,' she managed finally. 'When we know each other better.'

He seemed to understand, because he frowned, but the girl was already back to take their order. 'Tea, Casimir?' she asked. 'We haven't got any lemons but Dad has lemon balm in the garden. How about you, *miss*?' she said, the word drawled out slowly.

'Tea with milk would be lovely,' Rosie said, lifting her chin. 'What cakes do you have?'

'Scones, we've got a bit of jam. Or fruit cake.'

Rosie suspected that the scones would be very far from the light, buttery rounds her mother made, dripping with cream and fruit. 'I'll have a slice of cake,' she said, thinking of the one shilling and ninepence in her pocket, all she had left after her lodgings and stamps to write her daily letters to Cas.

'I too,' Cas said, then corrected himself. 'Me too. Thank you, Daisy,' then turned away from her.

Rosie could see that for him, Daisy didn't exist, no matter how pretty she was or how small her waist or curly her hair. He only had eyes for her. It was intoxicating, she couldn't help smiling.

'How has work been?' she asked. He had little to say in his letters about flying, except that he was getting very frustrated at not going on many proper missions. The whole country seemed to be holding its breath at what the Germans would do next, but the news coming out of France was dreadful.

'I have passed flying test,' he said, shrugging. 'Easy.'

'Are the planes similar to the ones you used to fly in Poland?' she asked. When he looked puzzled, she clarified. 'Same as?'

He laughed at that. 'Hurricanes fly very good,' he said, demonstrating with a hand. 'New planes. But upside down.'

It was her turn to frown. 'Upside down? You aren't flying upside down?'

He demonstrated flying a plane. 'Controls,' he said. 'Upside down.' He pulled back his hands and said, 'Go up. In Poland, go down.'

She grasped his hands. 'That sounds so dangerous.'

'No. Learn fast,' he said, grinning, squeezing her hands back. 'Very safe. Ready to fight now.'

'Have you had to fight at all?'

His expression changed, as if a memory of combat had come to mind. 'Not since France,' he said. 'Soon. Maybe next week.'

'Oh, Casimir. I'm so worried you'll get shot at.'

He shook his head. 'I worry too. You go' – he mimed an explosion – 'boom.'

She shook her head. 'It's all very safe. We have safety officers who go around every day.' She'd got used to telling the same lies in her letters home. *It's all completely safe.* She couldn't write about when one of the girls had inhaled some vapours that shouldn't have been there and collapsed, or the two girls who had been hurt when a box of guncotton ignited in transit. The sight of their burned faces had given her nightmares, but there was nothing in the local papers.

'Is war, yes?' he said, his voice dropping to a reassuring rumble. 'This why we get married.'

She couldn't help putting her hands on his again. 'But we hardly know each other.' He looked like he didn't understand. 'Too soon,' she explained. 'More time.'

'But soon,' he said and let go as Daisy brought over their teas. Cas liked his with sugar, which she had brought over especially. The cake was dry and lacking in both sugar and fruit, but was a nice change. She immediately missed the cakes she baked with Ma at home, her mother's apron, her father's laugh.

She looked down at her food to hide the unshed tears but he had noticed. He lifted her chin with one finger and dried her eyes with his napkin. 'Get married, soon,' he said. It wasn't a question.

'Let me talk to my parents,' she answered. 'I don't know. Give me more time.'

She could see he didn't understand, not the words but the sentiment. He looked like he would have scooped her off to a church there and then. But he nodded. 'Time. Soon.'

'And we need to see each other more,' she said, and that brought out a smile like the sun. 'You must tell me what days.'

'I tell you hours,' he said, looking at her hair, her eyes, her mouth as if he was filming her for his memory.

'Oh! And I want you to get a picture for me.' He shrugged and she mimed taking a photo. 'Photograph.'

'*Fotografia?*' he said, miming pressing a button on a camera. 'Yes. And you.'

She smiled back. 'Yes, I'll get a picture taken. *Fotografia*. I'll send it in a letter.'

15

PRESENT DAY, MARCH

The weather had kept Zosia indoors but she longed to get out in the garden. The back was dotted with sheaves of tall leaves and stars of yellow celandines. Out the front windows, low clouds drifted in, obscuring the tor and the hills, sometimes blanketing the house, the fog looking like cotton wool against the windows.

Zosia had been busy working inside Foxglove Cottage, cleaning, sorting through things to be donated or disposed of, and bringing old furniture and textiles back to life. She enjoyed time with Hazel, and the older woman couldn't have been kinder but she hadn't suggested translating her father's pages yet. Zosia loved dusting the silver-framed photographs over the fireplace, the images faded into pale greys. A handsome boy in uniform, cap pushed back from his forehead, grinning. A pretty girl, just a teenager, with wild curls and a neckerchief. Zosia asked Hazel about the pictures over their coffee break.

'Oh, that's the first picture my mother ever had of my father,' Hazel said, smiling down at the pictures, lightly touching the glass. 'They were so young. Eighteen and twenty-one.'

'They look so happy. Does he write about this time in his papers?'

Hazel's smile faded. 'Maybe we could find out. Perhaps we could start this evening?'

Zosia smiled. 'I'd like that.'

Zosia left early to pick up Krys and called in at the little shop.

'I was wondering what wine Hazel might like?' she asked the woman by the till. 'She's been so kind to us I thought I would treat her.'

The woman was short, and her dark bob was streaked with white. She stared for a long moment. Her badge said her name was Geraldine and she was the manager. 'Well, that's a kind thought. This is the one she normally picks.'

Zosia studied the bottle, which had a cartoon cat on the front. 'I normally pick wine by the label,' she said, filling in the silence.

'How you getting on with your neighbours at the bunga-low?' Geraldine asked after a long pause. 'I sometimes see one of the women in here with the children, but I'm always worried the kids are stealing something.'

'They aren't very pleasant,' Zosia admitted. 'Even the boys seem unfriendly. Rude, even.'

'They aren't from your neck of the woods, then?'

Oh. Zosia's stomach dropped and she felt like an outsider again. It happened at the school, too – everyone was very pleasant but they avoided conversation. 'No. I don't know where they come from. But it's not Poland.'

'Hazel's dad was from Poland,' Geraldine said, scanning the wine, then turning to take something off a shelf. 'Such a lovely man. Here, you'll want this.'

She handed her a large bar of chocolate.

'I don't know...' Zosia said, looking at it.

'Go on. My treat. The wine's eight pounds.'

Zosia stared at her. 'I don't understand.'

Geraldine handed her the bottle, wrapped in some pink tissue. 'If you're going to drink that bottle of Merlot with Hazel, and don't eat anything, you'll end up drunk as a fox in an orchard,' she said. She smiled at Zosia's expression. 'Welcome to the village, lovey. It takes a while for us locals to get to know new people, but we get there in the end. Your little boy is a delight, he's been playing with my granddaughter, Allie. I hope he can come round to ours to play with the animals one day. Allie's always talking about him.'

Zosia smiled. 'I thought he had started to make friends. He looks happier coming out of school.'

'Now those boys have been suspended again,' Geraldine said, holding out the card machine for Zosia to pay. 'They're proper tearaways. Allie's scared of them, I bet Krys is, too.'

'I'll keep an eye on him. But, yes, a playtime would be lovely. I'll talk to him and arrange a date.'

She climbed into the car feeling somehow lighter. The people in the tiny village had been... distant. Watchful, but always ready with a nod of greeting or a small smile. Now something had shifted. Maybe Hazel had said something, or perhaps Leon had.

At the school gate, one of the other mums approached her. 'Toby's having a birthday party next Saturday. I hoped Krys would come. We're at Cawsey Farm, just up the lane towards Holne.' She handed over a home-made invitation on colourful card. *Nell, Jimmy and Toby invite...* 'I'm Nell. Of course, you'll be very welcome, too. We'll sit and natter while the kids play in the haybarn and chase the donkeys.'

Natter. Not a word she knew but she smiled broadly. 'I'd love to. Should we bring anything?' Parties were more formal back in Newcastle, when Krys had started school.

Nell shook her dark curls out. 'Could you bring something for the mothers to share? Maybe something savoury, there's a lot of sweet things already promised.'

'I could bring some *pyzy*, steamed potato dumplings. I was going to make some for Hazel, I know her dad used to make them.'

'Dumplings would be lovely! I remember Cas's cooking at the school fetes, when I was a child! Doughnuts and angel wings. Amazing.'

Zosia looked at the card again. 'Who is everyone else?'

'Let me introduce you properly,' she said, turning to the other parents just as the children started to run out onto the small playground. 'Leila, Frankie and the dad is Pete, we all have kids in Krys's class, he's a complete sweetie. I'm picking up a couple of strays today – we often do a big school run.' She put her head on one side as Toby threw his arms around her middle. 'Hi baby, I gave Krys's mummy the invitation, and she's bringing him next Saturday.'

'I'm Zosia,' she said, speaking clearly enough to be heard by the others.

'We know, maid. You've been the biggest topic of conversation for weeks. It's nice to have someone new in the village.'

Zosia's eyes were prickling. 'Thank you.'

Back at the house, Zosia and Krys found Hazel sitting on the living room sofa gazing out at the rocky peaks and heathery slopes. She was surrounded by albums and loose photographs.

'I thought you and I might have a grown-up evening before we start on your father's pages,' Zosia said, brandishing the bottle. 'Geraldine insisted on adding a bar of chocolate as a gift.'

'That's a lovely idea,' Hazel said, her voice rough. 'I've just been looking at old pictures. Which is silly. It always makes me cry.'

Zosia sat at the other end of the sofa as Krys scampered upstairs. 'I think it's lovely,' she said. 'What are the photographs of?'

'Here, mostly. Did you know we used to live at Duke's Farm? After the war, my parents started their married life there. Then they bought this house at auction – it was an absolute wreck, burned out. Dad pretty well rebuilt it from the ground up.' She pulled out a picture of a tall man with bushy white hair, grinning into the camera. He had vivid blue eyes and a gap between his teeth. 'This was my dad, Casimir. He was about seventy then.'

'He came here during the war?'

'He was in the Polish Air Force, they had nowhere else to go to fight the Nazis after Poland was overrun and the rest of Europe surrendered. After the war he wanted to return but it was too dangerous.'

'The Soviets were in charge by then,' Zosia said. 'I was born after communism.'

'Of course you were. Where in Poland?'

'Just outside Chocz, Pleszew County.' She could picture their communist-era apartment, made of grey concrete. It had cracked windows, bright fabrics and painted wooden furniture handed down from her grandparents.

'Is that anywhere near Poznań? I think my dad was from there.'

Zosia mentally translated kilometres to miles. 'About fifty miles or so. I've been there a couple of times. I sang at the cathedral with the choir in a music competition.'

Hazel looked away, her eyes shining. When she looked back, her face seemed resolute. 'I'm looking forward to you reading my dad's pages. I don't know why he wouldn't talk about them to me, but I think it's time I found out. What's the worst thing he could have done? I know he fought in the Battle of Britain. He won medals for bravery.'

'I would love to help,' she said. 'But it might be a bit painful for you, he must have seen some terrible things.' Zosia remembered all the stories she had been taught at school, of the atrocities of the invasion and the heroes who fled abroad to fight the Nazis.

'In that case, it's a good job you brought wine and chocolate,' Hazel said, smiling. She had the same gap between her teeth that Casimir had in the pictures.

'Let's have a proper go tomorrow. I'll get all the papers on the table, and you can sort through them.'

Zosia left Hazel to fill the dishwasher and went upstairs to bath Krys. He was happily splashing around with his toy boats when she noticed something going on next door.

There was a lot of shouting, but it was sort of hissed back and forth between two men; they were repeating each other, getting angrier. She rested her phone on the frosted sash window, open an inch to let out the steam, and pressed record. One was shouting in English, the other arguing back in another language. She couldn't work out what it was. It was fired fast, like Italian, but she knew a bit of that language and it lacked something, and it sounded scared. She couldn't pick out one recognisable word, yet it sounded familiar.

She shampooed Krys's hair into a peak, and he giggled as she poured water over his head from a jug. 'Tickles!' he shouted.

The shouting outside stopped, and the English man growled, 'Just get inside!' She carried on pouring as some sort of scuffle ensued. The sound of flesh hitting flesh made her jump. Someone had been hit.

'Let's get the bubbles out of your ears,' she said over the sounds outside but Krys had already curled forward, dropping his chin onto his chest.

She finished washing off the shampoo. 'Do you want to come out now?' He did a little nod, and she reached around to the old radiator for one of Hazel's fluffy towels. 'Let's read some more Paddington Bear tonight,' she suggested, patting him down a little as he shuffled into her bedroom. 'Or the fairy tales.'

'Can I sleep in your bed tonight?' he asked, his voice soft and flat. She tousled his hair with a corner of the towel.

'If you really want to. Wouldn't you rather be tucked up in your own bed?'

He shook his head, spattering her with water. Curled into a ball, he looked younger than six.

Zosia retrieved her phone from the bathroom and shut the window, relieved to find that the men had gone inside, then collected the book from Krys's bedside cabinet.

'They're gone,' she said, pressing a kiss onto his forehead.

'Are they bad people?' he whispered, as if they could hear him. 'Mama, are they bad people like Daddy?'

'Daddy's not a bad person,' she said, her lip quivering for a moment. 'Daddy is an angry person. But not with you, just with me.'

'He hurt us.'

She put her arms around him, felt his head butt against her chest like a baby. 'Just once,' she murmured. 'He got too angry. That's why we moved away.'

He pulled away to look up at her, his long eyelashes clumped together. 'He shouted. He hit you. And me.'

This really wasn't the time she would have chosen for Krys to talk about the violent incident that had ended her marriage. A therapist had told her, just let him talk, but in the eighteen months since it happened, he had always refused to speak about it.

'He did, baby,' she said, her voice choked into a squeak.

'I don't want those angry men to come and hurt us,' he said, with more strength in his voice than she had. 'To hit you or Auntie Hazel.'

She sat with him in her arms for a long minute. 'I will ask someone to help if they get angry at us,' she said. 'Maybe they are upset about something. Perhaps they will move away. We just need to stay away from them.'

'I was sitting by my window,' he said, looking away. 'And one of them did a rude thing with his hand. And shouted something.' He demonstrated someone raising a middle finger.

'When was this?' she asked him, appalled.

'At the weekend. I told the *domowik*, then I felt better. Because brownies are magic, they look after us.'

He had been quiet on Saturday, sitting with them rather than playing with his toys upstairs. She had wondered if he was going down with something, and Hazel had baked cheese straws with him to cheer him up. It broke her heart to think he didn't feel safe at home.

'Krys, you need to tell me if anything upsetting happens. Straight away. You need to tell *me* as well as the brownie.'

He allowed her to pull a clean pyjama top over his head. 'I used to be scared when Max was yelling at the old house.'

Her neighbour in the rooming house used to get drunk, thump on everyone's doors and sing at the top of his voice.

'We don't live there any more. And we're never going back,' she said, with conviction.

'We might have to if the bad man is too scary,' he said, his voice small, as he pulled his pyjama bottoms on. They had steam trains on, they all had names but she had never seen them in Poland and couldn't name them. 'We ran away before.'

'We will not move,' she said, squeezing his shoulders gently. 'Auntie Hazel and I would call the police. And we have friends in the village now, I could call Father Leon to come over, he used to be a policeman. Did you know that? You'll like him. And he is super big, like a bear.'

That made Krys smile as he crept into bed, pulling up the quilt around his shoulders. 'Bigger than Paddington?' he said over a yawn.

'Bigger than the bear in the forest hut, from Auntie Hazel's book,' she said.

16

MAY 1940

At Northolt we were joined by two old comrades from Poznań,
Gabriel Walenty and Eckert Stanisław. Both were pleased to
see me, Gabriel was moved to tears to see someone he knew
from our escape from Poland. But they seemed afraid, too.
There were secrets they did not want me to talk about, and me,
I couldn't yet speak either. I have never spoken about what
happened in Hungary. We were all tainted by war.

— *EXTRACT FROM THE MEMOIR OF*
CASIMIR WOJCIK

The day after she met Casimir, Rosie was moved to another
section. She was so quick and deft they wanted her on the more
dangerous job of handling TNT, and she was told she would get
ten more shillings a week. The raw material was greasy with
acid and sometimes oily drops of nitroglycerine, depending on
the way it was made and the weather conditions. As the workshop heated up it became less stable.

Audrey was working alongside her for a change, but they
were forbidden to talk – not only to prevent them breathing in

excessive amounts of chemicals, but also because all their concentration had to be on their task of wrapping the pieces of explosive in protective paper. By the time they got out for the meal break, after six because they were doing the late shift, Rosie couldn't wait to talk to her.

'I met him,' she said, bouncing in the queue for food. 'I had tea and cake with Casimir.'

'Your Polish pilot? I thought he might have met someone else by now,' Audrey said, holding her hand as if she had an invisible cigarette. 'I wish I could have a ciggie.'

'Why would you think he would meet someone?'

Audrey made a face. 'My chap, you know, the man I was seeing before? He hasn't even written to me, after I sent him three letters.'

'Oh. I'm so sorry.' Rosie could almost feel the sadness in her chest at the thought of losing Cas. 'I did wonder a tiny bit. Not that he hasn't written, but there are so many women at the airbase. But he wants to get *married*.' She had lain awake trying to find the words for a letter to her mother.

'Look, you're young. If I had married my first chap, I'd probably have three children and a heap of debts by now. Take your time. Wait until the war is over.'

'But he might not make it through the war,' Rosie said, her voice small in her throat. 'They're flying every day now.' She could only nod at the woman serving the meals – shepherd's pie again with some olive-green peas. Something square was draped in custard and added to her tray. She stopped to pick up a large cup of tea; the safety officer always wanted the women to drink plenty in case they absorbed some poison. Rosie never took chances, she always used gloves, but many didn't, getting acid burns on their hands and goodness knows what else.

'Maybe he won't,' Audrey said, and tears sprang into Rosie's eyes. 'You've got to be realistic, it's a war. Or he might make it through and *you* might get blown to bits.'

'That just makes me think we should be married anyway.'

Audrey swallowed a mouthful of the lukewarm mash. 'So, marry him, then.' She looked bored. It wasn't the first time they had had a similar conversation but that was before she'd seen him again.

'My parents won't agree. I've got three years before I'm twenty-one.' Rosie attempted some of the grey rags of meat in gravy.

'You don't have to stand up in church to act married,' Audrey said. 'You could sleep together, even live together if you want. It's not illegal.'

'Oh, I couldn't,' she said. 'No one would rent to an unmarried couple, anyway.'

'Buy a ring. Call it practice for marriage. Try it out, see if you suit.'

Rosie was shocked at the idea, her heart skipping about in her chest. But the thought warmed her as well. 'My mother would never forgive me.'

Audrey pointed a fork at her. 'Then don't tell her. Just make sure you don't get pregnant.'

Rosie was sure she was bright red by now, her cheeks burning with heat at the thought of going to bed with Casimir.

'I know you're a virgin—'

'I lived on a farm, I do know how sex happens,' Rosie snapped back.

'I've got a leaflet. Marie Stopes, all that sort of thing.'

Rosie turned back to her pudding, so short of sugar it was almost savoury. 'The food's not very good today.'

'Juliet always does such a good job, but we've got Bronwen today.'

Rosie sighed. 'I just feel like we're wasting the little time we have together. We can't even be really alone. We went for a walk around the churchyard, we kissed...' The warmth returned to her cheeks as she remembered the kisses. 'But he won't respect me if I go to a hotel or something with him. He won't want to marry a girl like that.'

'Maybe he won't. Then you'll have learned a lot about him, won't you?'

Rosie pushed her plate away and glanced at the clock. 'Oh, look at the time, I'll hardly have time to use the bathroom.'

Audrey followed her to the ladies', with its long ranks of deep sinks that the girls used to scrub the chemicals off their skin before changing to go home.

On the way back to the workroom, Rosie made a decision. 'I suppose I could talk to him about it.'

'When do you meet him next?'

'I've swapped shifts so I can see him the Thursday after next.' She felt a jiggle in her stomach, excitement and nervousness. 'I don't want him to think I'm a...' She didn't have the right word. 'I mean, I want him to respect me. I just don't want to waste our time together.'

However much time we have left.

When she got back to the Parkers' house, she started a letter to her parents.

> *I have met up with Casimir. We went for a lovely walk by the church and for tea at a local café. You wouldn't have liked the cakes, Ma, a bit dry, but it's nice to have something different.*
>
> *I know you said we should just be friends until after the war, but things are so different here. Some of his friends have already had accidents in his planes, pilots have died. Time is so short for us, I feel we should be married in the time we have. Maybe it won't be very long, but I want to spend all the time we're not working, together. It would be lovely to cook together, or just spend a few hours on our own. We're closely chaperoned when we're at work or in digs, and he's working so hard,*

training in new planes, learning English so fast so he can understand commands.

The other pilots go on the town and meet girls, drink beer, go dancing, but Cas sits at home over his books, learning English and also all about the planes he will be flying. They are scrambled for ops – that's what he calls being sent up in his plane to look for enemy planes – more and more.

I miss him so much, and now I'm afraid that he...

She couldn't write any more without tears hitting the paper. She dried her face and added a final line.

I love him so much, Ma. I never thought I could love anyone as much as I do you and Dad.

17

PRESENT DAY, MARCH

The following evening, Zosia and Hazel had sorted through the first entries of Casimir's memoir. They were not about his childhood. It was as if Casimir's first important memories had been the invasion of Poland and crashing his plane in front of Rosemary Duke.

... *All I could see against the sky was a halo of hair and her eyes. Oh, my, her eyes, bright like headlights, looking down at me...*

'But what happened between the start of the war in Poland, and that crash? It was months.'

Zosia flipped through some of the papers. Many were held together with rusted paperclips, as if in chapters.

'I think he must have gone backwards and forwards in time,' she said. 'Look, this one is about living in Poznań, with his mother and father. Three sisters...'

'Sabina, Kasia and Angelika,' Hazel said softly. 'Kasia died during the war, he never said how.'

Zosia read the next few lines, her mind sorting out the grammar. He knew. *How do I tell this to Hazel?*

'He did find out eventually,' she said. 'He got the story in

1986. He wrote to Angelika, she was the youngest. She was still alive then?'

'She died ten years ago. He blamed himself for leaving his family, to fight for his country.' Hazel looked out over the garden. 'I know his father was shot in 1940. I believe he took up arms against the invaders, but I don't know whether that was the Nazis or the Soviets. His mother looked after her family as best she could.'

Zosia looked down at the yellowed, faintly typed sheets. They smelled of old smoke and tobacco and long-deposited dust. The edges were just starting to soften with use.

'It was a terrible time,' she said, remembering the history lessons all Polish children were required to take in school. 'My *babcia* told me what had happened to her parents, her family, torn in half by the war and the occupation afterwards. My *dziadek*, my father's father, was sent to work in East Germany and never came home.' She read through the next few lines. 'Kasia died when the Germans invaded.' She didn't want to put into words the agony Casimir had described, raw at discovering he had left his sister to a pack of ravening, rapist wolves.

Hazel put her hand over Zosia's, her strong grip warming her. 'Listen. I suggest you read one chapter at a time, maybe record your translation line by line. You can warn me when there's an especially emotional section.'

Zosia lifted a page up. 'This one is a happy one. They were trying to persuade Rosie's parents to agree to their marriage.' The two pages were filled with his recollection of complete happiness. 'He adored her. What would that be like, to have someone love you so much? I don't know it.'

'Me neither,' Hazel said, breaking off some of the chocolate Geraldine had given Zosia. She poured the remains of the bottle into two glasses. 'I've played the field, I even lived with someone for twenty years, but it's mostly been – what do they call it? Friends with benefits.'

Zosia could feel a little blush warming her cheeks. Her mother would have died rather than mention sex, but her own grandmother? She had been more open. She had never trusted Declan either; she had good instincts. Zosia wished she had listened.

'What happened with this twenty-year relationship?'

'Harry? He got so boring. He was a bit older than me, wanted to retire and settle down in the suburbs. That was when Mum and Dad were both running this place.'

Zosia couldn't help laughing. 'I can't see you settling down in the suburbs!'

'I went to teach English overseas for a year – South Korea – and I loved the culture. I loved the people, the place, the cities, I was even toying with living there. Harry broke it off when I suggested it. He barely said goodbye.' She grimaced. 'I think I only said that to get rid of him. Anyway, Mum asked me to come home and I realised Dad wasn't well. He was getting really tired, losing weight.'

'What was he like? As a man?'

'Kind. Loving and kind. But he carried something inside him, like a fear that it could all be taken away. He stored food. He had knives in the house, in case someone broke in when he was away with work or friends.'

Zosia nodded. 'My great-grandmother was the same. When she died, the care home said she was saving bread under her pillow.'

'The war was brutal, wasn't it? My mother always suspected there were things he couldn't talk about, horrible things.' Hazel finished her wine. 'There's some whisky in the dining room, if you want some.'

'I really would. Just a nip.'

As she returned with the dusty bottle, Zosia remembered the angry exchange between the neighbours. 'What do we really know about the men next door?'

'I know there are two main ones, two women who look half their age, and the two boys. Sometimes younger men visit and stay in the camper, and sometimes they drive it away for a day or two.' Hazel pointed into the kitchen. 'I make notes when they come and go,' she said. 'I don't trust them. I told Leon and he suggested we contact the police if they do anything.'

'I can't work out what language one of their visitors was speaking,' Zosia admitted. 'A romance language, I think, a bit like Italian.'

She typed 'romance languages' into her phone. 'The main ones are French, Italian, Spanish, Portuguese and Romanian. That's it! I *have* heard it before – we had a Romanian neighbour in the flats where I grew up, she used to babysit me.' She pulled up the sound file on her phone and turned the volume up.

Hazel leaned forward, listening intently, then flinching at the sound of the blow. 'You should show that to Leon. He might be able to work out what's going on. Maybe get a translation.'

'I don't want to aggravate them,' Zosia said, shivering despite the whisky. 'We don't want them to hurt us. I-I've been hurt. Krys saw – I don't want him to go through that again.'

'We won't let them,' Hazel said, squeezing her hand. 'But we will lock up the house every night. Let me talk to Leon, at least. *We'll* get the advice of a policeman, but all *they* will see is a hippy vicar.'

18

MAY 1940

I begged Rosie to marry me. I knew every mission could be my last, and I wanted us to spend as much time together as possible. Deep inside, I was scared of what would happen if the Germans did invade England. I knew what had happened back home, farmers dead in their fields, women pushing prams on the roads strafed by the Luftwaffe. I dreamed over and again of my mother and sisters trying to live under the terrible new regimes, first German then Russian. Only once had my rage overwhelmed me into violence, and I kept the details from my family, even my Rosie.

— *EXTRACT FROM THE MEMOIR OF CASIMIR WOJCIK*

Rosie's mother wrote back after a few days. Perhaps she had taken the time to talk to Dad about the idea of getting married. Perhaps she was shocked herself. But the letter was long and emotional.

I can't agree to you getting married at such an age, and in such circumstances...

Rosie folded the letter, written over several sheets, not able to read on yet. She was late for work, and if she delayed any longer she would be late. She tucked it into her pocket and ran for the bus.

There was a strange excitement on the street, and people were talking about planes taking off at dawn. With a lurch, she realised that as she had been sleeping, Cas's squadron could have been called out to defend the country from an attack. They had been declared fully operational now.

At the bus stop, she turned to a woman who seemed to know a lot. 'Is this the Northolt airbase people are talking about?'

'The Polish squadrons, yes, they all took off at six this morning. The airbase is half empty.' The rest of the people in the line were listening. 'My daughter works there, she's a telegraphist and phone operator. Sounds like the Jerries are coming.'

There had been so much in the newspapers about German forces massing on the coast after they had driven British forces out at Dunkirk. The fear of invasion was building.

When she got to the gunpowder mills, there was a new protocol. Break times were to be taken in the bomb shelter, all air raid warnings were to be taken seriously and the work had to be locked down at each siren. For Rosie, that meant packing all wrapped TNT in metal boxes with wheels, ready for one of the technicians to roll away into a safer area, while the raw material was placed elsewhere. It would slow them down to keep stopping, all while the ministry kept bombarding them with posters and messages about working harder and making more ammunition for the forces.

The first siren had them scurrying for safety, and Rosie could hear aeroplanes flying overhead. They weren't the familiar rumbles they were used to, these were sharper, more metallic, and sounded darker and more powerful.

'What are they?' she whispered to Audrey once they found a place on a bench underground.

'Julia says they're Heinkel bombers,' Audrey said, her face white. Rosie had noticed her getting paler over the last week and wondered if she was going down with something. 'If they hit the main stores, we're going to be blown to kingdom come.'

'They are spreading the new chemicals around a bit more,' Rosie said. 'That's what they said when they brought in the TNT this morning. In case a German bomber gets through.'

'TNT's not the problem,' Audrey said. 'I'm making nitro this morning. My hands have been shaking so much I'm going to blow myself up.'

Rosie squeezed Audrey close. 'Catering have rustled up some biscuits, that will help.'

'I'd kill for a cigarette right now. I might ask if I can go back to the changing room, have a quick fag.'

'You brought some with you?' Rosie was shocked. 'No, you'll get in trouble.'

'At this point, I don't care.'

Workers sneaking in cigarettes and matches could be fined or even imprisoned. You never knew how much explosive chemicals had leached into the work uniforms.

Rosie brought out the letter she had transferred to her overall pocket. 'I heard from my mother.'

'I'll bet she was shocked at your plan to get married. Or, you know, worse.'

Rosie opened the letter and scanned down the first page. *Dad would be so disappointed, it would be hard living with someone who doesn't share your values, language or religion...* She turned over the page.

'She's just really worried about me. She says I'm infatuated because I saved him from a crashed plane.'

'Maybe you are.'

Rosie took a moment to consider it before she shook her

head. 'I can't explain it. It's *him*. It was still there in the tea shop, and walking around the graveyard. We just fit together.'

'Does she know you might get together anyway?'

Rosie kept reading. 'I don't think so. But she does warn against getting carried away by a smart uniform.'

'She knows what you're considering,' Audrey said with satisfaction. 'She was young once.'

The writing on the last page was messier. It looped and scrawled as if her mother had written it in haste. *If you are really sure, really certain that you want to get married even over all of our concerns and arguments, then we must meet him first and talk about it.*

Rosie could hardly believe it. 'She might consent! At least, she will if I can prove how serious I am about Cas.'

Audrey took the proffered sheet. 'If you don't get blown up in the meantime.'

'I have a few days' leave coming at the end of the month. We could visit them then.' *If Cas survives his duties, if he isn't shot down and captured.* She hardly noticed the manager and safety officers coming in to issue the all-clear.

19

PRESENT DAY, MARCH

On Saturday morning, Zosia picked up the mail and was surprised to see something unmarked with a name or address. It just had a single letter on the front. Z.

She opened it, puzzled. Maybe it was something from the school; no one else knew where she was living...

'Leave him alone.' It was printed, just three words, but her knees gave way and she sat on the porch floor.

Declan.

She fought back a wave of bile in her throat, her heart leaping in her chest, her hands suddenly cold. Had he found her? Was he staying nearby, watching her?

Who did he mean by 'him'? Surely it couldn't be Leon? But there wasn't anyone else. Anyway, if Declan contacted her, surely it would be through a lawyer to get access to Krystof, just to drive her crazy. She pushed herself to her feet, smelling the coffee and toast Hazel was cooking, listening to Krys singing in the kitchen. She tucked the message into her pocket and composed herself, fixing a smile on her face before taking the rest of the post to Hazel.

. . .

After breakfast, Zosia opened the door to Leon, laden with a pile of boxes and a carrier bag that stank of onions. He handed the bag to her, and walked through the hall, calling to Hazel.

'If there's coffee on, I could do with some. I've finally totted up the church accounts. I hate paperwork.'

Hazel put her head around the kitchen door. 'I forgot to say, Leon is coming to help with the garden,' she said, unnecessarily.

Krys bounced down the stairs and stared after him. Zosia put her arms around herself, feeling cold. *He's a friend of Hazel's. He's a vicar.* No one could suspect her of having a relationship with Leon.

'This is my son, Krystof.' Her voice came out cool and formal.

'Mummy said you were as big as a bear,' he said, and Zosia could feel the blush creeping up her cheeks.

'I am. I play rugby sometimes.' He looked down at Krys. 'How old are you?'

Krys held up six fingers. 'I'm small.'

'You wait until you're twelve or fourteen. You'll be taller than your mum.'

Krys led the way into the kitchen.

'What is this?' Zosia asked, putting the bag on the table.

'Onions and garlic and a couple of giant leeks,' he said. 'We grow them in the church allotments.' He winked at Krys, who had followed her in. 'I was hoping Hazel could make soup for the gardening team.'

'Can I help?' Krys asked, his finger in his mouth.

'Help? You are *in charge* of the gardening team,' Leon said. 'Someone has to boss me around. Have you got any gardening clothes?'

Krys grinned up at her. 'Mama?'

She thought fast. It wasn't as if he had a lot of clothes. 'How about your old football shirt, the one you've grown out of? And the jeans with the big hole in.'

'You can see my pants through the hole,' Krys confided to Leon as he walked past. 'Mama was going to fix them.'

'I think they are past saving,' she explained. 'But they'll do for one day.'

'And you'll need wellies,' Leon called up the stairs.

'My pants have Thomas the Tank Engine on them,' Krys shouted back.

Hazel handed Leon a mug of black coffee. 'Perfect for the garden. There you go. Zosia?'

'I'd like to see if this still works,' Zosia said, walking over to her old but efficient coffee machine. 'Now I have this back, thanks to Leon.' She filled it up while she listened to Hazel's ideas for the garden.

'The thing is, I love the pergola,' Hazel said.

'The uprights have rotted off at ground level,' Leon explained. 'They would probably fall over if someone nudged them. They aren't safe. I'll keep Krys on supervisor duties until I've got them all down. Then we'll have to dig up the concrete bases, if you want a new pergola.'

'I always loved the shade the vine used to give, over the tables.' Hazel sipped her coffee, staring into it. 'Won't it cost a fortune?'

'Not if we do it ourselves,' he said, smiling at Zosia. 'With Krys and Zosia's help, we just need to re-dig the holes, concrete in some posts. We can connect them up with ropes for climbers, if you like. Or wood if you can afford it.'

Zosia left her coffee maker sputtering and hissing. 'I'd better get changed, then.'

She didn't have a lot of clothes either. They had left the family home with few belongings and money had been a struggle afterwards, living in emergency accommodation or at the shelter. She had some old leggings and an old T-shirt from her first year at university in the UK, before she had met Declan. They were a bit too small, but she was going to get covered in mud anyway. But she was excited to transform the sad garden, and a part of her had been warmed by just seeing Leon standing at the doorway.

The note, now transferred to a bedroom drawer, had rattled her. Had Declan found her, was he keeping an eye on her, would he risk breaking the restraining order? She had a feeling he would be more likely to hire a private investigator.

The smile on Leon's face as he looked at her in the kitchen confirmed that the impromptu outfit was very snug. She concentrated on making her coffee.

Krys barrelled back into the kitchen and Leon gave him a hard hat that slipped down over his nose.

'Oh no, it doesn't quite fit,' Leon said, ramming it onto his own head instead. 'Right, I'll do the dangerous stuff and you can help with the digging and move the rotten wood. Hazel, do you have gardening gloves in the shed?'

Hazel was laughing at the scruffy garden crew. 'Lots, all different sizes. Help yourselves.'

As Zosia passed, she smiled at her. 'Try not to bend too much in those trousers,' she murmured.

Zosia stalled in the doorway. 'Seriously, are they too small?' No one could see what was going on in the back garden, not even from the hillside behind, it was just them. But Leon was there.

'Very flattering,' Hazel whispered back. 'Probably not a bad thing, it's nice to see him looking so relaxed.'

As Zosia stepped out into the conservatory and through to the garden, she wondered what Hazel meant. She was soon busy attending to Leon's surprisingly quick-fire commands. Krys was parked on a short stepladder on the lawn, with a bag of tools to hand out when needed. Behind him, a backdrop of daffodils waved in the sun, buzzing with bumble bees.

Most of the upright posts were rotten through, and Leon sawed most of them short and dragged the heavy wood away to burn. A few times he was able to lift the wood right out of their concrete bases with Zosia's help, ready to cut in half. Zosia and Krys cleared a big patch of weeds off the patio beyond the pergola to build a bonfire. Between dry grass stems, tiny blue flowers ran in sprigs over the slate.

'We won't hurt the trees, will we?' Krys said, dragging over half a beam.

'They are far enough away,' she said. 'And we need to cut all these brambles back and burn them anyway.'

'I don't want to scare the fairies away,' he said, frowning at the tangle of wood, as Hazel approached.

'Fairies love bonfires,' she said, bringing out a tin of biscuits and a couple of mugs of tea. 'Here you go,' she said, extracting a box of juice from her pocket for Krys. 'Remember, the brownie lives in the fireplace, I bet he loves the log burner in the winter.'

Zosia loved to hear them laughing together after school, after Hazel had got him changed and done his reading home-work with him, leaving Zosia to concentrate on sorting the rooms out. She had been telling Krys stories and reading to him from the fairy-tale book.

Standing in the garden, eating a biscuit and sipping tea, Zosia closed her eyes and let the spring sunshine soak into her. Eighteen months ago she could never have imagined she would feel such peace.

'Hazel, which of these plants do you want to save?' Leon asked, holding up a bunch of sticks covered with bursting leaves. 'Is this a honeysuckle?'

'It's a clematis,' she said. 'Just cut it down to a couple of feet, it will regenerate and we can burn all those dead sticks. I've pruned the vine back, hopefully it will survive.'

He peered at the ground. 'I'll try and save it, but it's going to be tricky getting that lump of concrete next to it out.'

Zosia bounced on the slate slab next to the climber, feeling it move. 'This is a bit loose. Could we lift it to get access to the base?'

'That slate must be a metre each way but we can try. I'll get a crowbar from the shed and we'll have a go. Come on, Krys, let's look for the right tool.'

Two minutes later, Krys returned with a huge crowbar and Leon with an entrenching tool. Between them, Hazel holding Krys back firmly, they managed to lay it upside down on another slab. Underneath, creatures wiggled and wriggled away, through tunnels and holes. It turned into a nature lesson, with Hazel pointing out millipedes, centipedes and worms.

The wind still had a little bite in it, chilling the slight sweat on her forehead and across her shoulders and a thought made her shiver. They were safe and sheltered, who knew if she could find somewhere else. *If Declan is chasing us, we will have to run again.*

The soup they had for lunch was delicious, and Leon's enthusiasm for garden clearance was infectious. Zosia concentrated on tackling ropes of brambles and overgrown shrubs that snaked across what turned out to be another area of paving, surrounded by low walls holding back raised beds. Hazel had given permission to hack it all out, and the afternoon was filled with digging out roots, sawing off branches and listening to Krys and Leon laugh over their efforts. By four o'clock, Leon was a sweaty, muddy mess and Krys's jeans had finally fallen to bits.

He came down with clean ones on, while Zosia surveyed the scratches all over her arms and at least one on her forehead.

'Let's set fire to something,' Hazel said.

'Isn't it a bit early? I mean, antisocial?' Zosia asked.

'It's not like our neighbours have washing out, I doubt if they will care at all. I don't even know if they are home,' Hazel added. The camper van had driven off mid-morning. 'And we're half a mile from the village.'

That morning, after breakfast, Zosia had caught a glimpse of a face at a window, a young woman, unfamiliar, gazing at the garden then ducking down when Zosia waved. The girl looked young, barely in her mid-teens. And sad. Zosia recognised something in her face, reminding her how she had felt for months before she escaped Declan's control.

'There are women there,' she said, turning to Leon. 'What do you think is going on?'

He shrugged. 'Let me put a few cameras up while the neighbours are out. Maybe one in that plant that's growing all over the front wall—'

'The wisteria,' Hazel interrupted.

'The wisteria,' he finished. 'And one up by the telephone wires where they come into the house. I can probably reach from that window. And one in the conservatory to look over the garden.' He looked around. 'Where's Krys?'

'Bathroom,' Zosia said. 'Why?'

'I saw the old chainsaw, I'll take that away today. But there appears to be a gun cabinet behind.'

'*Gun?*' Zosia's heart lurched and she froze. She turned to Hazel. 'Did your parents ever have a gun?'

'An old shotgun of my granddad's, but that was donkey's years ago.'

'Did Casimir have a cabinet for it?'

Hazel looked uncertain. 'I knew there was a metal cupboard, I thought it was empty. Would a gun, if there was one, even work after all this time?'

Leon frowned. 'If you have a shotgun on the property, or even ammunition, you could be breaking the law.'

Zosia looked up at him, her heart skipping in her chest. 'You have to have a licence, don't you? My ex-husband had one – has one.' She shuddered. He had never threatened to use it, but often cleaned it and it was always on show, even when Krys started walking. It was as if he never wanted her to forget about it.

'You have to renew it every five years,' Leon said. 'I think we need to break the lock to make sure. I'll call the local police if there's anything in it.'

Zosia caught his arm. 'I don't want anyone to think we're causing trouble, or breaking the law.' Where she had lived in Poland she would have been very reluctant to call the police unless someone was at risk. 'Can't you just take it away for us?'

'Not legally.' He looked at Hazel and back to Zosia.

'We can go to the *komisariat*,' Zosia said, almost babbling in panic. 'Take it to the police station.'

'It's illegal for you to even carry it in the car.' He put his hand over hers, warming her fingers. 'They will want to do a full search of the house,' he said gently. 'A box of ammunition might be stored separately, and it could be very dangerous to a child. Why are you so scared? This isn't your fault, or Hazel's.'

Zosia's words stalled in her throat, caught between Polish and English. There was something so threatening about the men, even their children pushing past Krys on their way out of school, that made her want to run away. For a moment she was catapulted back into that room with Declan as his rage forced her to react... 'I don't know,' she stammered. 'The police are different here, more friendly.'

Hazel caught Krys as he bounced back into the garden, and Leon drew Zosia aside so Krys wouldn't see her face. She found she couldn't quite summon a reassuring smile for him. Leon bent his head down to speak to her, and she caught the scent of salt and tree sap. 'You've been hurt, haven't you?'

'Did you look me up?' she whispered back, suddenly terrified that he knew what she had done.

'No!' His sudden frown gave way to concern. 'Of course

not, I'm not a policeman any more. I just want you to know, whatever's happened, I do understand.'

She was breathless and light-headed. 'You must have met lots of people who have been – hurt.'

He looked over at Hazel, busy lighting some dried grass with a match, ready to add to the kindling they had arranged in a little wigwam. 'I've seen people beaten up, abused. I've seen them after they've been killed, too.' He looked back at her. 'Violence leaves a mark on people. But it fades over time. There are many more good people in the world than bad. You got away, and you saved Krys.'

'Too late,' she said, tears hot in her eyes, tickling her face. 'Krystof saw everything, at the end. He was hurt, too, I couldn't protect him.'

Leon moved to put his hands on her shoulders, the weight of his arms pressing down. Turned towards him she could only look up. His smile was kind. 'He saw you get away and create a new life. That's what he will remember, how brave his mother was, starting again.'

'That's not all that happened,' she whispered. She couldn't say what she had done, she couldn't bear to see his tenderness turn to disgust.

He waited for several breaths. 'When you are ready to tell me, I'll be here,' he said.

She could see Krys looking anxiously towards them and managed a tight smile. 'Let's burn the old pergola down,' she said, swallowing the tightness in her chest. 'A fresh start. Then, yes, maybe cameras would make us all feel safer.' At least they might pick up anyone who was watching them. Maybe even Declan, if he breached the restraining order. Or was posting notes through the door.

'I will break open the gun cabinet when Krys is in bed,' he promised. 'And get my friends at the police station to drop by casually, to check there's nothing illegal in the house.'

20

JULY 1940

I longed to get married to Rosie, to make a new family here while my own were lost, back in Poland. Maybe they were all dead, maybe imprisoned, I didn't know but the idea tormented me at night. I tried to channel that into the missions, shooting down several planes over the first weeks of the Battle of Britain, damaging several more. The thought of Rosie made me more cautious than some of my pilot colleagues, and I had to watch as one was shot down in front of me. I shouted, 'Spadochron! Spadochron!', not being able to recall the English word for parachute. The plane exploded into a fireball that one of my wings brushed through, leaving a scorch mark like a bird's wing on the paint. I asked the engineers not to wash it away when they polished. I added him to my prayers, but knew he had died a hero's death, fighting for our homeland. I could not imagine what Poland would be like after the war, but I wished I could take my beautiful Rosie there.

— EXTRACT FROM THE MEMOIR OF
CASIMIR WOJCIK

Having received her mother's refusal to agree to their marriage in the near future, it took two weeks for Rosie and Cas to get leave at the same time, to talk about it. Casimir had been intercepting fighter planes and bombers from the Luftwaffe every day. His plane had been damaged and put in for repairs three times, but he had always been able to fly back and land safely. Not all of his comrades had been so lucky. One had to crash-land on the South Downs, but at least had walked away with just a broken wrist. Another had parachuted into the sea and had to be rescued. One had died. Cas's letters were terse, he said he was tired.

They had met as before outside the tea shop, but Cas steered her away, towards the church gate. He was quieter than usual, and she could only imagine it was the daily battles that were wearing him down.

'Speak,' he said, in his shorthand English. 'Speak about us.'

She reached a hand out to his, squeezed his fingers. 'Cas, is something wrong?'

He stopped walking, and bent his head. She was horrified to see tears in his eyes, so uncharacteristic of him. Merry, optimistic Casimir seemed different. 'Josef,' he said, with difficulty, then a flood of Polish followed.

Josef was a flyer in his group from Czechoslovakia, who shared a room with Cas. She let the wave of words flow over her, holding his hand and looking into his twisted face.

'Cas,' she said gently, interrupting the flow. 'Is Josef... dead?'

'Not dead,' he said, shaking. 'Don't know word. *Spalony*.' He mimed something exploding. '*Płomień*. Fire?'

'The plane caught fire? Is he burned?'

Cas mimicked the sound of a fire engine. 'Go hospital. Bad.'

'He was taken to hospital? Is he going to be all right?' She pulled him to face her. 'Cas, that must be horrible for you.'

He reached out and pulled her close. She could feel him shaking, feel the tears on her neck. She just held him, feeling like she was a hundred years old. This war was pushing them so hard.

Only this week a girl had been injured when she dropped a firing cap in one of the sheds. It blew her foot off and damaged both legs. She had lost so much blood by the time the ambulance got there that she wasn't expected to survive. They had all been evacuated and given two aspirins and a strong cup of sweet tea. They hadn't witnessed it, but they had all heard the bang and the screaming. The sound of the girl's agony had still been ringing in Rosie's head at the end of her shift.

She longed to take Cas back to the farm, for them to walk along the stream hand in hand, to sit in the shadow of Combestone Tor and look up at the stars. The ponies would sway about in the moonlight, like ships at anchor, and the only sounds would be the wind in the tall sedges, and owls calling from the tors. Her mother would heal them with cakes and patient silence, give them hay bales to move and pigs to feed until the war fell away. She longed for privacy, to take time to tell him all of the thoughts that tumbled through her head at night, when she couldn't sleep.

When he turned his head to kiss her, it was different, dark, sad.

It seemed wrong to keep kissing beside a holy building and she pulled back a little. 'Cas?'

He pointed at the ancient stone front, the huge doors, one standing ajar. 'Come in,' he urged.

'No kissing, though,' she said, looking doubtfully at the cool, shaded interior. 'Not in a church.' He crossed himself before he walked right in, bowing his head.

'Get married,' he explained, as he showed her the front pews. 'Married, you, me.'

'We can't,' she said, looking at the worn slabs under her feet. 'I have to wait for my parents to give consent. They want to meet you first. They think we should wait.' She stopped, looked at him. 'My mother said we hardly know each other, really,' she said, as he stared back.

'I know I love you,' he said, in his strong accent. 'Love you, Rosie Duke.'

'I love you too, Casimir Wojcik.'

Every time she heard a plane fly overhead, she wondered if it was him, piloting his last mission. A sensible part of her told her that marriage was for life, that they didn't have much in common, not even a language. Another part of her couldn't stop staring at him, finding things she had almost forgotten – the tiny gap between his front teeth, a nick taken out of one ear, a few blond hairs curling out of the undone top button of his shirt.

He put out his hands and she walked towards him, to take his warm fingers in her own.

'We will get married,' he said, with complete certainty. 'I know you, I know me. Love you. Get *dom*, make life.'

She stared up at him for a long moment, a draught from the door just brushing his hair. 'We can't get married now. But we don't have to wait to be together.' She stared up into his puzzled eyes, and could feel the blush warming her cheeks. But she longed to be with him, to be able to kiss him and hold him in private. 'I want to have some time with you. Alone.'

'Alone now,' he said, but there was a wary look on his face. 'Get married.'

'We could just book a night or two in a hotel. When we have enough leave. We could just talk, like this.' She could already hear the footsteps of someone entering behind them. 'I trust you. We could get separate rooms, if you like.'

His lips were twisted, his eyes flashing with anger. 'No. Not that, like *prostytutka*,' he snapped with conviction, making her flush even more. 'You good girl. Get *married*.'

'I can't make my parents give consent,' she said. 'But if they knew I had been away with you, they might give in.'

He held her hands and spoke fast, in Polish. Then slowly in English. 'Lie to wedding man.'

'What?'

'Tomasz Kamiński, he marry girl. She seventeen, they lie.'

'What?'

He let go of her hand and reached into his pocket. He had a slew of documents, identity cards, some Polish. 'Change date on one.'

She didn't have her birth certificate in London but she did have a base ID card as well as a travel card. She opened her purse and pulled them out. The birthdate on her worn work card had been filled in with black ink, she could barely read it herself. The idea of lying, of breaking the law, made her heart race uncomfortably. 'I couldn't.'

'We can change.' He led her to a pew and they sat. 'When I get out of Polska, many borders. Many papers. Many soldiers.' He mimed having a gun. 'We had to make papers for Rumunia, Węgry, Włochy to Francja.'

'France.' She knew the dangerous, tortuous route he and many of the Polish airmen had taken to get to England. 'Do you think someone could change the date of one of my identity cards?'

'Man called Jan,' he explained. 'Is *notariusz* in Poland.' He mimed scribbling. 'He make birth certificate.'

'Notary?' she guessed. The idea made her feel cold. She had never broken a law. 'My parents would never forgive me. Ever.'

'They love. I love.'

She pulled back a little. She couldn't work out what he meant. Did he think she loved him more than her parents? Maybe she did. He was part of her world, she felt grown up in London, she had left the girl behind on Dartmoor.

He was nodding, pressing his hand to his heart. 'Your *mumia, tata,* love you. Still love Rosie.'

Her thoughts flew to the church where she had been christened, where her grandparents had married and their ancestors slept under the short grass of the graveyard. She imagined her mother in a silly hat, Dad stuffed into his suit looking proud, the family pearls around the bride's neck. Tig would be tied up in the porch. It had all been planned in her mind since childhood, not just by her but by her parents, too, fussing over their only lamb.

Maybe they would forgive her eventually. She looked back at him, at the pink nick out of his ear. She touched it lightly. He pulled back. 'Just shrapnel,' he said. 'Helmet loose.'

'When did you get hit with shrapnel?' Her voice was higher, louder.

He shrugged and looked away. 'When Josef shot, I went in to fight Germans. They...' He mimed a group of planes chasing Josef. 'Like vultures. Shot my cockpit canopy.'

She stared at him. In a few days, he could be Josef, barely bringing his flaming plane down, or worse, being killed. Or she could be the next girl to drop some unstable armaments.

She put her hands on his lapels and shook him gently. 'You're right,' she said, staring up at him. 'Yes. We should get married.' *We should be together.*

He curled his finger around hers and grinned at her. 'I sort out.'

21

PRESENT DAY, MARCH

It was a wet evening, rain pouring down the windows and washing the newly exposed slate patio clean in shades of blue and grey. Masses of wild strawberries had been revealed under the weeds, and a few tulips had popped buds above the leaves. Leon had promised to come back after Easter with two volunteers who wanted day work, to replace the posts that would hold up the new pergola, and Zosia was looking forward to planting climbing roses, a vine and some other climbers over the tables of the Fairy Café. Hazel had a summerhouse full of old fairy statues, faces and houses, all mouldy and some in need of repair, that she said used to peep out from flowers and climbers.

After a day of painting tables for the cafe, Hazel was sitting at one end of the vast dining room table, with a voice recorder waiting for Zosia to translate the next line. The problem was, Zosia didn't want to translate it. Hazel adored her father. But here he was describing acts of violence that shocked her, even though she knew what murderous chaos he had fled from.

'This bit is too...' She turned to the next page. 'Do you even want to hear this bit? I could write it down for you to read later, if you like.'

'I think I'd rather hear it from you,' Hazel said, pushing her glasses back up her nose and her hair out of her eyes. 'They were being chased by the Romanian police...'

'They were able to get to a farmhouse.'

Hazel stared at her, her eyes blue and piercing. 'Go on.'

'They weren't welcome. They – tied up the farmer and threatened his wife with a gun. They took food and stole clothes that made them look like farm workers. They took the couple's young daughter with them, promising to leave her in the town if they were not pursued. They said they would kill her if the couple called out the police,' she concluded.

Hazel's eyes widened then she turned away. 'Did they let her go?'

'He says they left her tied up in the porch of the church. Casimir agonised over it, but they had to. They tried to reassure her but they didn't speak the language. She must have been so relieved that they didn't hurt her.'

The tension seemed to leave Hazel. 'It was a war. They were trying to survive. How many girls were left safe and unmolested in that situation, do you think?'

'Not many back in Poland,' Zosia said, with a hard edge in her voice. 'There was a tragedy going on in Poland while you fought the Battle of Britain and invaded Normandy on D-Day.'

'We suffered, too. One of my English cousins was killed in the Blitz,' Hazel said softly. 'My mother worked in one of the factories that made bombs. My father's Polish family lived through the invasions in Poland, too.'

Zosia was immediately sorry. 'I know. It's just hard to think how scared that little girl must have been back then, at the hands of Poles.'

'It was war, maid. Nothing good 'appened in the war.' Hazel's Devon accent grew deeper when she was upset. 'Was that the worst of it?'

'So far. They had to walk over a hundred miles,' Zosia said.

'Through the foothills of the Carpathians, at the beginning of winter, dodging fascists. It took two weeks through the snow to the Hungarian border.'

'I think that's as much as I can manage,' Hazel said quietly, then switched off the recorder. Zosia was upset to see her eyes brimming behind her glasses, dimming her blue eyes. 'No wonder Dad kept my grandfather's old shotgun handy. Let's wander round the garden,' she added, finally. 'It sounds like Krys is asleep and it's stopped raining.'

They walked out, slipping into the boots kept by the back door. Hazel grabbed a shawl hanging on a kitchen chair then collected the lap blanket that lived on the rocking chair and handed it to Zosia.

In Zosia's mind they could have been two Polish women, a hundred years ago, going around the garden to lock up the chickens at dusk and check on the vegetable garden. Zosia could imagine their respective grandmothers putting their animals and smallholdings to bed along with their children.

'I've been weeding this raised bed,' Hazel said, in a quiet voice so she wouldn't wake Krys, nor draw the attention of the people next door who had returned in their camper. There was a smell of wild garlic from under the hedge, the sharpness of rosemary that had been cut back. It all made Zosia think of lamb, roasted with peppers and onions like her mother's recipe. 'I thought we could grow some aromatic plants, like herbs. And some edible flowers. I don't want to put prickly roses out here, but I love the scent.'

'There are roses without thorns,' Zosia said, remembering one she had planted in their first house together. 'I once had one called Eden. I planted it next to our garage, before Krys was born.'

Hazel walked to the edge of the straggly lawn, leading down to a hedge behind which were the three sheds. 'You don't talk much about your life before.'

'I'm ashamed of it,' she whispered in Polish before she looked at Hazel and continued in English. 'I wish I had done things differently.' She swallowed. 'I was like Casimir, who was young, frightened, fighting for his life. And having to survive the journey here with his comrades. Only I was fighting for Krystof.'

'He was abusive? Your husband?'

Zosia pulled at a stray dandelion flower that was growing between the slabs. 'I didn't understand at first. He liked things *just right*. I didn't get anything correct. He was patient but he would never back down. He was older than me, and I was quite new here, I thought this was how the British did things. Strict, regimented. But deep down, I realised it was *him*.'

Hazel sat down on the stone bench at the edge of the patio, revealed by the cutting of a forest of weeds. 'How did you know it wasn't right?'

'I sometimes worked as a translator for the police, and listened to women explaining how they had been beaten or terrified. I felt for them, but I kept thinking, why don't they leave? Most of them withdrew their complaints after a few days or even hours. I didn't think my life was like theirs.'

Hazel nodded and patted the bench. Zosia sat, feeling Hazel's warmth leaning supportively against her shoulder. 'What changed?'

'I was given some translations to do for charities, including a women's shelter. That was the first time I had really heard the words *coercive control*.' She looked down at her clenched fists. 'I was too afraid to do an internet search on our home computer. I knew he monitored it, and my phone. I hadn't really felt afraid until then. But then Krys needed to be fetched from his nursery.' She remembered using a fellow mother's phone, saying she needed to look something up for work, some silly excuse. But the woman's smile had been sad and kind in equal measure, and the few minutes of reading had been like a fire igniting in her brain. From then on, she thought about leaving all the time.

'And you left.'

'We did, even though I thought I still loved Declan, I knew we had to run away.' She shut her eyes at the memory of what he had done, what *she* had done. 'Something happened. We had to. We found a shelter, although I had to leave our dog behind.' The tears came then, dropping onto her hands as she wept. 'Declan got rid of him. I hope he had him rehomed but I couldn't find a record anywhere. I do not think a vet would put a healthy puppy down, do you?'

'I'm sure he's safe and happy somewhere,' Hazel said, turning to lock eyes with Zosia. 'Tell yourself that, OK? And you and Krys are safe and happy, too.'

Zosia grasped Hazel's big hands. 'Thank you.'

But the note she had received still niggled in the back of her mind.

Does he know where we are?

22

JULY 1940

While preparing for my wedding with Rosie I knew I had a huge stain on my soul which I couldn't bear to bring to our marriage. I made enquiries and found a Polish church just a few miles away. I spoke to Gabriel and Eckert and we agreed that we should go, confess, be absolved. And take mass in the proper, Polish style.

It had started back in 1939, on our third day walking in Hungary, when we were arrested to have our credentials checked. We carried few papers. Some of us had lost them in Romania, Eckert had burned his, as his mother was Jewish and anti-Jewish slogans were everywhere. We were led to a compound that had previously housed horses, and locked in. At nightfall, it was easy for a few of us, including myself, Gabriel and Eckert, to climb the fence and continue to walk towards France and freedom. But behind us we heard someone following, someone creeping along.

— EXTRACT FROM THE MEMOIR OF
CASIMIR WOJCIK

It took three weeks to manufacture a fake identity card and arrange an appointment at the register office, neither of them wanting to change their religion. Rosie hadn't given much thought about her mother's brand of Christianity until converting away from it became an option. Casimir didn't consider anything but Polish Catholic proper for a church, but was happy to have a register office wedding. 'Have marriage blessing in Polska, with *matka i siostry*,' he had said. 'Kasia, Angelika and Sabina, Mama, Tata. When we win war we will go back, make wedding.'

One of the factory girls had recently married in an old dress and Rosie borrowed it for the day; it fitted well except for the length so she tacked it up a few inches.

Audrey was looking pale, with dark shadows under her eyes, but wouldn't talk about why until she turned up the night before the wedding. She had brought a case full of hairdressing items including rollers, and a pretty blue necklace. It reminded Rosie again that her mum had a pearl necklet that she had promised to Rosie for her marriage, and the memory brought tears to her eyes.

'It's really lovely,' Rosie said, holding the necklet up against her skin as she sat in the bedroom chair, looking at Audrey's reaction in the mirror. 'Audrey, just tell me what's wrong.'

'You can't tell anyone,' she said, her hands stalled in Rosie's wet hair. 'Promise.'

Rosie ran her fingers across her chest. 'Cross my heart,' she said, trying to read Audrey's expression.

'Do you remember my chap, Albie?'

Rosie caught her breath. 'He's all right, isn't he? He hasn't been – hurt?' *Killed?* It was the thought that ran through her head every morning. *Is Cas all right?*

'No, nothing like that. I told you, me and him had a fling. Just light-hearted, I wasn't in love or anything. But he started to get serious about me.'

'Oh.' Rosie nodded encouragingly. 'Go on.'

Audrey took a minute to get the words out. 'He told me he was married. He said he wanted a divorce but you know how difficult that is, and expensive. He doesn't have that kind of money. So I told him, I was just having a bit of fun.' Tears started tracking down her cheeks in the mirror and her voice grew rougher. 'Only it turned out I did really like him.'

'Oh, maid, I'm so sorry,' Rosie said, turning around to look into Audrey's face. She stood and hugged her friend, who normally hated being 'wrinkled'. 'You could have told me,' she said as she let go.

'You had bigger problems,' Audrey said, sniffing back tears and dabbing at her make-up. 'With Cas fighting the Luftwaffe.'

The leaden feeling in the pit of Rosie's stomach returned. 'True,' she said, as lightly as she could. 'So, have you seen Albie again?'

Audrey started to comb Rosie's head of curls. 'I wrote him several letters and finally we met up. To tell him I got caught. You know. Pregnant.'

Rosie could see her eyes and mouth open wide in the mirror. 'Audrey!' she gasped.

'It's OK. The baby's gone now. By itself,' she added, meeting Rosie's eyes in the mirror. 'Maybe it's all those chemicals we breathe in all day.'

'You must have been terrified,' Rosie said, eyes watering as Audrey tugged at a persistent snag.

Audrey was silent as she carried on taming Rosie's mop. 'We'll put it in big rollers,' she said. 'Maybe we can get your crazy curls into waves.'

'Audrey...' Rosie started.

The hands trembled in her hair. 'It was horrible. At first it was like my monthlies, I was so relieved, I thought maybe the work had set me back a couple of months. But it hurt so much, I knew it was a miscarriage. There was so much blood.'

'That's daft. You could have died.'

Audrey shook her head. 'It was in the middle of the night shift, I was in the supplies cupboard in the bathroom block, I just waited for it to end. Or to die, I suppose.' She managed a shaky laugh. 'I'm amazed no one heard me, I was trying not to cry but... Then there was a sort of pop, and it came away. All of it. It was like a tiny puppy, it had a big head. I cried for ages.'

Rosie turned towards her. 'Oh, lovey, that must have been dreadful for you.'

'I didn't know what to do, or who to tell,' Audrey said, eyes shut, the tears drenching her face, hands clenched. 'I didn't know what to do – with it. I wish I'd buried it somewhere nice but I was so afraid someone would find out. I flushed it away.' Her words broke and she sobbed, dropping to her knees. 'It was so horrible.'

Rosie knelt down to hold her as she cried, great raucous sobs that sounded like they hurt her throat. The intensity of Audrey's feelings was terrifying. This is how she would feel if something happened to Cas. She rested her head on the top of Audrey's and let her grieve, not just for the baby, but for the pain and fear and loss of her love.

'Are you better now?'

'I'm still bleeding. I'm feeling really tired all the time.'

'You need to go to the doctor.'

'They might think I did something to myself.'

'But you didn't. Just tell them you've had a really bad monthly. My mother has those, she has to take iron tablets.'

Audrey blew her nose and got up from the floor. 'Your hair has started to dry,' she said, looking away. 'Let's wrap it up in a scarf until tomorrow morning.'

'You'll be there with me, won't you, with a few of the girls? Otherwise it will just be the boys from Cas's squadron, those that can come, anyway.' Cas's RAF senior officer had immediately refused when asked if he could get married. His Polish Air

Force commander promptly countermanded the decision and promised to attend.

'Of course the girls will be there with me,' Audrey said, tucking her handkerchief into her sleeve, smiling as if she was all right. 'It will be a lovely day. Then you will go off for your honeymoon and hopefully this bloody war will soon be over.'

It was magical when Casimir took her hand in his and looked at her with such love in his eyes. The church was huge, the wedding party in the first three pews, vases of marguerite daisies and cornflowers picked from the hedgerows. A few sprigs of purple heather made her think of home. He curled his finger around her ring finger. After the vows were read out in English then in Polish, they made their promises and he put her actual wedding band on. Just a scrap of gold, but more precious than any piece of jewellery she had ever owned.

Better than that, Josef was well enough to attend, in a wheelchair and covered with bandages, but he led the cheering as Casimir chastely kissed her cheek. The pilots sang the Polish anthem as the girls from the factory clapped and Cas kissed her on the lips.

Casimir struggled to speak. Overcome at first with emotion, he joined in the last chorus. 'You Polish wife now,' he murmured in her ear.

They retired to the local scout hall, where Audrey and a few of the other girls had put together a small tea, with a sponge bought from a bakery. There was a little beer and a couple of bottles of wine, which had to be drunk out of tea cups because the hut didn't have glasses. A few dance records were played on an old gramophone. Rosie danced only with Cas, and the two of them were lost in the luxury of being able to be together, in public.

The blare of a horn outside turned out to be their taxi to the

Rose Inn, far enough away that they shouldn't hear the planes taking off and landing. After their friends had wished them well and all the pilots had kissed the bride and shaken the groom's hand, they found themselves sitting on the back seat, in luxury.

'Got married today, then, mate?' the taxi driver asked, a cap pushed back on his head. 'Good day for it. How much leave you got?'

Rosie knew what he was asking; everyone had duties to go back to. 'Just two days.'

'Shame. Before the war you might have had a week by the seaside, like me and my missus,' he said.

A whole week by the sea. The idea was intoxicating. 'Maybe after the war,' she said, swallowing down the dread that there might not be an after the war.

'After war,' Cas agreed, grinning at her. 'We go to Poland, to see my family.'

'You one of those Polish pilots?' the man asked over his shoulder.

'He is,' Rosie piped up, snuggling into Cas's arm. His hand was laid possessively on her leg, and it seemed the most exciting thing he had ever done.

'Your lot are brilliant. Good on yer,' he said, pulling up in front of a white-painted building. 'Good luck to yer both,' he said, waving Cas's money away. 'I'm off home anyway, it's on me way.'

He drove off leaving them open-mouthed with surprise, Casimir still holding out the ten shilling note. He turned to her. 'Come,' he said, hand held out.

She took the note and tucked it into his pocket. 'Let's go up to our room.'

23

PRESENT DAY, APRIL

It was the Thursday before Easter, and Zosia was still uncertain if she was going to the family service. Without confession, she still felt the weight of her sins. No more notes had come through the door and she hadn't seen Leon all week. Krys wanted to go to the birthday party on Saturday, and then they would see Leon at church on Sunday. Zosia was up a ladder scrubbing down the conservatory walls when she heard Hazel come in.

'I dropped him off at school,' she called through from the kitchen. 'He's so excited for the last day of term, they all are. Next door's boys are excluded again. They are hardly ever there.'

Zosia craned her neck to look over the raggedy, neglected hedge – trimming it was another thing on her to-do list, but now the birds were popping in and out as if they had nests and she didn't want to disturb them. 'The camper van is gone again.'

Hazel came in and dropped her scarf and coat on one of the chairs and looked at the walls. 'Oh, my. I'd forgotten the conservatory was ever this colour, it's got so dingy and faded. It's going to need a few coats of paint.' She sat down. 'And I have some news. The council are sending an environmental health officer to approve us for serving drinks and cakes so we can revive the café.'

'Oh? So soon?' While Hazel had a range of stainless-steel-topped units and work surfaces around the sink, the rest of the kitchen was an old dresser, a bookcase full of cookbooks and half a dozen mismatched chairs around a rickety table. 'Will they allow the café to run?'

'I'm sure they will. But we'll need to wash up all the baking tins and crockery from the café, and scrub inside the drawers and cupboards. They haven't been used for several years, I'm sure they are full of spiderwebs and dried woodlice.'

'I'll get on it after I've finished in here.'

'I didn't mean now! They are not coming until next week. I thought, after you've changed, you could go for a walk.' She dropped her gaze to her lap. 'Actually, I'd like you to do something for me.'

Zosia stepped down the ladder. 'What do you want me to do?'

'This sounds silly – sentimental even – but every March I go up to where my father crashed and my mother pulled him out of his plane.' She looked up and smiled. 'I missed it this year. But I'd like someone to lay a few flowers on the place where they fell in love. While I live, anyway.'

Zosia smiled. 'I'd be honoured. These walls need to dry anyway. Did they really fall in love right there and then?'

'They always said they did. My mother just used to smile and say everything was different after that moment. I thought I'd pick a few spring flowers from the garden they planted, you could lay them there. I always put them on the mile marker beside the old track to Holne.'

Zosia followed Hazel through to the living room. 'How do I get up there?'

'I can show you out of the window,' Hazel said. 'There's a footpath on *this* side of the hedge. There's a stile, it's probably a bit overgrown. Then there's a sign past the churchyard and it goes right up to the tor. It's just over a mile. I'll probably be able to do it next year, but...' She looked at Zosia.

'Of course. We can leave painting the conservatory for a bit, then.' She smiled at Hazel. 'I'd love to. It's so sunny out the front and I've been stuck in the shade. Do you want me to pick some flowers for you?'

'I'd like to do it, there are a few cowslips in the hedge and some pussy willow. I might pick some daffs too. Go and get changed.'

Although she had taken Krys out on some of the shorter trails behind the large car park at Dartmeet, Zosia had never ventured out onto the moor in front of the house. The hedge, itself sprinkled with yellow stars and the odd daffodil, was patchy and rough in places where the wind had ripped holes in it. It was built on top of, or had grown out of a wall, with blocks of stone closely fitted together. A tiny bird flew out of one of the larger holes, twittering with alarm, and she recognised it as a wren. Hazel always kept feeders in the back garden, and they were sometimes covered in hungry birds.

At the end of the hedge, now curving towards the village, the signpost was faded and leaning, but clearly said Combestone Tor. There was the suggestion of a path through the carpet of grass, wiry and spotted with low flowers in pink and white, close to the ground. A hollow was filled with frost that wasn't touched by sun; it had probably been there since the last cold night. Rabbits launched themselves across the path, then sat up, as if believing themselves invisible in the heathers and sedges spiking out of the wet ground.

Zosia was intoxicated with the amount of sky, and she felt

as if she was rising into it as she walked. She could almost believe she was level with the clouds on the horizon. She put out her arms, as if catching the wind would make her lighter, lift her. Specks of birds flew around, ignoring her; a kestrel spiralled up on flexed wings then fluttered to look down. Ravens sounded like they were knocking on wood, she found them searching the grass ahead, in the shadow of Combestone.

The tor was much less a single pillar as several stacks of rocks, weathered like bricks from a giant, ruined house. She could see the signpost and track leading to Holne. She climbed up on the nearest weathered block. It wasn't huge like some of the famous tors, but from it she could see all around the moors. Distant slopes darkened with gorse, topped with the acid-yellow buds. Shadows of clouds tracked overhead. She spent some time taking pictures, noticing another walker far away to the east and another one north of her, from where she had just walked.

She started to walk along the track, only a hundred or so metres along from the tor itself, and found the mile marker, a carved block higher than her knees marked *Exeter 34 miles* in weathered writing. The corner was missing, perhaps broken by the plane crashing into it eighty years before, and lichens in yellow and ice white had covered the broken surface.

It was as Hazel had described, and she thought about how Rosemary and Casimir had visited every year until their deaths. Zosia was starting to feel like she knew Cas from his memoir, and from the small snaps he had sent his Rosie with a hundred kisses crammed on the back. Rosie had reciprocated, as she promised, a *fotografia* of Rosie and a taller woman squinting into the sun in overalls and cloth turbans, which were in the silver frames on the fireplace.

She laid the flowers on the stone, smiling through tears. 'For both of you,' she said, choked up. 'From Hazel. And me, too, and Krys, who would have loved to have known you.'

She spent a few moments breathing in the scent of the spring flowers Hazel had cut.

It wasn't until she turned to go back that she caught sight of one of the men who lived in the house next door, stomping up the hill towards her.

He shouted something incomprehensible at her as he came too close.

'I'm sorry,' she replied, pulling herself upright, trying to step back. 'I don't understand.'

He followed her. 'You called the police to the house.' He was shouting so loud some spittle hit her chin, and she stepped back, making herself even higher. 'You called the police, I saw them.'

'I did not,' she answered. 'Miss Wojcik found something illegal in her father's possession, they just came to take it away.'

'What was illegal?' he snapped, his eyes darting like a ferret. 'Drugs?'

'No.' She could see he was agitated, and she was a long way from help. 'It was an old shotgun. It belonged to old Mr Wojcik's father-in-law, Mr Duke.'

'I don't like police,' he snarled, unnecessarily. 'If we see the police again, you will regret it. Understand?'

Adrenaline made her insides wobble like jelly, her knees were shaking as if she was cold. 'I'm not afraid of you,' she lied, but her voice sounded small. 'You have nothing to fear from the police if you are not doing anything wrong.'

'You're not afraid, huh?' he said, turning his head and showing his teeth in a humourless grin. 'Not even for the old woman? Or the boy?'

There was a part of her that had already folded in on herself, as she had when Declan had ordered her about. *This meat is overcooked, this shelf is dusty, the boy is too loud.* Her heart was skipping beats, she felt sick. She acted on instinct to placate him.

'You can leave us alone,' she said. 'I have no interest in what you are doing.'

'No police.'

'No police,' she agreed, even though she knew what Hazel would say if she knew. 'Just leave us alone.'

24

JULY 1940

We ambushed the man following us, he was an Italian nation-alist and had been taking notes in the prison camp. He had a German-issue gun and identity papers. In his notes he had marked us as spies. We could not let him go.

Now, when I first stepped into the Polish church and knelt I was overcome with tears. I felt I could not sully this church, this priest, with my sins. And I could not bring this evil to my precious girl. I felt the old priest lay his hand upon my head, not gently, but firmly. As I knelt, bowing my head under the pressure, I felt something lift. I murmured 'Dzięki Bogu', praising God, and the priest answered with 'Amen.' After that it was easier to attend the mass, enjoy the Polish words to bless and cleanse me, before I confessed to my most heinous sins.

His name was Fabrizio Schiappacasse, I will never forget it, and he was an Italian Nazi party member. I remembered he babbled in German and Italian but I didn't understand much of it. It was left to me and Gabriel to deal with him, the others turned away. Eckert even went outside the barn. Gabriel kicked his legs from under him so he was on his knees, turned towards the wall, sobbing. Gabriel then turned to me, his eyes wet with tears.

'We have to put him down like a rabid dog,' he said to me. 'He will alert the police. They will not have any difficulty shooting us.'

'We could tie him up, they might not find him for days,' I said, but I knew it wouldn't give us enough time to get away.

The man turned sideways then launched himself at me. On instinct, I hit him with the butt of the gun, and he fell again. He looked up at me, blood running down his face. I could not do it, could not fire. He glared at me then in the low light from the barn door, his eyes gleaming with hatred, and I saw in his soul the kind of man who would shoot innocent civilians in Poland and conquer my peaceful country. In one second I pointed the gun and fired. He slumped, a shot almost between his eyes, blood dropping onto the straw.

That's how I got blood on my hands. I'm not sure it ever washed off.

— EXTRACT FROM THE MEMOIR OF
CASIMIR WOJCIK

Later, during their wedding night at the hotel, Rosie had woken up in Casimir's arms when he started shaking. He was whimpering and turning his head back and forth. She pulled away and turned on the bedside lamp. Far away, engines droned in the quiet of the night. They must have been miles away because the siren didn't go off, or maybe they were British planes.

Now he was muttering in Polish, his hands clenched, his face twisted.

'Cas!' she whispered. She shook his bare shoulder and he froze, opened his eyes, looking at her as if he didn't know her. 'Cas, please wake up.' Slowly, recognition dawned.

'Rosie. Beautiful Rosie,' he said, reaching out for her.

She had found that she could curve against his body perfectly. 'You were upset,' she murmured. 'Were you dreaming?'

'Planes,' he said, as if that explained everything. 'Luftwaffe.'

Of course he was having nightmares about the battle raging every day. It seemed so strange that the war between two huge countries had come down to a few thousand planes and their pilots.

His skin was cold, but a little damp, as if he'd been terrified. She hugged him, trying to infuse her happiness and warmth into him. She had known marriage would bring surprises, but this was the first painful thing. *For better, for worse...*

She could no longer block out the danger of what he was doing. Outside the reception hall, Audrey had pulled out a box of matches to light her cigarette. Josef, the Czech pilot who had been badly burned, and who had become Cas's close friend, had shouted with terror, flailing at his wheelchair to get away from her. Someone had blown the match out, and Josef's friends had rallied around to reassure him as he tried to apologise to Audrey for his terror. He'd held out his still-bandaged hands to her, and she had burst into tears, most unusual for Audrey.

Casimir had raised a glass to toast his fallen comrades by name. The list went on for a full minute. At that moment, Rosie prayed for his safety.

Now, as he woke from his nightmare, she felt more like his mother, holding him tight and whispering reassurance to him in English she knew he barely understood. But slowly his tremors subsided, and the chemistry that had grown between them turned their words to kisses and the comfort became something else.

They must have fallen back to sleep because he woke her with a word. 'Food!' he said, standing by the bed, naked. 'Is time!

Breakfast.' He had a prodigious appetite. When they did manage to find somewhere to live together, Rosie wondered how she was going to find enough rations to fill him up. She didn't know where to look, and blushed.

She was too shy to slide out of bed in front of him, not least because he stared at her and grinned. But her clothes were in her case, and she snatched up what she needed and scooted into the bathroom.

Her one set of decent underwear was strewn somewhere in the bedroom. She and Casimir hadn't worried about folding their clothes the evening before, and she was sure he must have lost a couple of shirt buttons. But that had made her giggle and him laugh and made everything else seem so natural and easy... Now she blushed at the thought of their night together as she straightened the lace on her best blouse, the one sent by her mother, and smoothed down her skirt. Her only pair of nylons had hopefully survived the wedding but she'd have to find them. She stared at herself in the mirror. She looked like a Sunday school teacher.

'I'm here,' she said. 'Let's go down to breakfast.'

At least he was dressed in a nice jacket and trousers and a clean shirt. He was smartly buttoned up but hadn't bothered with a tie. He took her hand as they walked out into the carpeted corridor of the hotel, and down wide, shallow steps that looked better designed for rich Victorian crinolines than her narrow skirt. The dining room was bright with bleached tablecloths, and they were shown to a freshly laid table with a full teapot and a miniature milk jug and sugar bowl. Around them, lots of other couples were holding hands, and she imagined many were newlyweds. She turned her ring around on her finger; it seemed strange to have it there and it was a tiny bit loose.

'Sir, madam,' the waiter said, handing them both a menu.

The breakfast was included in the astronomical cost of the

room, so she ordered for them both. 'Full English for two, please,' she said, smartly bypassing the suggestion of a continental breakfast. 'And may we have some more hot water for the tea, please.'

He smiled and walked away.

'Is *English* food?' Casimir asked. He and his fellow pilots often talked about their Polish breads and sausages and how much they missed them. Rosie wondered if she could find a recipe book.

'Lots of food,' she answered, reaching across the table to hold his hand. '*Angielski,*' she explained, before realising she didn't know the word for breakfast. 'Toast, eggs and bacon.'

'*Becon?*' he said, then screwed up his face and did a good impression of a pig.

'That's it!' she said, and oinked back. They were still laughing when a silver toast rack with brown triangles was placed on the table along with a plate of minute butter pats.

The breakfast was delicious, and it was lovely to eat something off the rations for a change. The kitchen topped up their tea and then brought a fresh pot and more toast. They were both starving, and Rosie smiled at the thought that the night had given them an appetite.

'Where shall we go next?' she asked, smearing a scrape of butter over her last piece of toast. 'We could go to the park, it looks like it's going to be sunny. I don't have to be back until six tomorrow.' Reality hit her like a bucket of cold water. To her cold, single bed in a shared room, and a week of late shifts while he was fighting overhead. 'I don't want to go back,' she whispered.

'What do you say?' he asked, but when he saw her face he took both her hands in his. 'I have surprise. Wedding present.'

'You don't have to give me a present,' she argued, but he was already pulling her to her feet. She left a shilling as a tip, it was all she could afford, and they walked together upstairs to pack.

At least Casimir had taken advice from his fellow pilots and she was protected from having a baby. She tucked the rest of the card-wrapped packet in his suitcase, and he smiled at her, pulled her close for a long kiss. She wondered when they would be alone again.

'So, where is this present? she asked, looking around.

'You see,' he said, kissing her hand. 'In taxi.'

25

PRESENT DAY, APRIL

Reading about Casimir's actions as he and his friends fled across Hungary to avoid being recaptured was heartbreaking. Zosia had struggled to say the words, as each sentence seemed almost a blow to Hazel.

'Poor Daddy,' she had whispered. 'He must have been so afraid, so desperate.'

When Zosia had translated the description of the killing of the Nazi spy, Hazel burst into tears. All Zosia could do was hug her, cry a little herself and wait for the storm to pass.

'He was only twenty-one years old,' she said to Hazel.

'You didn't know my dad,' Hazel said. 'He couldn't kill a rabbit with myxomatosis, my mother had to do it. He wouldn't kill a spider.'

'It was different, then,' Zosia said, putting her hands on Hazel's shoulders and shaking her a little. 'He must have been so shocked and traumatised after the German army invaded.'

Hazel had wiped her eyes and tried to catch her breath. 'I knew there was something there, something dark. Maybe that's why he kept the gun.'

'Maybe. Perhaps to protect his family if war came again,' Zosia had said. 'Feeling better?'

Hazel sat up straight. 'Do you know, I think I might go to church after all. Maybe I'll have a word with Leon. He's great at putting things in perspective.'

Zosia couldn't put the current threat out of her mind. On the Saturday before Easter Sunday, the day of Toby's party, Zosia got up early to distract herself with scrubbing surfaces and furniture. She had been rescuing old chairs from the garden and giving them a coat of wood preservative. There were jobs she wanted to get done if she had to run away, if there really was a threat to Krys. The man's words rang through her head many times a day. *Afraid for the old woman. Or the boy.*

Hazel tried to show her the security camera footage but she found herself making excuses for the neighbours, saying she felt uncomfortable invading their privacy and that it couldn't be easy integrating into a new country.

In private, she did review a little of the footage, hoping no one was stalking them. There hadn't been another note but she was on edge from two directions now. She spent a few hours at night searching for new jobs on her phone, trying to get ahead of the threatening neighbours and their vile threats to Krys. The note still puzzled her but she dared not show anyone.

After breakfast, she cooked the promised steamed rolls, and as she put them out to cool she was surprised to hear Leon's voice from the hallway, talking to Krys.

Her son was, by now, in love with Leon. He treated him half like a favourite uncle and half like a climbing frame. They came in, Krys dangling from his forearm.

'I've just got to find a wet, muddy place to dump this monkey,' he said, walking through to the garden as Krys shrieked with laughter. The garden had now been declared safe and all weapons and dangerous tools either removed or locked up tight. Krys ran off to fetch his football from the long grass.

'I could strim that lawn down, maybe get a mower on it if you like,' Leon offered, coming back in as she finished loading the dishwasher. 'So he can really play football.'

'You should ask Hazel,' Zosia said. 'It's her garden.'

He leaned up against the doorframe, watching her. She dumped the empty baking tin in a bowl of water, scrubbing it clean in the bubbles. The rolls were dripping with butter.

'What's wrong?' he asked, his voice dropping to a rumble.

'Everything is *fine*,' she enunciated carefully. 'Nothing is wrong.' *Except I'm scared Declan will know I like you.*

He carried on watching her until she had scrubbed the tin unnecessarily hard and dried it thoroughly.

'Only you haven't looked at me once.'

She turned to him, stared into his eyes and spoke again. 'I am busy. I have a birthday party to go to with Krys.'

He nodded slowly. 'You'll probably be glad to know neither you nor Hazel will be arrested for having a gun without a licence.'

She had to look away as she put the baking tin away in the freshly washed-out drawer. 'The police called and told Hazel we were OK,' she said, turning the rolls over to cool down evenly. 'If that is all, I have to get changed.'

'It isn't all,' he said, as she walked to the door into the hall. 'You don't look yourself.'

She shook her head, clenching her hands. 'You don't know me very well. I am tired, I am busy. I don't have time right now.'

'The police are concerned about a teenaged girl they tracked into this area. She was trafficked to the UK but they've lost track of her. Have you seen anyone like that?'

The face she had seen at the window next door popped into her head, along with the grimace on the face of the man next door, snarling at her about how he would hurt Krys. 'I have seen women next door, no one special stands out.' The look on the girl's face had been terror, and the thought made her chest feel tight.

'Well, if you see anyone, let us know.'

She turned at the bottom of the stairs. The banister was curved and warm in her hand, like it had been made for her fingers. 'You sound like you are still a police officer.'

'I was in the police for a long time,' he said. 'It's a mindset. I'm sorry, I'll go back to being the parish priest. I came to ask you to bring Hazel to church tomorrow. I think she would, if you and Krys came.'

'I think she might go.' She bit her lip, feeling the weight of unconfessed sins, especially after reading Casimir's account of wartime horrors. 'I don't know – I am Catholic. I don't know what to do in your church.'

'All are welcome. No matter what your version of Christianity, I think you will want to celebrate Jesus's rising from the tomb.' She could remember the pageantry from her home town, the early morning mass, the wonderful songs from the choir. She looked up at him, his smile faded and his eyes were warm with compassion. 'Come to church and be with your new friends in the village.'

That made her eyes prickle with tears. 'I will talk to Hazel,' she promised. 'Krys wants to come anyway because all his friends are going.'

'And we will have an Easter egg hunt afterwards.'

She hadn't even painted traditional hard-boiled eggs, as she had done when Krys was little. She couldn't bear to buy a foil-wrapped chocolate egg if she couldn't celebrate as she had when she was a child. Święconka, baskets of food reflecting the Easter feast, blessed by the priest... The memory of helping her mother and grandmother in the kitchen made her homesick. She managed a small smile, and headed upstairs. She could feel his eyes on her, puzzled by her reserve. It made her heart ache.

. . .

The birthday party was more relaxing than Zosia had expected, the mothers and a few fathers ranged on picnic tables in the warm sunshine, the children tumbling in and out of a barn half filled with bales of hay. Toby's mother Nell introduced her around again, which helped because she hadn't recalled all the names.

One mum she hadn't met previously was the wife of Pete, one of the parents at the school gate. Jennie sat in a bit of shade feeding a baby that looked just a few weeks old. Zosia couldn't keep the smile off her face, they looked so comfortable.

'Come and keep me company,' Jennie said. 'Drag up a chair, or a hay bale. Or some other piece of farm furniture. It's lovely to speak to someone new.'

'I didn't realise you had another child,' Zosia said, enchanted at the glimpse of a tiny face, eyelashes fanned over perfect, pink cheeks. 'Boy or girl?'

'It's a boy. We've called him Rowan but don't get my mother started on the name, she hates it.'

'I think it's a lovely name,' Zosia said. 'Hazel – I'm living at Foxglove Cottage – has two rowans in her garden.'

'He was premature, born early. He was in hospital for two months after he was born,' Jennie said, never taking her eyes off the baby. 'It's lovely to have him home at last.'

Zosia sat back, trying not to show her shock. 'He looks so well.'

'He is. He's made amazing progress.' She looked up at Zosia, tears filling her eyes. 'Sorry, I'm still a bit emotional.'

'That must have been so difficult. Will he be all right, now he's home?'

'He has Down syndrome,' Jennie said. 'I'm still struggling to explain it to people. We are just thrilled he's here, and alive, but it's hard to deal with other people's reactions. They don't know whether to congratulate you or commiserate, especially when he was so ill.' She pressed her lips to the blond fuzz on the top of his head. 'We think he's *perfect*.'

'He really is,' Zosia said, her arms aching with memories of Krystof as a baby. Rowan let go of the nipple, his mouth dribbling a little milk. 'You did amazingly well to breastfeed through two months in hospital,' she said.

'He had a heart defect. He used to go blue when I tried to feed him at first. They fixed that a few weeks ago and now, as you can see, he's making up for lost time.' She discreetly covered up and buttoned her clothing. 'Do you want to hold...?'

'I would *love* to,' Zosia said, taking him. He was a warm presence, swamped by his blanket. 'Oh, he's beautiful, so tiny.'

His downy little cheeks were round and his chin wobbled in his sleep. She propped him up a little on her shoulder, and found herself rocking him. She was rewarded by a delicate little belch.

'I feel like I'm being defensive all the time, like he's going to face rejection or discrimination, and I want to protect him,' Jennie said.

'I suppose there might be a bit of that, from ignorant people,' Zosia said. 'But I don't think it's going to bother him for a while yet. By then, you'll be more relaxed.'

'Maybe.' Jennie stood up, stretched. 'Are you all right there for a moment? I need to pop to the loo and grab a cup of tea. Feeding him makes me so thirsty.'

Zosia smiled and nodded, and carried on rocking baby Rowan. The first few weeks of Krys's life were about the happiest she could remember. Declan had been stressed and difficult during the pregnancy, but she put it down to first-time dad nerves. Afterwards, he couldn't have been more attentive. It was only after a month or so that he started to add suggestions that turned to insistence and finally were regimented demands. The baby should be on a routine, weaned, not carried or comforted or played with *too much*. As if there could be a too much for love and attention.

Someone blocked out the light and when she looked up, it was Leon, watching her.

He crouched down next to her, smiling at the baby. 'You look so comfortable there,' he said softly.

She looked at him, the few grey hairs at his temples, the healing scratch where a bramble had almost caught his eye when they were doing the garden. 'I'm sorry if I was rude,' she whispered back. 'This morning. I'm just a bit stressed at the moment.'

'You know where I am if you want to talk. In confidence, if you prefer.' He smiled at her, and the baby snuffled in his sleep. His smile vanished. 'Oh, don't let me wake him up, I'll be in so much trouble.'

Zosia resumed the rocking. 'He'll be fine. I didn't expect to see you here.'

'Parish duties on the farm next door,' he murmured. 'And I knew there would be cake. Those rolls you made smelled amazing.'

'We *will* come to the church tomorrow,' she said. 'All of us.'

'You will both be very welcome.'

Looking around at the parents on their garden chairs or hay bales, all smiling and most of them looking at her, she finally felt it, the welcome from the whole community. Which made the idea of being driven away even more painful.

26

JULY 1940

Every time I met a new Polish flier, I questioned him about Poznań, about my family, and he would tell me what he knew, and he did the same to me. Did we walk through some village or town, did we see the motor car garage or the restaurant by the railway station? I could never reassure them, nor them me, but we tried anyway. There were no letters, no contact with home. We had seen people machine-gunned in the fields, strafed on the roads, trying to flee the invasion. For all I knew my family were dead.

At first, I thought about going back to Poland, a conqueror, a hero, where all acts of war would be forgiven. Until I married Rosie Duke. I couldn't imagine how she would fit in to my home, the language, my family. I know they would love her, but she would seem like a fragile flower to them, I thought, in my early ignorance. I had not yet seen the strength of my wife, because with me, she could be young. We both could just be young and in love, until we went back to our war work, when we remembered the horror of war. But the memories haunted me.

I knew my Poland was gone.

— *EXTRACT FROM THE MEMOIR OF*
CASIMIR WOJCIK

Outside the honeymoon hotel, Casimir lifted both cases into the taxi and handed the driver a piece of paper. 'In, in,' he said to Rosie.

She moved across the seat for him to join her. 'Where are we going?' she asked.

'That's going to be a couple of quid,' the taxi driver said. 'You got it, mate?'

'I got it,' Cas said, showing the man a few notes. 'Is surprise,' he said to her, kissing her cheek.

The car wove its way between the occasional heap of rubble or workmen mending pipes, but mostly the town seemed to be intact. 'You're stopping the bombers getting through,' she said, holding one of his hands up to her cheek.

'Not all,' he said, staring up at the buildings with slates blown off or windows gone, curtains trailing out in the light breeze. 'We try stop all planes.'

'You a pilot?' the driver said, glancing back at them both.

'He is,' Rosie said, hugely proud.

'I thought you was German for a second,' he said. 'No offence, mate,' as Casimir started forward, his cheeks going brick red.

'He's from Poland,' she explained. 'He really doesn't like the Germans.'

The man gave a cough of laughter. 'I'll bet. He's been up recently? Churchill's calling it the Battle of Britain.'

'He is,' she said, glancing at Casimir as he sat back. 'He's been flying back-to-back missions. We just took two days off to get married.'

'Oh!' He seemed very pleased. 'Cheers, girl. You're not from around here, either, are you?'

'I'm from Devon.'

'Beautiful part of the world,' he said. 'My cousin's nipper's been evacuated down that way. Newton Abbot.'

'That's not far from my home,' she said, as a wave of homesickness rolled over her.

'Well, maybe you and your new husband will get some leave back to Devon, soon. It's not like he can take you home to Poland.' He laughed at his little joke, which she thought was in terrible taste. The car started to move outside of the city, along the edge of parkland.

Casimir held her hand, lifting it to his lips a few times. 'Not far,' he said. 'I see this place from—' He seemed to run out of words. 'From plane.'

'Oh?'

'It's near Epping Forest,' the driver contributed. 'I saw a Messerschmitt shot down there a week ago, my fare made me drive over to see it on fire. Caught some of the trees, too.'

All Rosie could think about was the pilot. She hoped he'd got out, even though he was an enemy.

'This place, Loughton. Has bus,' Cas explained.

She pulled him around to face her. 'What is this all about?'

'Our home,' he said, his eyes wide. 'We need home. You live there – go work on bus – I get leave. Come home.'

Her heart felt so full she felt dizzy. It was everything she wanted. 'Is it a room?' she asked, as the driver pulled into quiet streets in terraces of narrow houses.

'Is...' He placed his hand in the air, put his other fingers on top. 'On shop.'

'A flat?' The thought of getting away from her miserable, draughty digs was intoxicating. Here they could spend their free nights together; she could cook him meals. She didn't care what the place was like, it would be their first home.

The driver checked the paper and pulled up on a street

with a small row of shops. 'Looks like it's over the barber's,' the man said. 'That's a guinea, mate.' Cas didn't seem to understand the reference so she pulled out a pound, a shilling and an extra two shillings for a tip. No matter how insensitive he had been, he seemed genuinely pleased for them.

'Can you wait until I make certain we can get in?' she asked.

'A couple more minutes won't hurt,' he said.

She walked to the door beside the shop. 'Do you have a key, Cas?'

Casimir smiled and hammered on the door. It opened almost at once to reveal Audrey at the bottom of a flight of stairs, cigarette in hand, smart trousers cinching in her waist. She handed over a front door key. Her coat hung at the bottom of the stairs and she took it down.

'I don't want to play gooseberry,' she said, leaning forward to hug Rosie and kiss her cheek. 'The girls had a whip-round to get you started. See you tomorrow, chick, on the evening shift.' She smiled at Casimir and walked to the taxi driver. 'Are you available? I need to get back to the Waltham powder mill.'

The man immediately smartened himself up, tugging at his collar and sitting up straight. 'Certainly, duchess,' he said, winking at Rosie before they drove away. Rosie realised her mouth was still open.

She turned to Casimir, her eyes brimming with tears. 'You did this?'

'I ask Audrey,' he said, grinning. 'Come, in house.'

'Wait,' she said, pulling him back. 'In England, it's good luck for the groom to carry the bride over the threshold.'

'Good luck?' he said, sounding the words out as if trying to understand. 'This, good luck?' And he swept her off her feet into her arms and stepped over the doorway.

He started up the stairs, making her shriek with laughter. 'No, Cas, not up all the stairs! Put me down.' He kissed her before he did, then went back for the cases. She climbed the stairs to a tiny landing.

The whole flat was floored in old linoleum, cracked and torn in a few places but serviceable in a floral pattern that was wearing away in places. One door led to a small room with a gas cooker and lamps, a table with two chairs, and in the corner, two fireside chairs that looked almost child-sized. A dusty window looked over the road. Directly opposite the stairs was a cupboard with a WC and tiny sink squeezed in beside it. The last door opened into a bedroom, with a high metal bed and a rag rug in bright colours at the end of the bed. A simple chest of drawers sat against the wall, and the window looked over the back yard of the barber's.

Casimir had stopped beside her, staring into the room. 'Here,' he said, holding out an envelope. Inside was a card with the best wishes of her friends and colleagues, and she put it on the tiny bedroom fireplace. The expression in his eyes changed, like storm clouds coming in. 'Bed,' he said, not commanding her but just stating a fact. 'Eighteen hundred hours.' His next shift.

She kissed him and walked backwards into the room until she reached the bed. 'How long will it take for you get to the airbase?'

'Two hours, train,' he said, groaning as she undid his shirt buttons. 'One hour taxi.'

'Taxi then,' she said, laughing, before he lifted her onto the bed.

Audrey had set up the kitchen. His fellow pilots had given them a basket of bread, and an ornate pot of salt, and they toasted each other with a small bottle of fiery spirits Cas called *wódka*, before he dressed to go back to the base.

'Love you, Rosie Wojcik,' he said, staring into her eyes as they stood at the bottom of the stairs.

'Love you too, Casimir Wojcik,' she said.

He bent his head to kiss her hand, then stopped. He circled her loose wedding ring. 'This finger, *Angielski*.' He slipped the ring off, over her tiny protest. He moved to her right hand and slid the ring onto her third finger. 'This finger, *Polski*.' It fitted perfectly.

27

PRESENT DAY, APRIL

Zosia curled up in the armchair in the corner of the living room to phone her mother in Poland. She really didn't want to be overhead by Krys or Hazel, both of whom could understand much of what she was saying.

'Mama?' she said when the house phone was answered.

'Zosia? I thought it was your sister.' Her rapid-fire Polish rattled down the phone. After so many years speaking English, Zosia struggled to pick it up straight away.

'Which sister?' Zosia asked, to buy time.

'The stupid one,' her mother said. 'How is my beautiful grandson?'

'He's fine, he's doing so well at school.'

'And you have moved, yes? Again? Are you at least in a nice house?'

'Very nice. It's owned by a lady whose father fought the Germans during the war. A Polish family.'

'All Poles fought in the war,' her mother said, her voice sharp and high. 'And your husband? Have you spoken to him?'

'He's not my husband any more,' Zosia said. 'And I haven't spoken to him. I don't feel safe with him.'

Her mother shouted something to someone, probably her father.

'How is Dad?' she asked, tears prickling. Overprotective, calm, kind Dad who had visited after they broke up, who had held her hand as she signed the divorce papers.

'You know. Scatterbrained. He's been helping out in the community garden, he never forgets anything about plants but he can't find his way to the shop.'

Zosia frowned. She had noticed something odd about him last time she had seen him. A bit vague about detail. Forgetful about glasses, keys, time. 'Maybe you shouldn't let him go out on his own.'

Her mother snorted down the phone, half in jest, half in frustration. 'How do I stop him? Why did you call me? You don't speak to me for months, then suddenly a phone call.'

'I was wondering about coming back home.'

'Bringing Krystof back for a visit? That would be lovely. We have room now your sister has moved out.'

'Not just a visit,' Zosia said, the words coming with difficulty. 'Maybe to live again.'

'What about your husband? God has put you together, you can't just run back home. And what about Krystof? A boy needs his father.'

Zosia couldn't explain. 'Well, just a holiday first, to see you and Dad. We could talk about it.'

She was very aware of Hazel and Krys laughing in the kitchen.

'You have that kind of money? Just to come for a holiday?'

'I have a few savings. We only have to pay for the travel, if you can put us up.'

'But we always come to you. We stayed in your lovely house in Newcastle. I remember when Krystof was just born, we stayed, Declan was so kind. So polite. And we met your mother-in-law, Crystal. How is she?'

I have no idea. Zosia tried to change the subject. 'I've been doing some translating again, the memoirs of a Polish Air Force pilot.'

'We can come over to England in the summer, when Krystof is home from school. I can get new passports.'

'Mama, I don't have anywhere for you to stay right now, and I'd really like to show Krys Poland. Declan never wanted to go but I am really missing home.' She couldn't explain that reading Casimir's agony of homesickness had infected her with similar longings.

'You can all come, it would be better.' Zosia could hear her mother digging in. 'You and Declan could talk to a priest, maybe get some counselling. Patch up your difficulties. You always had a bad temper as a child.'

'Mama, I just wanted to bring Krys for a few days to see you, to have you to ourselves. That's all.'

She could hear the hiss of her mother's frustrated breathing. 'You know we would never say no to seeing you,' she said begrudgingly. 'But you should see a priest. You can't neglect your religion as well as your marriage.'

'Well, we're going to church tomorrow,' Zosia said, managing a smile. 'And I *will* be talking to a priest.'

The Easter service was nothing like the ones Zosia had grown up with. The tiny church had a door open at the back and children wandered in and out with two Sunday-school helpers and a Labrador. There were a couple more dogs asleep under chairs. The music was a surprise, too – musicians with guitars and a piano played modern hymns full of joy and celebration. A couple of what she guessed were more traditional ones were sung with passion, and Leon spoke from a full heart about Easter bringing the community together. Hazel stayed awake;

she hadn't brought a book as she had threatened to, but didn't sing along.

Zosia tried to. 'Are you all right?' she whispered, after the first song.

'I'm not comfortable with all the religious stuff,' Hazel whispered back.

'Why did you come, then?'

'Chocolate,' Hazel said and winked at Krys. 'And because Leon wanted me to.'

Even though one of Leon's messages was that Easter was not all about chocolate, it featured prominently in the egg hunt all over the church, the grounds and the hedge. A separate collection was made for the school in Zambia that Hartford was twinned with, and a video call had been set up so the children could talk to the community in Kabwe. It moved Zosia seeing Krys and Toby chatting with a boy and girl in a school far away, Krys as confident as he had ever been. The children finally ended their calls, collected their eggs and got ready to go home. As they were walking to the car, Leon called after her.

'Zosia, wait.'

'Oh. W-we were just going,' she said.

'I know. I just wanted to see if you were all right. You seemed distracted.'

After the threatening conversation with the man next door, she had struggled to relax around people.

'I'm just tired. I'm thinking of visiting my parents for a few days, maybe in the summer.'

'I'm sure a holiday will be good for you both.'

She waved at a couple of the mums from the school gate. 'Maybe.' She made a face. 'My mother is very religious. She doesn't believe in divorce.'

'Catholic?'

'She just doesn't understand.' She looked at the ground.

'My father's been getting very forgetful over the last couple of years. I think I should go and see him.'

His smile faded. 'How old is he?' he asked, his voice low and gentle.

'Not old enough to have dementia,' she snapped, then immediately shut her eyes. 'I'm sorry. I'm tired, I've been busy...' She felt him take one of her hands between his and looked up.

'Don't apologise. You can say anything to me.'

Suddenly shy, she pulled her fingers away. The warmth of his palms lingered. 'I'd better go. But thank you for a lovely day, and a magical service.'

He smiled again. 'Any time. We're here every week.'

She could feel the pull of attraction to Leon as she walked towards the car for the short drive home, past hedges full of fragrant blossoms, and birds singing.

28

JULY 1940

Rosie's work seemed mundane to me at first, she described it as mechanical. Cutting cordite for various bullets and shells, keeping the factory clean and safe. Apart from a German bomb breaking through, I didn't think there was as much danger to her. But that idea was to protect me, I see that now, as I protected her by saying we were just patrolling the skies in case a German bomber got through. She couldn't lie about the booklets of regulations and procedures she had to learn to make explosives. I couldn't read the words, but I saw the pictures, grey images of protective clothing and terrible accidents, first aid for catastrophic injuries. I confronted Rosie, I made her read them to me, and finally I saw the dangers she faced. Like a pack of Focke-Wulf 190s or a Messerschmitt Bf 109s circling like deadly crows. I found myself praying for her to be safe, to be well, not to be injured or killed.

She cried when I cried, and we promised not to keep any more secrets. But I still couldn't tell her about the red rage that made me a better pilot, the rage that bloomed as I remembered the corpses on the fields and roads as I fled my homeland.

Rosie's first shift back at work after the wedding held a few surprises. The more direct bus route was one: it gave her another twenty minutes in bed. Audrey had organised all of her belongings to be transferred to the flat, which meant she didn't have to say goodbye to the Parkers, who had never been friendly and Connie had already been transferred closer to her parents' house. The manager of her section waved her over her as she came in.

'You have to fill in a form,' he said, smiling. 'Congratulations, you're being transferred to bombs. You'll be making RDX. There's an extra eight shillings a week for you.'

The form was short, just relaying her new address and name – the first time she had had to spell out Rosemary Wojcik – and a line where she was supposed to put her next of kin. Was that Cas now? She couldn't bear the thought that her parents wouldn't be contacted if something happened to her. She put Casimir's name down but felt increasingly uneasy as she moved to the new section. Her parents still didn't know she was married. The biggest thing to happen to Rosie in her young life and she hadn't told Ma and Dad.

The bomb section had different rules. Heavier overalls, rubber boots and a hood with a glass window to be used when pouring or working with the acid. An older woman showed her how to tuck her hair entirely away.

'You might be better cutting it short,' she advised. 'The chemicals burn it off anyway.' Her own forehead had no hair growing low down. 'A smear of Vaseline along the hairline helps too,' she said, showing Rosie where it was kept. Her hands were covered in tiny brown splotches. 'Acid,' she said, showing Rosie the backs. 'They say you have to wear the gloves, but they are so thick you can't pour accurately.'

Rosie was so anxious her own hands were shaking as she tucked her hair up. 'Is it all right to wear my wedding ring?' she asked.

'Oh, that's what that is, on your right hand? They send the girls up here a lot, after they get married. Maybe they think you'll be more careful. It's better to leave your ring in your locker. If you get acid underneath it will burn longer.'

Despite all the dire warnings, the staff were friendly and explained she would be doing just one part of the process: measuring and mixing the acids from glass carboys, giant jars that weighed forty pounds. The trick was to stop them splashing – or foaming up into a mist – while adding them to the reaction tank. Rosie was careful, but when there were colleagues lining up behind her with a backlog of chemicals, it was harder to be careful *and* fast, but she soon got the hang of it. Break time required her to change out of the protective clothes, especially to air out the hot and damp cowl, and it only left a few minutes for a sandwich and a cup of tea. To her surprise, all workers were required to drink a small glass of milk, which was luke-warm and not too fresh. There was little conversation. Her shoulders and neck were already aching; she wondered how bad they would be at the end of the day.

That night, her muscles stiffened up as she tried to sleep in the new bed without Casimir. The blackout curtains didn't meet in the middle, so she couldn't read in bed. Eventually, overwhelmed by tiredness, she fell asleep, only to be woken up a few hours later by the barber's shop opening early morning. Men, it seemed, visited the barber on their way to work. She could barely lift her arms to get dressed.

Audrey – thank heaven for Audrey – had left a little food in the pantry. It was enough for breakfast, because she hadn't had time to queue for food or register with local shops for their rations. She looked at her new list of shifts and couldn't see a time when she'd be able to make it to the shops. Her next day off was Sunday when the shops were shut, and she knew Cas didn't have time to visit until the following week. She caught the early bus, hoping to catch Audrey before her shift back at the cordite building.

She swept Rosie into a huge hug when she saw her. 'They moved you!'

'They did,' Rosie said. 'I miss you. I miss all of you.'

Audrey tucked her hand into Rosie's arm as they walked to the changing room. 'So, how is married life? Now it's been nearly a week?'

Rosie couldn't help it, her face heated up. 'Married life is lovely, thank you. Living on my own is difficult, though. I don't have time to shop or cook and I can't imagine doing laundry.'

'One of the girls in my dorm has just left,' Audrey said. 'Why don't you stay with us for a few days, until you get set up in the flat? You can pop back whenever you want. The food is dreadful but at least you don't have to cook it. We have a laundry room. And the company is good.'

Rosie thought rapidly. That would give her a few days to get everything right for the next time Casimir had leave. 'That's a lovely idea,' she said, hugging Audrey again. 'I'll pack a bag and stay with you tomorrow.'

She walked back to the workshop. There were two huge banks of earth built between the bomb section and the rest of the campus, and rabbits scampered up one side. A few birds were singing, and it took her back to memories of the farm.

Her last letter from her mother included news of their three evacuees. Fred, Bridget and Howard had arrived from London after their house near the docks was condemned. They had immediately let the chickens out, stolen from the pantry and threatened to run away. It sounded like Ma had got the better of them with a combination of kindness and strictness. Withholding pudding seemed to be an incentive to wash, dress and behave. It seemed as if her mother was enjoying a return to parenting.

They don't know the meaning of work, though,' she had written.

> *Farmers' children always know where food comes from, and you helped as soon as you could walk. Bridget likes collecting the eggs, and Fred doesn't mind stacking straw bales and bedding down the animals. I kept a room free for you, I can't wait for you to come home on your first week's holiday...*

Which was soon and would create a huge problem. She wanted to spend as much time as possible with Casimir. But part of her longed to breathe fresh air, step out on the springy grass and heather around the farm, smell Ma's apron as she was hugged like a child.

While she worked, she started forming the letter in her head, trying to find the words to tell her parents that she was a married woman, even if they had broken the law to do it. As she tried to form the sentence that explained why she had forged her papers, her hand slipped. A splash of acid hit her glove and a small part of her wrist above it and she screamed. She hung onto the carboy, grinding her teeth with the effort of holding on to it. She emptied it slowly but the acid burned like a lit candle and her glove was smoking. The safety officer was on her way, and Rosie put the empty carboy down and staggered away from the tank.

The woman grasped her elbow and dragged her towards the sink, safely situated thirty yards away. Water getting into the acid tank itself could make it boil or explode. She pulled off Rosie's glove with her other hand, and ran the tap over the whole of her arm. There was a dark yellow burn on her wrist more than an inch across, the skin creased like old leather, and the cold water running over it made it burn even more. She struggled to catch her breath.

After several minutes, the woman moved her over to a first aid station beside the sink. 'There,' she said. 'It's not too bad. You did well not to drop the bottle on yourself.'

'It was such a shock,' Rosie said, her voice coming out thin and breathless, her hands trembling.

The woman smeared a white paste over the burn and the rest of her wrist. 'This is just bicarb, it neutralises the acid. I'll put a bandage on it and you can go home. But you need to learn from this – you must concentrate.'

'I was a bit distracted,' Rosie whispered. 'I'm trying to work out how to tell my mother I got married.'

The woman smiled, and Rosie realised she was quite old, half her teeth missing and wisps of grey hair peeping from under her cowl. 'That would be distracting. Take my advice, dearie, tell her straight. She'll forgive you.'

'How do you know?' Rosie said, turning to look at her.

'I've got five girls and a boy. Eventually you forgive them everything,' she said, her eyes narrowing as she laughed. 'And if she doesn't, have a baby. That will *definitely* do it.'

Rosie managed to smile, although her wrist was now throbbing with pain.

29

PRESENT DAY, APRIL

'There's a letter for you,' Hazel shouted up the stairs. 'And Leon is popping in this evening to measure up to order the wood for the new pergola.'

Zosia jumped at the thought of another note. She slid into her dressing gown and went downstairs. It wasn't another message, it was an official-looking letter in a heavy envelope. She sat on the stairs to open it, hoping it wasn't a tax demand or something she had overlooked. It was much worse.

Declan was applying to the courts for visitation rights to his son.

Zosia felt physically sick. The hall tiles blurred in front of her and she clung to the banister. Her own solicitor had been given the Dartmoor address and now she wanted to know what Zosia's instructions were.

Her first instinct was to grab Krys, bundle him into a taxi and run away. She had a few hundred pounds saved from her work with Hazel – she could just disappear. Maybe she could replace the passports Declan had kept, get them back to Poland...

Her thoughts spun around and around, like a terrified bird

in a trap. She needed to stand her ground. Her solicitor had made it plain that in hiding from Declan she was strengthening his case.

She went back to the letter. ... *provide access to Mr Armitage with a social worker's supervision... at the moment he is not asking for custody... Mr Armitage is being reasonable...*

Zosia knew just how reasonable Declan could be. She staggered a little when she stood up, and walked into the kitchen. Hazel stared at her.

'It's not like you to come down in your pyjamas,' she said. She laid a hand on Zosia's forehead. 'Are you feeling ill? You're freezing cold.'

'It was a bit of a – shock,' Zosia said through chattering teeth.

'Come and sit in the rocking chair. I'll get you some tea.'

Zosia couldn't even argue that what Hazel called tea – probably some brew with nettles and lemon balm in it – wouldn't help because it often did. She rocked in the chair, clutching the letter to her chest, before unfolding it and reading it again. It barely made sense to her. But once she was given the tea, sweetened with honey, she handed the letter to Hazel.

It tasted as bad as she expected but she sipped it anyway, as she watched Hazel lean against the table and read it through.

'My goodness. How did you leave things with Declan?'

Zosia swallowed too much hot liquid and choked. When she stopped spluttering, she croaked, 'He was in prison for actual bodily harm and I was in a women's shelter.'

Hazel sat in the chair opposite her. 'Tell me, maid. Don't worry about it, just explain it so I can help.'

Zosia was too tired and shaken to hide it any longer. 'He had always been controlling. I didn't want children so early in our marriage but he insisted. I just felt like I had to be careful around him, all the time.' She kept slipping into Polish, but Hazel seemed to understand. 'I tried hard to make him happy. I became so afraid of making him angry. One day he got so angry he lashed out at me for the first time. Just a tap, what he used to call a play slap. But it hurt and I pushed him away. I'd never fought back before.'

She recalled the way his face had contorted into something she had never seen before. His next blow was a punch that knocked her onto the floor. She banged her head on the kitchen island, knocking a chair over and splintering it. 'Declan, no!' was all she had been able to say.

He was enraged, kicking at her, pulling her up to sitting, punching her so hard she couldn't think, her arms up to protect herself.

'Mama!' Krys was four years old then, standing in his favourite jumper, eyes wide. Declan hated that he called her that; he always wanted him to call her Mummy. Krys ran forward to her as Declan pulled back his arm, his elbow smashing into their son and sending him flying.

Zosia had ducked the next blow in her effort to get to Krys, while Declan's fist slammed into the wall, punching a hole in the plasterboard. She had dragged herself up against the kitchen island, trying to see around him to where Krys lay, silent and unmoving.

Then something broke inside her, a wave of rage, and she grabbed the nearest thing to hand – a heavy wooden knife block – and swung it towards Declan with all her strength. In that moment, she didn't care if she killed him. It connected with his temple. He was felled instantly, and she ran to Krys, grabbing him off the ground. It was then that she heard the dog's frantic howling from the garden, jumping up at the kitchen door.

Krys was breathing – she had ripped his jumper up to lay her ear on his chest. When she took her head away she saw the blood she'd transferred to his skin from her face. He moved in her arms, and she grabbed her keys and bag and fled to the car.

As she started the engine, she looked back. Declan was reeling, swaying in the doorway, blood pouring down his face. His mouth was a scarlet scream as she backed the car out of the drive, heedless of the traffic, and locked the doors with a shaking hand. Krys was still on her lap, clinging to her like a monkey. She drove off the estate and down the main road until she judged she was far enough away, then peeled Krys off and put him safely in his car seat, hoping that Declan wouldn't run up behind her. Her hands were shaking and blood was trickling down her face and neck as she drove towards the police station with exaggerated care. She was dizzy, her vision was obscured by blood, she felt sick. A street short of her goal, she knew she was going to faint, and just managed to take the car out of gear and put on the handbrake as the world spun into darkness.

Hazel listened and waited, as Zosia tangled Polish and English to tell the story, flipping backwards and forwards in time as she rambled.

'So, what happened after you stopped the car?' she asked, her voice gentle, putting a hand on Zosia's for a moment.

'A kind person saw me slumped over the wheel and called an ambulance. I managed to explain what had happened, or tried to, anyway. Krys started screaming that Daddy had hurt Mama, and when they took me to hospital the police were already there. I was much more hurt than I thought, they were amazed that I had driven the car that far.' She put the empty cup down and hugged herself. 'Declan had already called the police, said that I had gone mad, attacked him and stolen his son. They thought...' *that I had tried to hurt him, that I was violent.* 'I was arrested for assault at the beginning. I felt so awful. I still do. I could have killed him.' Zosia flinched before she looked up, afraid at what Hazel must think of her.

But there was no judgement. 'In self-defence.' Hazel's eyes filled with tears. 'You must have been terrified.'

Zosia found the words flooding out. 'Those leaflets I had translated told me what to say, how to explain. I had a cracked and dislocated jaw, talking was agony. I'd broken a collarbone and my wrist when I fell, yet I could carry Krys to the car and drive. They put Krys in the bed next to me in the emergency department, but he kept climbing out to get to me.' She choked on a sob. 'In the end, he cuddled on me like a baby while they checked him over. He had a concussion, we both did. The police officer told me Declan wouldn't be allowed near me until everything was cleared up. We had one day in hospital before he caught up with us.' She took a deep breath. 'He claimed I had attacked him – it was his word against mine. He was quite badly hurt. It wasn't until the investigation that we could prove that I had hit him just once. But I had a dozen injuries, cracked ribs, bruises, fractures. They dropped the charges against me.' She shrugged. 'Krys was completely clear about what happened and – I did lie about one thing. I don't think he meant to hurt Krys but he said Daddy hurt him deliberately and I let it go. I got sole custody, he got eighteen months in prison although he was let out after eight.'

'And you've been waiting for him to make contact?'

'I've just kept moving since the refuge,' Zosia said, holding her hands out. 'I've never taken a penny from him because I don't want him to find me.'

Hazel took her hands in her strong fingers. 'You have to deal with this,' she said. 'You can't keep running and hiding.'

Zosia shook her head. 'I thought he had found me. There was a note. It had a Z on the front.'

'What did it say?'

'Just: "Leave him alone." I thought it meant Leon. Declan was always insanely jealous, thinking I was looking at other men, contacting them.' Tears filled her eyes. 'It's not just me, I have to protect Krys.'

Hazel let go of Zosia's hands and stood, stretching her back. 'Maybe he did mean Leon. Which makes it all the more important we talk to him and get his advice. Are you sure the note is from Declan?'

Zosia thought it through, her heartbeat becoming steadier. 'I couldn't think who else would do it.'

'This Declan sounds like he would have banged on the door,' Hazel said.

'There's a restraining order,' Zosia said. 'If it was Declan, I thought he would be a lot angrier, swearing a bit. But he wouldn't want to announce himself, he hates being caught in the wrong.'

Hazel looked over the garden, up the hillside to the tor, dotted with sheep and lambs in the distance. 'I think we'll have to be careful to keep the doors locked, anyway. And don't worry about the solicitor, I can help you out with the fees if you need it. Let's go on the offensive, and keep Declan away from Krys.'

30

JULY 1940

Duke's Farm, when we visited from London for the first time, was astonishing to me. The moorland that Rosie loved so much was a patchwork of colours in summer: bracken like a chestnut pony, gorse as dark as seaweed, covered with butter-yellow flowers; grass tipped scarlet as if dipped in blood. The ponies were wandering over the moor, the land wild and beautiful. I had to remind myself that this was a land without bears, wolves and lynx, that the deer and sheep had nothing more to worry about than foxes. The land was free to graze. The Dukes only had a few enclosed fields close to the farm, nestled into a valley. I leaned on the farm gate. A low, slate-roofed building with several sections was snuggled into the hillside, a few hens pecking by the door. In my heart, I was terrified that they would greet me with disgust and anger, that their daughter had wasted her love on me, just a refugee from the war.

— *EXTRACT FROM THE MEMOIR OF CASIMIR WOJCIK*

Rosie hefted her bag and Casimir's too from the bus stop in the village. The lane was hot and dusty, long grass dropping seeds all over the ground, the hedges overgrown. He was dragging his heels a little, and she turned to look at him. 'It's not far,' she said, looking at the pale face.

'Your parents will hate me,' he said, wincing as he walked, leaning on a crutch. A bullet, one of hundreds that had drilled through his plane and put out his engine, had hit him. One of Cas's friends had brought the news that he had crashed on a beach in Sussex, barely bringing the plane down in one piece. Ricocheting through his thigh, onto his instrument panel and clipping his wrist, it had missed all of his vital organs but he had needed several days in hospital and a blood transfusion. She had felt like she would die too until she had rushed to the hospital. She was allowed to see him for a few minutes, muzzy from the anaesthetic, still covered in blood spatters on his face and hands. It reinforced to her that they were right to marry. The time they spent together was magical; she felt like someone else in his arms.

He had been given a week to recover, so Rosie took the opportunity to bring them down to Devon for a long weekend.

She had written to tell her parents she was married. They had answered with a very guarded letter expressing their disappointment. She suspected they were more upset that she had lied to them than they were about her marriage. Ma and Dad lived on moorland farming time, season by season, not day to day in the factory or in the air.

'My parents won't hate you,' she said, but she could hear a little doubt in her own voice. She cleared her throat. 'They will understand, even if they would have preferred me to wait.' She let him catch up with her, smiled up at him, reached to kiss him. 'You have three days for them to get to know you. Then they will love you, too.'

'They know about – this?' he asked, shaking the crutch.

But Rosie had kept that detail back. She hoped that his injuries, gained in his duties, would speak louder to her parents than anything. Time was precious, the war was savage and heartless.

She caught a little movement out of the corner of her eye and swung around to see her father, stick in hand, pushing a stray pig back into the enclosure. He shut the gate and secured it before he turned to face them. He looked a little stooped over, as if with the extra work, and his long face had a few more lines.

'There, maid,' he said as she ran to him. He hugged her as if he would hardly be able to let her go, lifting her up onto her tiptoes. He pulled her back a little, looked into her face. 'You look pale.'

'We don't get out in the fresh air much,' she said, her voice small. 'Dad, this is Pilot Officer Casimir Wojcik. My husband.'

Her father turned to look at Cas. 'Oh, I know who he is. You've grieved your mother bad, chick, that's all I'll say.'

'I know,' she said, tears tickling her throat. 'I know, Daddy.'

Her father put out his hand, looked at Cas's sling and pulled it back. He offered the left, Cas managing to prop the crutch up against himself and shake it. 'Thank you for seeing me, sir,' he said earnestly. He had never looked so young as he did with cropped hair sticking up, leaning forward on the wall to support his bad leg. 'Very kind.'

'You'd better come in and sit down,' Dad said, smiling his lazy, slow smile. 'I've got a one-legged cockerel who walks better than you do.' He turned to Rosie. 'Your ma's rubbing the horses down. Go and see her, chick, she won't want to cry in front of everyone.'

Rosie's heart dropped at the thought of upsetting her mother. She smiled at Cas, patted his good elbow and said, 'Go with Dad. Get some tea on.'

Her mother was brushing Bella's flank vigorously, wearing

old overalls that Rosie had once worn. 'Ma?' she said with a wavering voice.

Marion turned to look at her, her round face crumpling, and began to weep. Rosie couldn't bear it. She dropped the bags and darted forward to hug her mother. 'I'm so sorry,' she said, her words tumbling out. 'I never wanted to hurt you, I'm so sorry, but I had to—'

'No. I'm sorry,' Marion mumbled, pulling away to dry her cheeks. 'I didn't listen to you, I still thought you were a little girl. And all the while—' It wasn't working, tears were still pouring down her face. 'I'm sorry I didn't know what to write, either. Did you bring – him? Casimir?' It sounded funny with a Devon accent, Cazzimeer.

'Dad's taken him indoors. We caught the earlier bus, we were lucky with the train.'

'And you've both got leave?'

Rosie caught her breath for a moment. 'I've got leave. Cas is off sick. He had a crash-landing.'

Her mother gasped. 'What happened?'

Rosie tucked her arm into her mother's. 'He managed to glide back to the coast and put down on a beach road. Did I tell you he learned to fly on gliders before the war? But he got shot, by just one bullet, through his thigh.'

Her mother pulled her to a halt outside the back door. 'He could have been killed.' Looking into her eyes was like looking into a mirror, blue like a summer sky.

'Yes,' Rosie said. 'But he didn't. It's his job.'

'And you got injured, too?'

Rosie unconsciously put one hand over the healing burn on her wrist. Her mother reached over and gently pulled it away. She didn't say anything, but turned towards the house. 'Goodness, I can't go in in these overalls, they smell of horses and I'm covered with straw.'

'He won't mind,' Rosie said, smiling at her suddenly flustered mother.

'I'll nip up the back stairs and change,' she said, and disappeared into the scullery. Rosie walked round into the warm kitchen. The smell of baking made her mouth water. Cas was sitting in the chair beside the stove, looking wide eyed, leaning forward with his hands clenched together. Ma had put the best cloth out, a tray for tea and Grandma's wedding cups and saucers.

'His English in coming along well,' Rosie said, smiling down at him. She sat at the table, her hand taking his. 'But it's still hard when he's anxious.'

'I suppose he had to learn all the words for flying first,' Dad said, putting the big teapot, part of her history, handed down for three generations, on the tray. Her mother had chipped the spout as a child, and Rosie was the reason the lid had been glued back together. 'Your ma's put you in the spare room. There's a big bed in there, we needed your old room for the evacuees. They'll be back from school shortly.'

And that dealt with all of the questions she was too shy to ask. 'How are they getting on?'

'The oldest, Fred, is a bit of a tearaway, but he'll settle. Bridget's a good little thing, more or less does the chickens by herself except cleaning out. Howie's just a little scrap, he's five. Loves riding the horses.'

'And the pigs, if he gets a chance,' her mother said from the door. Casimir made an effort to stand up but knocked his stick over with a clatter and fell back. 'No, no,' Ma said, rushing forward to pick up the crutch. 'You sit down, now. You look pale enough. Rosie said you had to crash-land your plane? Is that what hurt your leg?'

He stared up at her in amazement. 'You look – like Rosie,' he stammered. 'Just like.'

Ma looked at him, a big smile on her face. 'Well, you'll find out we're quite alike, but we have our differences. She hasn't got my hand with scones, that's for sure, and she can sour milk just by scowling at it.'

Rosie looked at Casimir, who hadn't really understood all of this. 'Ma, this is Casimir Wojcik. My husband. My Cas.'

'So I see,' she said, holding out her hand, then changing it just as Dad had done. 'Well, you are very welcome, my dears. No matter how you ended up here.'

31

PRESENT DAY, APRIL

Zosia had received another note a week later. It was definitely about Leon, and was crudely suggesting that they were having sex. It warned this could ruin his career, and would create a local scandal in the press.

The unfair thing was, she wasn't sleeping with Leon and had no way to prove it.

The note had been vicious. 'Leave him alone' had been the theme. It *must* be Declan, but she couldn't work out how he was getting the notes delivered by hand. No one came up the drive except the postman and Leon – a stranger in the village would have been noted. Maybe he was paying someone to follow her. He had employed a private detective after their separation, and sent her a long list of places she'd been, men she'd been innocently seen with, moments when she had let go of Krys's hand or told him off. He had those resources. Part of her longed to talk to Leon about all of it. Another part held her back from showing him that vile note, talking to him about their unspecified but warm friendship.

Leon had 'just dropped in' a few times this week, this time to install something he'd been given – a bright orange slide for the garden. Zosia had been covered in mud and grass from weeding and planting when he arrived.

'My friend's kids have outgrown this,' he'd said, and he spent the next hour putting the slide together with an overexcited Krystof. Hazel and Zosia had been gentle around each other since they had talked about Declan, and also reading Casimir's accounts of his history. It was as if he skipped back and forth through his life, depending on what his mood was. A snapshot of his joy at Hazel's birth was mixed up with the agony of finally hearing from his family in Poland after the war.

Zosia's nerves were raw, but seeing Leon playing with Krys was soothing, though she was keen to avoid talking to him. Hazel had suggested she went for a long soak in the bath. Zosia knew that Hazel wouldn't say a thing about Declan.

The next time Leon came to the house it was to mow the lawn again and kick a ball around with Krys and Toby. At the end of the week, he had called Hazel, rather formally, to ask to speak to Zosia on the phone.

'I'm taking one of my older friends to the garden centre tomorrow,' he had said. 'I need someone to go with us.'

'As a chaperone?' Zosia joked.

He laughed. 'Maybe. I got my bottom pinched at the pensioners' Christmas dinner two years ago. No, Mags recently had a stroke, she walks with difficulty but she refuses to use a wheelchair. I just need help to steady her and in case she needs the loo.' Zosia's thoughts, as they did during dark times, had reverted to Polish so it took a few moments to translate all of this. Before she could answer, he added, 'It's an hour, maybe two, she just wants to plant up some pots in her garden. It's all she can manage now but she used to win "best-dressed garden in the village" prizes. We could pick up the shrubs Hazel wants, too.'

Zosia finally found her voice. 'That would be OK,' she said cautiously. She'd felt raw since she'd received the lawyer's letter, since she'd been threatened out on the tor. She didn't want to blurt her entire history out to another sympathetic, kind soul. 'But I want to get back early for Krys. I promised we would do some cooking.'

'We won't be long, and thank you. I'll pick you up about half past nine.'

Zosia smiled to herself. She *did* want to see Leon again.

'I'll see you then.' She put the phone down and walked through to the garden. Hazel was leaning on a fork dug into the ground, where they had taken out the most overgrown shrubs. 'Oh, let me do that! That's what you pay me for.'

'No. I pay you to clean up the garden and kitchen, to get through the environmental health inspection so we can run the café,' she said, but she relinquished the tool. 'You work so hard. I just thought we could put a row of lavender plants along there. I promised to drop Krys at Toby's farm to meet up with his friends for the morning, if you remember.'

'I did,' Zosia said, smiling at Hazel. There was so much she loved about the older woman, her fearless enthusiasm for life, her determination to live it on her terms. 'But your physio said *light* gardening for four more weeks.'

Hazel huffed. 'This is light to me. I once built a stone wall to grow succulents on. It's still there, buried in that buddleia and that stupid evergreen.'

'Do you want me to choose some lavenders tomorrow?' Zosia asked. 'I'm going to the garden centre with Leon to help one of his friends.'

'English lavender, please,' Hazel said, 'and not those little cuttings they grow for hedges. Let's have big, chunky plants, so we get the scent and the flowers this year. I ordered some roses, too – they should be ready to collect tomorrow. I took your advice and got thornless ones.'

Zosia was moved, yet again, by the way Hazel was consulting her about the design of the house, the garden. In her dark moments, when she dreamed of fleeing into Europe or applying for other jobs, she felt disloyal but it was more than that. She would miss Hazel, a woman with a completely different life and experience, who was more than twice her age. She respected Hazel's enthusiasm for life, her wisdom and resilience. Zosia aspired to be like Hazel one day, even as she felt weak and frightened, thinking about running away.

Zosia hadn't slept well; the crudities of the last note had run round and round in her head. By the time she came down to breakfast she felt tired and stressed. Everything Krys did seemed to be a bit louder than usual. Maybe he sensed there was something wrong because he clung to her a little.

Leon looked tired, too, when he rang the doorbell. He was driving the large estate car he'd taken down to the city, and in the front passenger seat was a tiny woman who stared at her with interest. Her face was a mass of loose wrinkles over a bird-like skull, her nose jutting out like the prow of a ship and bright scarlet hair projecting from under a hat decorated with artificial fruit.

As Zosia got in the back of the car and waved to Hazel and Krys, the old lady twisted around to see her, to study her closely.

'You don't look very old,' was her only comment, in very deliberate received pronunciation, like the late queen. It took a few seconds for Zosia to catch what she was saying.

'I'm nearly thirty,' Zosia said, defensively.

'*He's* forty,' the woman said, loudly, the way deaf people speak sometimes.

'I'm sorry,' Zosia said, equally loudly, 'I didn't catch your name. I'm Zosia Armitage.'

'There's no need to shout,' she replied. 'I'm Marguerite Carmichael. Like the flower. Nice to meet you, Mrs Armitage.'

Zosia was amused by the game. 'How do you do, Mrs Carmichael.'

Leon started along the main road. 'This is all very formal, Mags. Can't you just call her Zosia?'

'What kind of name is that? Young people have made-up names all the time.'

'It's Polish,' Zosia said. 'It's not made-up at all.'

There was a long silence. 'Well, that's all right, then,' she said. 'You can call me Mags.'

Within ten minutes she had talked all about the war she'd lived through as a child, the lack of proper flowers at the garden centre and identified exactly where Zosia had grown up. Her voice had softened, taking on a Dartmoor accent which was just as hard to understand, although Zosia was becoming used to it. Mags told her she had kept the car when her husband had died, and had only recently given up driving herself, after a 'silly stroke'.

Zosia could see how the stroke had affected her when she helped her out of the car. She was bent forward with age, with a slight lean to the left. Holding onto Zosia's firmly with one hand and holding a walking stick in the other, she was ready to go.

'I don't suppose you would like a wheelchair?' Leon suggested at the sliding doors, but Mags and Zosia both laughed at him.

'I am barely keeping up,' Zosia said, catching his eye. His expression was intense, and she paused for a moment, causing Mags to snap at her to keep going. Leon had looked at her with so much – warmth. And interest. The latest note spiralled into her mind, cutting the smile she had made in return. She turned back to Mags.

'Where's the blessed petunias?' the old woman said, as Zosia guided her to an array of plants, some starting to flower in bright colours.

'I don't know which ones you mean,' Zosia said. 'We have

petunias in Poland, but I don't know what their leaves look like.' Her father was really the gardener, filling their balcony with pots.

Leon joined them, pushing a wide trolley. 'What are you after, Mags?'

'Petunias, busy Lizzies, marigolds and begonias,' the old lady scoffed. Clearly, the stroke hadn't affected her gardening knowledge. They browsed the plants, Marguerite choosing by colour rather than species, filling up her trolley. 'Now then,' she said to Zosia. 'Steer me to a table in the coffee shop and you can get the plants for Hazel. She told Leon she wanted a few.'

'She gave Zosia a list,' Leon said, parking the trolley beside Mags. 'We won't be long.'

As soon as Mags was comfortable and a pot of tea ordered, Leon followed Zosia into an area filled with perennials. He touched her arm, startling her into turning to him. 'What's up?' he asked. 'What's wrong?'

She looked up into his dark eyes, the concern in the wrinkles on his forehead. 'Nothing, really. I'm just tired.' She could feel the pressure on her arm and pulled away.

'You've been tired for a while. Are you ill?'

'No, nothing like that.' She turned to look for the lavender plants Hazel was after, rows and rows of different-sized pots. 'It's just an – adjustment.' She was pleased with the word, she knew it but had never used it. 'New home, new job, new people.'

'You were more relaxed before Easter,' he said, following closely. 'Please, let me help.'

The words were spoken so passionately, with such feeling, she almost caved in. 'You aren't my priest,' she said lightly.

'Do you need to see a priest?'

She glanced back at him, surprised. 'No. I told you, I'm not that religious.'

'I wasn't really speaking as a priest. I was speaking as a

friend.' His shoulders dropped and he looked away. He was hurt.

'We don't know each other that well,' she said lightly. 'I'm fine, really. Do you think these are big enough to make a hedge?'

'Zosia—' He touched her arm again and this time she pulled away quickly.

'Look,' she hissed, her heart racing with the thought that some investigator was lurking nearby, taking pictures, gathering evidence against her for Declan. 'You are Hazel's friend, you are a kind man and a vicar, but that's all. I hardly know you. OK?'

His expression changed and he pulled back. 'Absolutely. Message received. I think Hazel wanted the big ones. She gave you a couple of hundred pounds, didn't she?'

Zosia lowered her eyes, she didn't want to meet his gaze. She put half a dozen of the more mature plants at the front of the shelf. 'These, I think,' she said, adding another two to be sure.

He got another trolley and handed her Hazel's list. 'She wants big plants,' he said coolly, 'to fill in the gaps where Krys and I hacked the old ones out.'

She lifted one into his trolley, a philadelphus a metre high with an eye-watering price. But he was right, she had enough money and it would look good for the opening of the café.

'Thank you,' she said, as he arranged the plants.

Two roses were sitting by the door with Hazel's name on the label.

'If you pay for these, I'll put them in the car. You can go and sit with Mags. I'll leave plenty of room for her plants, too.'

By the time Zosia had got herself a coffee and sat with Mags she was close to crying, although she couldn't say why. Nothing escaped the old lady.

'Lover's tiff?' she snapped, her hand shaking as she topped up her own tea.

'We're not – we're not lovers,' she said, her voice coming out flat. 'I haven't been here very long.'

'You're divorced, I hear,' Mags said, the words clinking out like a spoon on china.

'Yes,' Zosia said, and bent to sip her coffee.

'He was a bad 'un, then,' Mags concluded. 'He hurt you.'

Zosia sat back, her heart skipping beats in her chest. 'How did you know that?'

'Why else would a kind, sensible woman get divorced?' Mags said, then struggled to lift the cup to her lips, sipping cautiously. There was a fair bit of tea in the saucer. 'Pop that back in my cup, will you, maid?'

'Some men are unfaithful,' Zosia said, tipping the tea back for her.

'Well, that's the thing that hurts the most, doesn't it? Was that his problem?'

Honestly, the elderly think they can ask anything, say anything. Zosia sighed and sat back. 'Nothing like that.'

'Then he *was* a bad 'un,' Mags concluded. 'Not like Leon. He doesn't have a mean bone in his body. He got taken advantage of, I reckon. Some woman hurt him, he's got the mark of it.'

Zosia knew that Mags was right, that she had seen it in him. Some shadow of pain in his kindness, in the warm way he treated Krys and Hazel and everyone else. With her, he'd been gentler, like he understood she was wounded. She couldn't help wonder about the sort of person who would hurt someone like Leon.

32

AUGUST 1940

The Germans increased their attacks on the factories, and it was hard to fly over London to defend other targets while Rosie was in danger. One bomb and the site would go up like a firework. I breathed easier when she was not at work. What little we saw of each other was difficult. I could not hide the injuries, the tiredness that was taking a toll on all of us. Stray shrapnel parted my hair, the odd bullet found its way into the plane, mercifully usually missing me. I was so tired one night I fell from the cockpit, spraining my foot.

Rosie grew pale, stuck indoors in all the chemicals, having to concentrate every day. I could do nothing but kiss the burn that was scarring on her wrist. There were marks on her forehead, the hair bleached and falling out where her scarf and hood didn't always cover. She was being seared and poisoned away. Sometimes, she was so tired she would just fall into my arms and cry that she needed to sleep, and that was the best I could do for her. I knew she slept better with me, even as I lay awake and worried. She had a cough, her voice was a little raspy, but she said everyone had those on the section. I wondered if she would ever heal. Part of me wished she would

*go home to the farm, but every time I had leave I wanted to be
with her again. My selfishness tormented me. I thought maybe
I was being punished for my terrible crime. I longed to tell her,
to get her absolution, but dared not talk about it.*

*— EXTRACT FROM THE MEMOIR OF
CASIMIR WOJCIK*

Working on the bomb section was dirty, difficult and required a
great deal of concentration. Wearing the hood and gloves made
it unbearably hot during a warm summer. Rosie started feeling
weak when she woke up, tired even when she had a day off. She
started to flinch every time she heard a plane fly overhead. The
losses were shocking, and not all reported in the newspapers.
Cas didn't want to talk about it; he was losing friends to capture,
crashes and the battle. By the middle of July the squadron had
been bolstered by new recruits, many of whom struggled with
the hot-headed Poles, all of whom were grieving the loss of so
many of their comrades.

Rosie woke one Monday for the six o'clock morning shift
and couldn't stand. She struggled to the bathroom on her hands
and knees and was horribly sick.

Am I pregnant? It was a frightening thought since they had
been trying so hard to prevent a child. Part of her longed for a
baby one day, and now she was so terrified she would lose
Casimir, she wanted something of him to keep. But her joints
ached, and she felt sick and very tired. She stumbled down to
the barber's shop to call work to say she would be late, but one
of the barbers rang for a doctor instead then helped her back
upstairs.

The doctor diagnosed her with chemical poisoning and
ordered her to have extra milk – the base would provide – and
to take some horrible black linctus that stained everything. She
was also ordered to sleep and drink lots of tea.

A safety officer came from the base, delivering two pints of milk and extra tea, and to make sure Rosie was well enough to take the regimen herself at home rather than going into hospital.

She couldn't bear to tell her parents, and she knew Casimir would worry terribly and want them to come and get her. But she needed to be near London, if – it happened.

Just two weeks ago, she'd seen a plane, a German Heinkel, surrounded by Spitfires, close to the factory. It turned turtle and crashed upside down in a fireball. The image haunted her every day. The pilot wouldn't have been able to escape. Although he was her enemy he was just a pilot, just a man like Cas, fighting for his country. It broke her heart to think that he might have a wife, mother, children who would mourn him. When she shut her eyes to get her prescribed sleep she saw it again, and ended up sobbing herself to sleep.

Eventually Cas missed her daily letters and was given emergency leave to check on her. She woke to hear him bouncing up the stairs, shouting in Polish and English.

'I'm here,' she said, realising she hadn't spoken to anyone for two days, her sore throat making her hoarse, her mouth ulcerated from the poison. She had fallen asleep curled up in one of the small armchairs. She realised she hadn't brushed her hair, she hastily ran her fingers through the tangles.

'You *are* sick,' he said, dropping to his knees and framing her face in his large hands. He kissed her as if she was fragile. 'Look white. See doctor.'

'I saw the doctor. It was one of the chemicals,' she said. 'I must have breathed too much in.'

When he was upset he always struggled with English, now he shook his head. 'Go hospital.'

'No, Cas, the doctor comes here.' She stroked his face, too, feeling the beard, knowing he hadn't shaved since yesterday. 'You've been flying.'

'Much flying,' he said, kissing the palms of her hands. 'Tired.'

'When do you have to go back?'

He made a face as if he didn't want to say the words. 'Four hours.'

She tried to form a smile, but tears bubbled up anyway. 'Take me to bed.'

He did carry her into the bedroom, made the bed and laid her in it. 'I sleep,' he said, fiddling with the alarm clock. 'You sleep. Too white.'

He curled up behind her, fitting himself against her, and she put her feet between his warm calves. 'I love you,' she said, tears dripping onto her pillow, but now the whole world seemed right...

When she woke up, she was alone. A note on her pillow said, in his terrible print, 'Go Duke's Farm.'

Whether it was the reassurance of seeing him or a week of milk and medicine she didn't know, but she had a little energy to at least do a little cleaning, to make herself a small meal. She looked different in the mirror. She was thin, pale, her lips pale. She took the last dose of her medicine and went to the telephone downstairs to arrange some leave with her manager.

'Rosie!' There was something different about her mother when she flew into her arms. 'Oh, my dear, you look so tired.' Her warm, curvy mother had become thin.

Rosie pulled back to look at her. 'Are *you* all right?' she said, looping her arm through her mother's.

'It's been hard,' Ma said. 'I've been a bit sick. Then I was worried about you...'

Rosie's heart was rattling around her chest. Her mother was never ill. 'Ma, what's wrong?'

She hugged Rosie fiercely. 'I don't think anything's wrong,

we just have a lot to do. But you, you look so pale. You aren't – you've not fallen, have you?'

'No, Ma, nothing like that. I'm on the mend and I'm going back to the cordite section with my friend Audrey.'

'And Casimir?' Marion pulled up, put her hands on her shoulders so she could see into her eyes. 'Tell me, lovey. How's he doing?'

Rosie's eyes immediately filled up. 'Just bumps and grazes, he says. But his friends – all those lovely young men who came to our wedding. Almost half are gone or badly hurt. He was so tired one night he hurt his ankle getting out of the plane.'

'We've seen so many mentions of all the pilots in the news,' Marion said, pulling her through the open back door and into the kitchen. 'Especially the Poles and the Canadians. They have been such heroes.'

'Cas says it's because they are fighting for England *and* Poland,' she said. 'And they mustn't lose.'

'I'm sure you're right. Now come and sit down, lamb, and rest. Do you have any medicine to take?'

'Just fresh air, good food and not too much sun, my skin is still sore,' Rosie said, turning to the window to look out at the small back garden, full of flowering herbs. 'I'll sleep better here, too. I can't hear the planes overhead. I always wonder if this is the last time...' Tears sprang into her eyes.

'He'll come through,' Marion said with such conviction that Rosie almost believed her.

33

PRESENT DAY, APRIL

Zosia was woken in the night by a high-pitched wailing. It sounded like an animal caught in a trap, and for a moment she thought she had dreamed it. It came again, then trailed off into what sounded like sobbing.

'Mama?' Krys was standing at the bottom of her bed, holding on to the bedpost. 'I'm scared.'

'Did you hear the funny noise, too?' she asked, pulling back the quilt for him to slide in next to her. 'It's probably a fox. They make the silliest noises.'

'It sounds like a person,' he said, as he settled into her arm. 'I don't like the dark.'

She didn't want to put the light on, in case the neighbours saw one window lit up. 'We'll never get back to sleep if we put the light on,' she lied. 'It's stopped now.'

The man from next door had filled her nightmares enough already, along with that girl's face at the window. She had looked so afraid. Again, she was racked with indecision. She wanted to help but she couldn't put Krys at risk.

'Auntie Hazel is going to put some things up to stop bad

stuff happening,' he said, in a small voice. 'Fairy things her daddy made. He was from Poland. He could see fairies.'

'Could he? Well, you're half Polish, maybe you will see them, too.'

'Do you believe in fairies?'

Zosia smiled in the darkness. 'I did when I was six. The tooth fairy, the fairies in the garden, the naughty brownies moving stuff around when I was asleep around Christmas.' That was her father's doing, encouraging her belief in other worlds and magic until school friends dissuaded her. 'You know I've been reading Casimir's book? He talks about fairies in there sometimes.'

She'd recently translated a piece he had written about his grief that he and his wife couldn't have children. Rosemary had tested positive for an infection carried by sheep after the war, which reduced her chances of getting pregnant. Casimir had had all sorts of ideas for improving their chances, from prayers to female saints to hanging coloured glass in sunny windows, while Rosie had accepted their situation and concentrated on building up the bakery and café. It was a good job Casimir hadn't caused a fire, the sunshine poured in the bay window every morning through crystals, filling the room with rainbows.

After two heartbreaking losses, Rosemary had managed to carry a single child to term, Hazel. She had grieved that she wasn't the boy Cas thought he had wanted, but once he held that tiny baby, he wrote in his pages that he had been overwhelmed with love and joy for his little girl. He had seen the best of both of them in the baby's tiny, crumpled face. They kept trying for a second child, but after another miscarriage, they gave up, centring their lives around the baby and their new businesses.

Minutes passed and Krys relaxed and turned over. Then another thin cry shattered the peace outside. Zosia looked at Krys, but he was asleep. She crept out of bed, trying not to move him, and knelt by the window, lifting the lace curtain. One light in the bungalow was on, and there was another one in the camper van. Another scream, quickly muffled, echoed from the van.

Zosia pressed her hands to her ears, but she couldn't keep them there. Someone was being hurt, and they were frightened.

She couldn't ignore it any longer. She knew it was happening. The next cry came thirty thudding heartbeats later, and this time it sounded like pain. She could hear a woman pleading in the liquid language she recognised as Romanian.

Zosia was out of the room and down the stairs before she thought about the consequences. She rammed her boots on, snatched up a long coat to cover her pyjamas and opened the door to the porch. She marched down the drive, hearing Hazel's voice calling her back. She walked straight up to the camper and hammered on the door.

'*Przestań ją ranić!*' she shouted, before realising she was talking in Polish. 'Stop hurting her, let her go!'

There was some swearing before she heard the door latch click. A door opened in the house, too, footsteps sounding behind her. Her outrage had given her courage, but now it was fading away and she just felt cold. She pulled her coat around her and turned to see the man who had threatened her closing the gap. He grabbed her and shook her.

'None – of – your – business!' he shouted, poking her painfully in the chest with each word.

'I can't just leave her, she's in trouble,' she shouted back, but terror flooded her, making her knees shake.

'His wife is angry, it's just a domestic,' he snarled.

She could hear Hazel's voice over the hedge. 'Should I get the police?'

The door to the camper van swung open and a woman, barely more than a girl, fell out. She collided with Zosia and both fell to the ground.

'She is useless,' a man shouted over their heads. It was the other man, his fat belly hanging over unbuttoned jeans. 'Get rid of her.'

There was a quick exchange over their heads as Zosia tried to get the slight, blonde girl to stand up. She was wearing only a T-shirt and was pulling it down to cover her nakedness. Her face was swollen, whether with tears or blows, Zosia couldn't be sure, but she could barely stand, and her collarbone jutted out like she was half starved.

'No police,' the man yelled. 'You can take the useless...' The word he used was unfamiliar but the girl flinched as if under a blow.

'Come with me,' Zosia said, afraid now that he would attack them next. Her hands were shaking as she guided the young woman by the elbow. 'You're safe.'

Hazel met her at the road, holding her phone. The light was on in Zosia's room, and she hurt at the idea that Krys had woken up and was scared by all the shouting. 'Shall I call the police?' she asked.

'Let's see what she has to say first, please,' Zosia said. 'He says it's a domestic row.' She knew how many domestic violence charges were withdrawn by terrified partners.

'Well,' Hazel said, tucking the girl's arm into hers. 'We know where *that* can end. Maybe we should just call 999, right now.'

'No police!' the girl whispered.

'No! No, and he threatened to hurt Krys,' Zosia said. When Hazel raised a curious eyebrow, she mouthed 'later'.

They walked up the drive and the girl hung back. 'It's all right, my dear,' Hazel said firmly. 'Nothing bad is going to happen.' She turned to Zosia. 'This is ridiculous, we must tell the police. We should have caught it on our cameras.'

'Just wait. Please, Hazel. Please.' Zosia's terror must have communicated itself to Hazel, who looked uncertain in the porch light.

'Let's look after the walking wounded first, then we'll talk about it,' she said, nodding to Zosia, looking down at her leg. Zosia realised her fall onto the gravel had scratched and bruised her bare knee. 'But we should call first thing tomorrow. No one can be allowed to threaten us.'

Zosia lent the girl some underwear and a pair of leggings, and she put Krys back to bed. She was a bit impatient as he tried to explain that the fairies would come and look after them and the bad men were trolls, but in the end, she tucked him in firmly with his two favourite teddies.

'No more fairies,' she said firmly. 'If the stories scare you, we will stop telling you them. Everything is safe, everything is fine. But you need to sleep.' She kissed his forehead, then both cheeks. 'OK, *kochanie?*'

'OK, Mama,' he said, his eyelids drooping.

Downstairs, the girl was tucked up on the sofa with a blanket and pillow, already asleep. She had acne, a red cut over one eye and a bruised lip; she looked like a child. Hazel pushed a large hot chocolate towards Zosia, and put an empty mug in the sink.

'Poor girl, she was drugged up with something,' Hazel said, looking out of the kitchen window at the black outside, the kitchen reflected in the glass. 'He tried to force her, she said. He'd done it before. She told me her name, Alina, but she wouldn't give me a surname. She seems terrified about something. Maybe everything.' She turned to Zosia, who was pulling the leg of her pyjamas up to see if she'd missed a bit of grit in her shin. 'We *have* to call the police, Zosia, they are literally rapists and criminals, and they are living a few yards away from us. They have to talk to her.'

'No! She won't talk. Look, I worked with lots of recent immigrants when I was a translator. Lots of illegals, too. They can't go back – either they have a huge debt or their families back home will suffer. Maybe the traffickers will take another child or threaten parents, grandparents.'

'You're telling me, but it's not like that here.' Hazel's arms were folded, her smile gone.

'Yes it is!' Zosia said. 'It is like it anywhere people have no money, no hope, even in England.' She leaned forward to convince her. 'I have worked with the police, I have translated for trafficked women, women who marry English men, sex workers who are being controlled by pimps.'

'Traffickers?'

'All sorts of criminals. English, German, Polish, Romanian, Greek... not just men, cruel women, too. There is money in young girls and boys, modern slavery.'

Hazel sat at the table. 'Surely the police can help them?'

'They disappear. They run off to someone else, or get sold like cattle.' Zosia looked at her hands, at the crooked finger where Declan had knocked her to the floor with such violence that her bones had broken. 'I was in a women's shelter, there were some there. They were desperate, they had family who were in danger. Younger siblings or even their own babies in the hands of criminals, forcing them to work in drugs or in the sex trade.'

'But the police *must* be able to help.'

'On the moor, that day I laid the flowers, one of the men threatened us,' Zosia said, pressing her hands to her chest. 'You and me, and they have said they will hurt Krys. I'm not with him every second of every day. Someone could take him, hurt him. I can't take that risk, not again.'

Hazel frowned. 'But, here in England—'

'You don't understand. These bad men, they work for bigger gangs.'

For a moment, despite all that she was saying, she longed for Leon to be there, to advise.

'Well, I'm sorry. I know the police will keep Krys safe once they know. We have to tell them, and we can't keep that poor girl locked up forever.'

Zosia was too tired to argue about the police. 'How long do you think it will be before Declan finds out Krys is a target, and uses it against me? Maybe to apply for custody or take him away from me?' She sank into a chair, exhausted. 'I'll pack in the morning, see if I can find a room, somewhere I haven't stayed before. Then maybe Krys and I should go home to Poland, to stay.'

Hazel stared at her for a long time, as the clock in the hall ticked loudly. 'I don't want you to go,' she said baldly. 'We can fight Declan. I have resources, I have lawyers.'

'I don't want to go either,' Zosia said, her eyes filling with tears, blurring Hazel's outline.

'Tomorrow morning, we will send for Leon and we will tell him everything. *Everything*,' she said, putting up a hand as Zosia drew a breath to argue. 'He will know what to do, he knows far more about crime than we do. If you still need to run away, well, then you and I and Krys will go on a nice holiday somewhere, while the police deal with these criminals.'

Zosia covered her face with her hands as the tears flowed. No one had made her feel more looked after or more loved, since she was a little girl. She managed to nod.

'Well then,' Hazel said, putting out some of the lights. 'We'll let poor Alina sleep off whatever drugs she's been made to take, and we'll sort it all out in the morning.'

34

AUGUST 1940

My constant dread was ditching in the sea. I had never learned to swim, and although we had stayed near a lake as a family, none of us had learned. I knew that the biggest danger was being dragged down by the parachute canopy in the water, or the cold. The English Channel is cruel. My life preserver had to be inflated once I was in the water, but I doubted being able to swim long enough to blow it up. My natural ability to glide made me overconfident, perhaps, that I would always be able to land somewhere, or even land on the water and get out safely. Battle is chaos, instinct and violence. I was naïve, stupid. When my engine failed, I fought to steer towards the wide, sandy beach of Norfolk. Anything to stay out of the sea.

— EXTRACT FROM THE MEMOIR OF
CASIMIR WOJCIK

After her shift, Rosie expected him to be waiting at home, ready to go for a fish supper or at least cook some of the groceries she had picked up on the way. But he wasn't there. The flat was cold and dark, and it had never felt so empty. An official-looking letter lay on the mat.

Her knees began to shake, and she put her hand on the wall for support. She tried to bend down but ended up sitting beside the envelope, the word *Important* typed across the top. Was this how her love story would end? Surely one of the other pilots or the base commander would have contacted her?

She picked it up; it was absurdly light. There was nothing underneath it, like a letter from Cas, and she hadn't received one at the farm, which was so unusual. Since he'd started at the base, Cas had written every day for months, then every other day when he was on operations.

It was a strange feeling, sat between the glorious joys of her meeting Cas, their love, their marriage... and something else, dreadful, that would start when she read the letter. She had seen a few telegrams sent to workmates. *We regret to inform you...*

She held it a little longer, caught in the quiet place between worlds, before she slid her finger under the flap, breaking the seal.

We regret to inform you... the words blurred in front of her, *that Pilot Officer Casimir Wojcik is missing. His plane was hit, being lost off the coast of the North Sea. We will keep you informed of further developments.*

That was it. It was a better than a confirmed death, but terrifying. She jumped to her feet and ran down the stairs to the barber shop.

'I need to call the base,' she said to the owners, clutching the paper. 'Cas has been shot down.'

'When?' one of the men asked.

She hadn't thought to look, it all felt like it was happening now, today. She scanned the telegram again.

'Yesterday,' she said, tears thickening her voice, running down her face. She fumbled for a handkerchief.

'Go, go,' he urged her, waving towards the phone and handing her some coins.

She made the call to the base and was put through to Group Captain Jeffries straight away.

'Cas? We don't know, but the engine was definitely hit. Josef kept the Jerries off him while he took off along the shore. No one's seen him since but the navy have patrol boats out. We'll let you know as soon as he's found.'

If he's not already drowned. She had never thought to ask if he could swim.

By the next morning, Rosie felt she would be better being with people than brooding in the empty flat. She had an appointment with the base medical officer before she was declared fit for duty, and was put back to cordite processing with Audrey. Many of the girls there were new, but they were all friendly and it was nice to be able to talk a little between batches, and go back to the same canteen. Audrey had given up smoking and was argumentative and grumpy, but she was gentle about Cas.

'That boy will pop back up,' she determined, without knowing any of the facts. 'Look what he's survived already. Marching across half of Europe, fighting for Poland, for France, now us. I'd be surprised if we don't hear shortly.'

'You can't know that,' Rosie said.

'Joe saw him get away, not far from shore,' Audrey said.

'Is Josef all right? I was hoping to speak to him.'

Audrey had a little spot of colour on each cheek. 'He might be. He was when I saw him last week.' There was a studied indifference in Audrey's voice, and she had tilted her head back to look down at Rosie.

'You saw him?'

Audrey dropped the haughty act. 'If you must know, we went out to dinner. It was a very nice restaurant, too.'

Rosie couldn't imagine the two together, the quiet Czech and the worldly, upper-class Audrey. 'Is he all right?'

'He's getting better, I think, he says flying is easy. He still can't stand heat anywhere near his burned skin, has to bathe in cold water, he says.' She made a face. 'Horrid, although the water in our quarters is lukewarm at best anyway.'

Rosie stared at her friend as she finished her stew. 'Are you and Joe – a couple?'

Audrey answered without looking up. 'Would that be so terrible?'

'No, of course not!' Goodness knows how many times she'd had nightmares about Cas being locked in a burning cockpit, and it had happened to Joe. 'After everything he's been through, he deserves a little happiness.'

'He's not Henry Berrington-Gifford, of course,' Audrey said, wiping a piece of bread over the plate and smiling up at Rosie. 'But then, I don't really like Henry Berrington-Gifford.'

'Who on earth is *he*?' she asked, unable to finish the gristly stew. She still had a pasty and some home-made biscuits from the farm for when she got home.

'The man my parents think I should marry. Well, at least go home this weekend and look him over. Like a horse I might want to buy.'

Rosie smiled at the thought. 'But you're not going home?'

'Dear child, I am going out all weekend with Josef, to the West End. I intend to see a show under blackout conditions, and eat at Claridge's. My treat.'

Rosie shook her head. 'I didn't think you would end up with someone like Joe,' she confessed.

'I'm not going to "end up with him", as you put it. He's twenty-four years old and may not make twenty-five. I just want to enjoy myself – enjoy ourselves – while we can. And yes, we're staying at the hotel together.' Rosie couldn't think of anything to say, but she found she couldn't judge Audrey at all.

There was something in her voice that made her suspect she really loved Joe.

'Then I hope you have a marvellous weekend,' she said, tears choking her, as they did more and more these days.

'We will,' she said, her smile lopsided again, as if caught between hope and sadness. 'And I hope you do, too, when Cas turns up.'

35

PRESENT DAY, APRIL

Zosia slept badly for a couple of hours but by dawn, she was up. The sky was pink, purple clouds on the horizon. She slipped into clean clothes, ran a brush through her hair and crept downstairs. Krystof was in his own room and had surrounded himself with soft toys, like he'd done whenever he'd felt afraid of Declan. Her chest hurt at the thought that she had let him get so upset. The idea of running away to Poland now filled her thoughts.

She put her head around the door into the living room, but Alina was gone.

'She stole some money,' Hazel said, from the kitchen door. 'It wasn't much, sixty or seventy pounds. Maybe enough for her to get away, poor girl. I wish she'd let us help her.'

Zosia nodded, looking around. She couldn't see anything else missing.

'Leon will be here soon. He's with a parishioner, but he's asked the police to come out. He'll come over as soon as he can.'

Zosia immediately felt guilty that she would think of trying to run away, leaving Hazel with her trouble to sort out. 'Any more noise from next door?'

'Just the camper van leaving,' Hazel said, switching the kettle on. 'It woke me up. I'm glad they've gone. I had their number plate but I saw them fiddling with it a couple of days ago. Maybe they've changed it. Hopefully they won't be back.'

Zosia sat down with a bump in the chair. 'Changing the number plate is an offence, isn't it?'

'Maybe.' She poured hot water into a couple of mugs. 'I think what happened to that poor girl is a much more serious offence. I know you don't like tea, but I thought you might like a pick-me-up.'

Zosia smiled at the expression, which she hadn't heard before. 'Thank you. I'm getting used to tea.' She was hit by a sudden longing for Leon, for his warm presence, for the way he looked at her. 'I'm glad you called him,' she said in a small voice, remembering how cool she'd been with him in the garden centre.

'I explained what happened last night, and he said we have a responsibility to inform the police. It was the right thing to do. If the girl is gone, there's not much they can do except look for her. We'll give them a description.'

Zosia stood up and looked through the conservatory at the back garden. The lavender plants were thriving already; Hazel had been watering them and mulching them with bark. Mulching, another new word. Zosia felt like one foot had taken root in this place, in Hazel's house and garden. Reading Casimir's journals had connected her with Hazel's father as well, his longing for his homeland but also his love for the wild moor and his family. He was a man who had balanced both.

She slipped her garden shoes on and took the steaming mug out onto the patio. A carved wooden face sat by the door – one of the fairy faces Casimir had carved and placed around his garden. She had scrubbed and varnished it herself. It was sticking its tongue out; maybe it was warding off the neighbours.

She walked alongside the hedge, listening for any signs of

the men. A few minutes later, she heard a car pull up at the front. Her heart lurched with the hope that it was Leon, and she shook off the idea by deadheading the roses, fragrant petals sliding through her hands.

She made her way inside and found two police officers sitting in Hazel's kitchen, looking at the security camera footage. They hadn't captured much, in the dead of night, just Zosia marching next door, the van obscuring what had happened. There was a fuzzy record of Zosia walking back with the terrified girl, and a few words of Hazel's on the recording.

'I wouldn't have recommended you confront them. You should have called us,' one of them said, rewinding the footage and looking again. 'We could have taken the girl into protective custody. How do you know she didn't go back to the men?'

Hazel, leaning against the work surface, answered briskly. 'On the front camera, you can see her running down the drive and heading for the village,' she said. 'Time stamp 05:41. I imagine she was going for the early bus. She's wearing my fleece and Zosia's trainers.'

They checked the footage again and started making notes, muttering to each other. When the front door banged, Hazel nodded to Zosia. 'That's Leon. Can you tell him what's going on?'

He had pushed his way in the front door and was waiting for her in the hall. 'What on earth happened?' he growled. 'You should have called the police. Or me.'

'How's your parishioner?' Zosia said. She saw his face. 'Oh.'

'Out of pain, I thank God,' he said, his expression changing to something vulnerable. 'It was a hard illness but a good death, in the end.'

Zosia hated seeing him upset. She reached her hands out to him and he caught them. 'I'm sorry,' she said. 'We were all safe, and you needed to be there for him.'

Leon sniffed, coughed, looked away. 'I know,' he said. Then

he looked straight at her, and she moved towards him, towards his bear hug and wrapped her arms around his waist. He rested his head on hers, and she shut her eyes in the warmth of him. After a moment, he let her go.

'Friends again?' she said, her voice coming out huskily.

'Friends. But you have to tell me what's going on. It's driving me nuts, thinking you would run away and we'd never see you again. Either of you.'

She shook her head. 'There's just a lot – I can't talk about it much.'

'Don't think I don't have stuff that's hard to talk about, too,' he said.

'I do have some things to show you,' she said, leading him into the kitchen. 'And Hazel. I was scared to show anyone.'

She went upstairs to retrieve the notes she'd received, to show Leon and the police.

'This is why you didn't want to be seen with me in public,' he said. His eyes scanned all the words, even the ones Zosia couldn't bear to read again. 'You were being warned off seeing someone. Why would you think it's about me?'

'You were the only man I ever spent time with. I have an angry ex-husband,' she said, stumbling over the English words, her heart skipping her ears. 'A violent man. Maybe he had paid an investigator to follow me here.' She brought out the solicitor's letter, creased from so many reads, so many returns to the envelope. 'See, he wants visitation rights.'

Leon scanned the letter quickly. 'Why hasn't he asked for visitation before?'

Zosia had to breathe deeply to find the words. 'He was in prison.'

'For hurting you?' His voice was strained.

'For hurting both of us,' she said. 'I can't talk about it now. I just need us all to be safe.'

'Come and stay at the vicarage,' he said urgently, putting his big hands on her shoulders. She liked the weight of them. 'All of you, while we sort this out.'

'No.' She thought back to the notes. 'I think that would make Declan angrier. And Hazel's right, we mustn't give in to bullies.'

'You don't know it's Declan,' he said, staring down, his eyes dark.

'Who else could it be?' she asked.

For a moment, he opened his mouth to answer, then shut it again. 'OK. But no more secrets. If you can't tell me, tell the police.'

By the afternoon, the police had finally got a warrant to go inside the house next door, and had come out with bag after bag of rubbish. Hazel saw many yellow bags, and the police had explained that it was drug paraphernalia. The men may or may not have been selling drugs but they were certainly using them. The officers reassured both women that the men wouldn't return.

Zosia had been shown dozens of sheets of photographed faces. Only one stood out to her, the man who had shouted abuse at her on the moor.

'We know who he is,' a police officer had told her. 'And we know who he works for.'

Zosia frowned. 'So, who was that?'

'He's a human trafficker,' he explained. 'He deals in modern slavery, drug running and prostitution. Most of their victims end up working for terrible wages in unlicensed places, in debt to the people who smuggled them in.'

'Was the girl Romanian? I recognised the language.'

'Maybe. The trade is global, we have people and drugs here from all over the world, carried and sold by all sorts of people. We just arrested a group of middle-aged women peddling diet pills and injections in a beauty clinic.' He had smiled grimly. 'Even the Botox wasn't pure. Who knows what harm they could have done.'

'And the girl?'

His smile faded. 'We see thousands of trafficked girls and women either moving drugs or in the sex trade. We're doing everything we can to find her.'

Zosia had been left with Hazel and Krys, able to wander around the garden, feeling safer now the men had gone. Once the police had locked up the bungalow and left, the sounds of the moor took over. Wind rustled through the short, spiky grass down into the valley then whistled back up to the tor. Birds seemed to sing louder as the spring progressed, protecting their nests, perhaps, or just singing for the joy of it.

Zosia spent the next few days toiling in the garden, weeding and sweeping soil away from the patio, getting ready to open the café for the summer holidays. She had sanded the surviving tables and benches, and the kitchen had passed the safety inspection. After five days, Leon arrived with a truck full of wood and two men, who put up a new pergola. Zosia painted the inside of the conservatory, and Hazel cleaned and mended a hundred pixie, fairy and gnome figures they had found in odd corners and shelves in the sheds. She had repainted and varnished them with Krys's help, then put them up all over the garden, the corners of the house, the trees and even inside the porch by the front door.

The day Krys went back to school for the summer term, Zosia left her painting to pick him up. She noticed straight away something was wrong. He was subdued, walking with his hands across his belly, eyes streaming with tears.

'He says he fell over in the playground,' Toby said, helping

Krys by supporting one arm. 'But he's been crying since lunchtime.'

His teacher, Miss London, walked across carrying his bag. 'I'm really sorry, I don't know what happened. No one saw him fall and he won't let us check his tummy. I was wondering if he had a virus.'

He pressed himself against Zosia. 'We've had a difficult few days,' she said. 'With the police. It might have brought up bad memories.'

'Well, there's one odd thing,' Miss London said. 'I thought I saw your neighbour's older lad today, outside the school boundary. I thought his family had moved on. I could have been mistaken. It was just a glimpse before he ducked behind the hedge. We told the police, they said they would look out for him, he really shouldn't be out of school.'

'I think the whole group have gone,' Zosia said. She really couldn't think of them as a family. 'What about the women who brought them to school?'

'I haven't seen them for weeks. When the boys did attend school on and off before Easter, one of the men dropped them off.'

Zosia rubbed Krys's back, like she had when he was younger and Declan had been shouting. He shuddered in her arms. 'I will get Krys home and find out what is going on. Has he been all right in class?'

'Just very quiet.'

She felt his forehead but he didn't seem to have a fever. 'Come on, let's see what Auntie Hazel has got for us. And we have a surprise for you in the garden!'

He didn't look up, just shrugged. He still wouldn't let her pull up his T-shirt and jacket to take a look while she fixed him into his car seat. 'No, Mama!'

But his demeanour had changed by the time she pulled up

outside the house. When she reached in to unlatch his seatbelt, he leaned forward for her to carry him.

'Oof, you have grown!' she said, letting him cling to her with arms around her neck and legs curved around her waist. All of a sudden it felt like he was four years old again, after the beating from Declan, after moving into the shelter. 'You must tell me, *kochanie*,' she whispered into his ear.

'I know,' he said, and twisted awkwardly in her arms. 'I got hurt.'

As he lifted the hem of his T-shirt she gasped at the bright red marks, the blue bruises above his waistband. 'What on earth happened? Who did this?'

'The big boy,' he said, dropping his T-shirt and burrowing closer. She could feel the tension ease out of him. 'He came back, behind the forest classroom. He said we shouldn't say anything. *Anything.* Then he used a rude word.'

She carried him in, took him through to the kitchen and sat him on the work surface. When he finally allowed her to move his clothes she found three distinct blows, two with shoe prints suggested in the bruise.

'We need to go to the doctor's, my darling,' she said, brushing away at the tears streaming down her face. 'Just in case you have bruises inside your tummy, too.'

'Like you had,' he said, his eyes dark, his words flat. 'Like Daddy did to you.'

She caught her breath. 'But this wasn't Daddy.' She stared at him, trying to read his thoughts as he looked away. 'Was it? You haven't seen him around, have you? Daddy?'

He shrugged, then winced and put his hands over his body. 'I saw a lady in our garden a few times, but that was ages ago.' Ages to Krys could mean the day before yesterday, but she couldn't get him to narrow it down.

'But the lady didn't hurt you today, did she?'

'No,' he said slowly. 'But she did watch.'

AUGUST 1940

I stumbled in the shallow water, cutting away my parachute and dragging it behind me to a group of women, their skirts tucked up, with rakes and baskets full of shells. They were shouting, beckoning to me. As I looked back, I saw my plane half in the water, already being swamped by the tide. I felt my spirits rise, even as the water and soft sand dragged at my legs, as I had survived yet again.

— *EXTRACT FROM THE MEMOIR OF*
CASIMIR WOJCIK

Rosie had still heard nothing from Casimir, nor his base. She lay awake, the minutes ticking into hours instead, wondering what it would be like to create a home, looking over the heather and bracken of the moor, cooking for guests with Cas. *When he comes home. If he comes home...*

Getting ready for her shift, she turned at the sound of a letter coming through the door. She started to shake, her heart drumming in her ears. Her hands were cold. *Suppose it's the official letter?*

She half ran down the stairs. For a moment, it felt like her heart had stopped. It *was* a telegram, but it didn't have the War Office stamp on the outside. She ripped it open.

My darling Rosie...

She slumped onto the bottom stair, trying to catch her breath. His words typed in three lines. It took a few moments to clear the tears and focus on the three lines. *Rescued by fishermen Norfolk. Love you, Casimir.*

Rescued. The word she had been praying for, hoping for, in little moments of optimism in a sea of fear. Even now, she wondered if he was safe, travelling back. Back. She couldn't go to work, she couldn't miss him! But the telegram had been sent from Norfolk early this morning. He couldn't be home before evening. She tucked the letter inside her clothes, against her breast, and ran for the bus to the factory.

She put her wedding ring safely in her purse and headed out to the cordite factory. Audrey was looking tired, but still smiled at her. 'What – don't tell me he's OK? You're beaming.'

'I can't stop smiling,' Rosie admitted, settling into her chair. As the safety officer was already scowling at her, she whispered, 'He's on his way back from Norfolk.'

'I'm so glad for you! We'll talk about it at break,' she added, out of the corner of her mouth. 'Strict Hilda is coming.'

Audrey always seemed to have rude names for the staff. Rosie really liked Hilda – she was warm and friendly when she wasn't trying to get them to concentrate on their dangerous work instead of gossiping. Talking meant they breathed through their mouths, inhaling more of the toxic dust into their lungs. She pulled her cloth mask up and started work.

It was hard to focus. *He's coming home!*

It was so hard to concentrate that she didn't notice a batch of solid cordite, not quite dried. It smelled much more of acetone than normal, which only registered through the mask too late to avoid unwrapping it. It glistened with oily liquid. *Nitroglycerine.*

'Alarm, alarm!' she shouted, stepping back and bumping into the girl working behind her. 'Nitro!'

The shed evacuated briskly in an orderly fashion. These events happened two or times a week but they had never happened to Rosie before. She waited by the door. The safety officer came over. 'Is the batch still there? You didn't put it into the cutting machine?'

'I-I left it...' she stammered. 'I forgot what I was supposed to do.'

'You did the right thing,' she reassured her. 'Go to the canteen and get a cup of tea. I'll get another safety officer to help me sort it out.'

'It might be the whole batch,' Rosie said, as she was shooed away.

Audrey had saved her a seat, and once she had washed her hands several times, she went over to sit beside her. A few of the girls toasted her with a cup, probably glad of the break.

'Just digestives today,' Audrey said, pushing a plate over and pouring her a cup of tea.

'It was such a shock,' Rosie said, clasping her hands together to stop them shaking. 'All I could hear in my head was that safety film – that one teaspoon can blow you up, and there it was, all over the paper.'

Audrey dumped a spoonful of sugar in her tea, normally reserved for shock. 'You look like you need it.'

'It's not just that,' Rosie said, reaching for the telegram only to realise it was with her clothes. 'Cas is on his way home. I can't believe it, I'm so excited but I'm scared something will happen to him now. Maybe the train will crash or a bomb will fall on him.'

'Once you see him, you'll feel better.' Audrey smiled but it was strained. 'Joe will be pleased to see him, too.'

'How is he?'

Audrey shrugged. 'Not so good. His scars need regular treatment, his skin is healing up too tight. It's very painful, but he doesn't want to miss any missions.'

'But you're still seeing him?'

Audrey shrugged. 'When I can. But what's the point, Rosie? I'm not an optimist like you. He's twenty-four, he had a girl-friend back in Bratislava. He's not for me, it's not like Cas. Even if he survives, he'll probably want to go back when the war ends.'

'But you love him.' The thought that Cas would want to go home haunted her some nights.

'At the moment he's desperate to go home. And he loves me. I'm here and I give him what he wants and make him happy – but what happens if he dies? Or goes back?'

It was a question Rosie had never found the answer to. 'I just think, if Casimir died, how much worse it would be if I hadn't spent all my free time with him, loved him, got to know him,' she said. 'That's the best I can come up with. We just have to live for now, and worry about that when it happens.'

Audrey pursed her lips. 'And that made you feel better when everyone thought Cas could be dead?'

'No. It was horrible. But over time, once you know for sure, I'm sure grief eases.' It had when her grandfather had passed away, when her school friend died of tuberculosis, when her favourite animals had been put down. 'Death is part of life, Audrey. My dad says to truly live you have to accept death.' He'd said that the first time he'd sent her lambs – her bottle-fed baby lambs, who grew into rambunctious sheep – to slaughter.

'They want us back on the line,' Audrey said, standing. There were dark smudges under her eyes. 'So I should visit Joe and accept that one day, my heart will be broken?'

'Isn't it broken already, when you don't go and see him?' Rosie asked softly, so the other girls didn't hear.

Audrey smiled back. 'Maybe. Ask me again when you get your Cas back from Norfolk. Hopefully in one piece.'

PRESENT DAY, APRIL

After four hours at the hospital, Krys was given the all-clear. He had no internal injuries or broken bones, but he was badly bruised and shocked. The hospital suggested he stay in for the night, but he became so upset they agreed that she could take him home after another couple of hours of supervision.

That gave her time to talk to the police officer, then the social worker. It was an uncomfortable conversation, and she had to explain the end of her marriage in some detail, almost within earshot of Krys.

'Who does Krystof say hurt him today?' the man from social services asked. He was wearing a lanyard with a name, Terry, with a large sun on it. It was mesmerising, she couldn't stop staring at it.

'He said a neighbours' boy did, one of our neighbours up until a few days ago. Two of their children were getting into trouble at school, Krys knew them better than I did.'

'And they've recently left? Do you have a forwarding address?'

Zosia could feel her temper heating up as her face did. 'They were possibly drug dealers who may have been human traffickers. You should ask the police.' She shut her eyes. 'I'm sorry. It was such a shock seeing him like that. I thought he just had a tummy ache.'

'I'm sorry, too,' he said, and when she looked up, he did look sympathetic. 'It must have been terrifying. I have to get all the facts, because your ex-husband's solicitor will ask for the details.'

'A boy from the school hurt him. Isn't that enough?' She looked back at Krys, who was laughing at something a nurse was doing. 'The boy told him not to say anything. Krys is too little to know what he meant. That message was for me.'

'But you are fully cooperating with the police.' He wrote something down then looked back at her. 'They will know he told you, and they will know you are working with the investigation.'

'I have to. We don't have a choice. We can't lose our home.'

He checked his notes. 'You haven't been there long. I see your previous address was a hostel. Could you go back there for a short time?'

'It was completely unsuitable. No, Hazel has made us so welcome, the whole village has. We want to stay, if she'll have us.'

He smiled then. 'Since she's waiting in reception, I assume she wants you to stay, too. She's ready to take you home. If you have any other concerns, let us know.'

She hesitated as he gathered his papers. 'There is one thing,' she said. 'There was a woman. Krys says she's been watching the house, and she saw him get hurt. She didn't intervene when he was attacked.'

He sat back again. 'That's odd. I mean, it's human instinct to protect a child. Do you think she was acting for your ex-husband?'

'I think she might be a private investigator. Maybe she's come to prove I can't protect my son.' The words were hard to say. 'I'm afraid my husband is trying to build a case against me, to take my child back.'

'Under the circumstances, it's very unlikely that he would succeed,' he said. 'But I'll make a note, in case he, or his legal representatives, get in touch.'

'Thank you,' she whispered.

'Was there anything else?'

'I've been getting poisonous little notes, warning me off seeing a friend.' Her face warmed up. 'A male friend.'

'Are your local police aware?'

She nodded.

A nurse came over with a bag of medication. 'Right, you're all ready to go home,' she said, smiling. 'Here are some painkillers in case he needs them. They are some very nasty bruises, but he'll heal.'

'Thank you,' Zosia said, clutching the bag of medication. 'And thank you,' she said to the social worker.

'I'll need to do a home visit but that's just standard. So you can show me your house, young man,' he said, smiling.

Krys was walking towards them, looking tired but no longer pale. 'You can see the pixies and fairies, and the garden,' he said, as he walked into Zosia's arms. She picked him up, feeling like she would never want to let him go.

'Mama!' he protested, but he didn't try to get down, just lay his head on her shoulder. 'Where's Auntie Hazel?'

'Waiting for us outside. I don't know how she got here. We took her car.' She hadn't even asked, just accepted the keys from Hazel's hand and left.

'Maybe Leon brought her,' Krys's sleepy voice said. 'I hope he's outside with her.'

Me too. Her heart bumped a little harder at the thought. 'Let's go and find out.'

Leon *was* there, and Krys wanted to clamber from her arms

to his. He carried him out to Hazel's car and strapped him in his seat.

'You're growing out of that chair,' he said, adjusting the headrest that Zosia had been wrestling with for a week. 'Hazel desperately wanted to come, I hope that's all right. She's becoming a proper grandma.'

'She's fabulous,' she murmured to him, leaning in so Hazel wouldn't hear as she chatted to Krys. 'Better than his actual grandmothers. Don't let her hear me say it, though. She has a very youthful attitude, she might not appreciate being called a good grandma.'

'I think she'd make an exception for Krys,' he said, laughing. His smile faded and his expression grew intense. 'I'm glad he— that you are all OK. I worry about you out there on the edge of the village. The offer still stands, the vicarage has spare bedrooms.'

'The police will keep an eye on us. They can monitor our cameras remotely now.'

'Call it copper's instinct, but I'm worried that you've become known further up the chain, that the gangs could threaten you. They had no reason to hurt Krys unless they want your silence.'

Zosia put her hand on his arm, feeling the warmth of the muscles under her fingers. 'Silence about what?' she asked. 'We don't know anything. We can look after ourselves,' she said, smiling. 'But maybe you should have left the gun.'

'That old thing,' he said, pulling back to look at Hazel. 'It would have blown up if you'd fired it. You three had better get on the road, you all look tired. I'll follow in my car, in case you get into trouble.'

Zosia drove Hazel and Krys through the city streets. Once they got out of town, Hazel told her to stop, to step out and get in the back with Krys. She was too tired to argue, and let Hazel drive home. Occasionally, Leon's headlights crept up behind them, lighting up the inside of the car; it made her feel safe. She fell asleep next to Krys before they got home, waking with a jolt as the car crunched over the gravel drive.

Hazel unlatched Krys from his car seat and guided him up the steps. 'Let's all have a good night's sleep,' she said, taking him to the foot of the stairs. 'I'll bring you some supper on a tray in bed, like my mother used to do, when I was ill or hurt.'

'Can I have hot chocolate?' were the words that floated back down to the hall.

'I'll sort him out,' Hazel said. 'You go and sit down. Unless you want to go straight to bed?'

'With hot chocolate and toast,' Zosia said, laughing. 'It does sound lovely.' Hazel's hot chocolate was a local legend, and Zosia hadn't yet worked out why it was so good. 'Will you tell me your secret?' Zosia said, as she folded into the rocking chair.

'Certainly not!' Hazel said, laughing. 'Well, not until we open the café, anyway,' she conceded, and put out two hand-made cups from the local pottery and a mug in the shape of a teddy bear for Krys.

I love that he has his own cup here. 'Word from the village is that you put chocolate buttons in it,' Zosia said.

Hazel shook her head and smiled. 'Do they, now? I'll just take this up to Krys.'

Zosia let her mind wander as she shut her eyes.

The smell of hot chocolate and toast roused her a little while later. 'I must have fallen asleep again,' she said, yawning. 'What a horrible day. Poor baby, he's dealing with it very well.'

'He's just worked out he's a hero,' Hazel said, but her lip was shaking. 'He doesn't know that he could have been hurt much worse, or even died from internal bleeding.'

The thought that had been troubling Zosia was like a chill wind down her collar. 'Should I take him away? Somewhere safe?' She bit her lip. 'I thought I might take him on a holiday to see my parents in Poland.'

'We'll talk it over tomorrow when the police get back. Did you know, they have a possible address for the camper van? Soon both those dreadful men will be in custody and then they'll find the boys.'

'I wonder what happened to the girl, Alina?' Zosia said, sniffing the froth on the top of the drink. 'I hope she's all right.'

'They haven't found her. I looked at hundreds of pictures with the police but I couldn't identify her. They think she's just a teenager. Anyway, we're here now, the house is locked up tight – yes, even the outside door – and Leon will be over tomorrow with the police.'

Zosia's sleepiness had fled. 'Leon.'

'Yes, Leon.' Hazel looked at her with such understanding, Zosia's eyes began to prickle with tears.

38

AUGUST 1940

I was interviewed by the local Norfolk police, then moved up to military police, then finally someone called my squadron. As I drank cups of tea and told my story again and again – my English wasn't good back then – slowly people started to help me. A secretary there helped me write a telegram for Rosie, and with my last shillings, she was able to send it.

The train journey was slow, held up by air raids, slow on damaged tracks through to London. My impatience was painful. But I knew as the day went on, she would be waiting for me. I prayed she had not been too scared.

— *EXTRACT FROM THE MEMOIR OF*
CASIMIR WOJCIK

Casimir arrived home late in the evening after Rosie's shift. He was too tired to use his key and just knocked on the front door. She flew down the stairs in her slippers and housecoat.

He was leaning against the doorframe as if falling asleep. He smiled at her, kissed her, then limped upstairs dragging his bag. It wasn't until he got into the living room that she realised his arm was in a sling. He didn't speak, just hugged her, dropped his coat and kissed her once again. He was sweaty and smelled of railway dust and coal smoke.

She led him to the bed and helped him undress and climb under the blankets. He smiled as he fell asleep, and she watched over him for a while. Having been so brave through the last few days, now was the time for tears, and they flooded out as she washed up her dishes, tidied up the books she had been reading and cleared the grate. She sat curled up in the chair for an hour, sobbing until she felt empty after the storm. Finally, she crept into bed, finding a spot where she wouldn't jolt his arm, and put her arms around him.

Despite the tears, or perhaps because of them, she fell asleep, and when she woke up she was curled up in his good arm. 'You have to wake,' he said, kissing her. 'I need bathroom.'

A quick glance at the clock brought back the horrible realisation that she had to leave for work soon. Even as she argued with herself that she couldn't – *wouldn't* – leave him, she threw on her clothes. She knew the work was so important that even one worker missing a shift could throw off a whole line.

'I have to go to work,' she shouted through the door.

'Go,' he said, his voice sleepy. 'I wash, sleep. See later.'

She was buzzing when she got to the changing room at work, and, for once, wouldn't take off her wedding ring but asked for tape to cover it. Audrey was late as usual, barely making the line for the factory, still stuffing her hair into her cap.

'He came home!' Rosie said, ecstatic.

'Joe said he was on his way back,' Audrey said, out of breath. 'He was rescued by the cockle fisherwomen.'

'You saw Josef?'

Audrey made a funny little face. 'Of course I saw Joe. He isn't getting enough time to eat properly, let alone sleep. At least a night in a hotel means he can get both. How's Cas?'

'Tired, dirty. His arm is in a sling, too, he didn't say why. He just went back to sleep.'

Audrey started up her machine, ready to cut the cordite strings to length. 'They're saying the RAF has got the Luftwaffe on the run.'

Maybe by the time Cas returned to active duty, the Battle of Britain would be over. 'I hope so,' she breathed as one of the safety officers walked by. 'I can't believe the Germans will just give up though.'

'Concentrate, ladies. And look out for quality issues, the warm weather has made some of the cordite too dry.'

Cutting and packing was boring but less dangerous than most of the processes in manufacturing cordite, much of which was left to older women with grown-up children.

Too wet made it liable to explode, too dry or too hot made it inflammable. Rosie wondered what too cold in the unheated sheds would bring over winter.

39

PRESENT DAY, MAY

Over the next week, Zosia painted the new pergola a hyacinth blue, and Hazel – able to walk without her stick now – did some pruning and weeding. They spent time cleaning and repairing the customer loo, accessed from outside in the garden and now visible behind a wall of chopped-back bracken. Zosia could see how the café would look, and was inspired to hang some fairy lights from the new pergola. Hazel also ran up a couple of sail-like squares of nylon fabric on an old sewing machine, to hang between the wooden uprights for shade.

The conservatory was repainted a cheerful pale blue, almost like the sky, and a high-powered hose had cleaned off the glass roof, letting in lots more light. On rainy days, it would be a pleasant alternative to sitting among the herbs and shrubs on the patio. They had arranged the china figurines from the house on a set of shelves Zosia had made from an old bookcase. She took the first payment for the café, from one of Hazel's friends, who had come to book the space for her crafting afternoons.

They didn't see anyone in the neighbouring property after the police had done their search of the house. As far as they knew, there was no sign of the young girl, or the woman Krys had talked about.

There was also no sign of Leon, which Zosia tried to convince herself was a good thing.

Hazel and Zosia rewarded themselves for their hard work by heading for the garden centre after they had dropped Krys off at school.

'What exactly are we looking for?' Zosia asked, as Hazel pulled into the car park. 'Apart from apple cake and coffee.'

'House plants, for the conservatory. You know, to bring the outside in, lush and green.' She looked up at the scudding clouds. 'There's a proper blow coming in.'

Zosia, who liked gardening but had never managed to keep a plant alive indoors, was doubtful.

'Declan never liked plants in the house,' she said. 'He always said I would kill them. His mother used to give them to me but they all died.'

'So Declan's words came true,' Hazel said, looking back at her. 'But you're not with Declan any more. Maybe he stifled your green thumbs.'

Zosia glanced at her hands. She had never heard the expression but could guess what it meant. 'Maybe he did. He always told me I was holding Krys wrong, feeding him badly, stopping him developing. He told me I walked the puppy wrong, that he would turn vicious if I spoiled him.'

'And did he?'

Zosia thought about it as Hazel locked the car and got a trolley. 'No. But he was scared of Declan. We all were.' She smiled, without humour. 'Maybe the plants died from the unhappy atmosphere.'

'Maybe he just killed them,' Hazel said, prosaically. 'To make a point. You said he never wanted them. Why did you get a dog?'

'His mother gave us a puppy when her dog had a litter.' She

thought back to Crystal's house. 'Even she acted a bit nervous of Declan. Very – is the word – deferential?'

'It is, if you mean a bit timid, giving him too much power. Maybe you could get in touch with her now, if you want to. She *is* Krys's grandmother.' She headed over to a huge display of plants, some in bud with brightly coloured flowers. 'Although I feel a bit territorial about Krystof,' she confessed. 'I do love him. What about these?'

They filled the trolley with flowers and a few colourful pots, before Hazel said, 'I just need a sit down,' and settled herself on a nearby bench.

As Zosia turned to manoeuvre the trolley, she almost ran into Leon. 'Oh!' she said.

'Is everything all right?' He seemed a bit distant, cool with her.

'We're just stocking the conservatory,' she said, gesturing to the plants. 'For the Fairy Café.'

'Hazel said she wanted to open to the public by the summer holidays,' he said. He looked over at her, and waved.

'We're just getting it ready. You should come and have a look.' She felt her chest tighten at the thought that she had just asked him over. His behaviour was so up and down, she didn't know how to read him. One minute she was pushing him away, now he was pushing her... She didn't trust her instincts any more. 'We've missed you recently.'

He smiled briefly, then changed the subject. 'How is Krys doing?'

'Apart from checking his bruises day and night to watch them change colour, he's well. I think he feels like the worst thing happened, and now we're OK, and the bad boys have gone.'

'They've caught the men that were operating out of your neighbours' house,' he said. 'Did they tell you?'

'Yes. We've left the cameras up, just in case.'

He looked at Zosia, his expression cool. 'Don't let me hold you up.'

She caught his forearm for a moment and he froze. She let go. 'Leon, what's wrong? I thought – you said we were friends.'

'We *are* friends,' he said, gazing into her eyes as her heart jumped. He looked away. 'I know you've got your history with your ex, but I have some issues with mine. That's all.'

Maybe he is getting back together with her. For a moment, the garden centre seemed cold and grey.

She nodded. 'I'm sorry. It was nice to see you.'

'I will come and see the garden. Soon. I just need to sort some stuff out at the vicarage.'

'Of course.' Her voice had come out small. 'Goodbye, Leon.'

He nodded to Hazel and left, without any shopping, she realised. Maybe he would have to come back later when she wasn't there. That made her feel worse. He was the first man since Declan that she had liked, and she had thought the liking was growing into something more – or maybe she really did have terrible instincts about men.

'Where's Leon going? I thought he might stay for a coffee.'

Zosia sank into the chair next to Hazel. 'He seems to be avoiding me.'

'Last week he virtually threw me into his car to come racing after you when Krys was hurt.'

'Well, today he's talking about his ex. Maybe splitting up with her was a mistake?'

Hazel put her hand on Zosia's smaller one, squeezed. 'I doubt it. He barely got away from the woman. He left his job, his life back in Kent, everything to get away from her.'

'Like I did,' she whispered.

'Just because he's a big bear of a man, don't think he's invulnerable, or any more able to deal with an abusive partner than you were.'

Zosia's eyes opened wide. 'Abusive? He spoke about it?'

'A little. When he visited me in hospital after he rescued me from my broken hip. His ex-girlfriend, I don't think they ever married, was obsessed with him after they split up. She used to stalk him, make complaints about him to the police, blame him for things going wrong. He never spoke about her again, but I could see it had hit him really hard.'

Zosia could see now how low he had been. 'Do you think we should do an intervention? Get him over, cheer him up? I know Krys would love to see him.'

Hazel laughed. 'We could certainly try. Let me call him. I only have to hint that you are a bit sad or need something and he will probably come over. How about next Sunday lunch, after the service? I might even go to church.'

'Really?' Zosia said. 'Well, if you do, Krys and I will come, too.' She couldn't explain how much being in the community church with the villagers all around her had cheered her, now she knew them. Despite the different style of worship, she felt peaceful and safe there. But mostly the appeal was the man leading the congregation.

By the evening, both women had worked hard in the conservatory, picked up Krys, enjoyed long showers and were settled in the living room. Hazel didn't watch much television, but they sat down to enjoy a romantic comedy together with a bottle of wine and Hazel's customary bar of chocolate to share. They were almost all the way through the film when the power to the house went off.

Zosia jumped, her heart hammering in her chest.

'It's OK, it's just the wind,' Hazel grumbled, and rummaged around for something.

It didn't take long for Zosia's eyes to adjust to the darkness, aided by the moonlight coming in the window. Hazel always left the curtains open, she loved to get the evening view across the moor and up to the tor, which would turn scarlet red with the last rays of the sun.

A torch flicked on and the room lit up a little. 'I told you it was going to be windy today.'

'Why does the wind make the power go off?'

Hazel lit a match and a candle in a glass jar flared into life. 'There are overhead lines into the village,' she said. 'It will probably be fixed by morning.'

'I don't want Krys to be frightened,' Zosia said. She didn't like the dark herself and the sunset was now just a warm glow in the dark sky.

'Well, since we won't able to watch the end of the film, we may as well go to bed. I've got lots of candles in jars around the place, we can put one up high on Krys's wardrobe, if you like. That's what my dad did when I was little.' Hazel handed her the glowing jar. 'We're always the last house to have the power restored.'

Zosia watched her light a small lantern at the bottom of the stairs and hang it out of Krys's reach. She lit the way up the stairs with the torch then lit another at the top.

'Thank you,' Zosia said, following her up. 'I thought I might have to sleep with Krys but I think he will be all right.'

Hazel lit a small lantern in Zosia's room, then, unusually, reached out to cup Zosia's face and kissed her cheek. 'Goodnight my dear. I'm glad you decided to stay with me. I think we make a good family. We can fight this ex-husband, between us.'

Zosia smiled, and walked into her own room, her face warmed by Hazel's touch. It was wonderful to feel like she belonged in a family again.

40

SEPTEMBER 1940

Two weeks after I had crash-landed in Norfolk, I was attacked again. A hundred bullets tore into my wing, and my engine spat smoke and fire before I lost power. I bailed from my plane as it dropped sharply, a few hundred feet from the surface of the sea. My chute barely opened before I was plunged deep underwater, thrashing towards the light. I was trapped under the wet parachute for a minute, flailing to keep my head above the water until my knife was out of my pocket and hacking at the lines. I started blowing to inflate my life jacket, and managed to get the last of the cloth off my head. I had never felt closer to death, gasping little breaths with the cold, puffing into the tube. Half inflated, the jacket lifted my face just above the water. My hands were white, shaking, I had been in the water two minutes and I was already so cold my knife slipped from my frozen fingers, disappearing into the green. I looked up to see two of our fighters engaging three of the enemy, close down. A line of bullets zipped by me, a few feet away. Josef, I was sure it was him, came in hard and shot the tail fin off the German plane. A thread of smoke dragged itself across the sky as it spun away. I looked around for my plane, but there were just a few fragments, a few flames smouldering and the darkness of oil seeping to the surface. In the distance was a small boat, bright blue, fishing in the green water, unconcerned about the life and death dogfight above. Beyond, a castle sat on an island a little way from the shore. I wondered if I could paddle all that way before I froze to death.

Hope warmed me up, as I splashed towards the nearby shore, thinking of Rosie, our little home, the farm. Anything other than dying of cold. The planes were much higher now, whizzing around like gnats and wasps high in the atmosphere, but I had another problem. As I swam slowly towards the fishing boat I saw a plume of water from a German patrol, which was approaching fast enough to create a white wake behind it. It curved around the smaller vessel, and headed straight for me. All I could do was play dead, resting face down in the water with just a sideways gulp of air, and hope to be washed onto the rocky shore. I prayed to God to see Rosie again.

— *EXTRACT FROM THE MEMOIR OF*
CASIMIR WOJCIK

Two weeks after Casimir had crash-landed in Norfolk, he was flying missions again, sometimes back to back. One morning, the base called Rosie at the barber shop to say Casimir had been shot down again, this time off the coast of France. In her agony of waiting, Rosie called her mother to come up from Dartmoor. She arrived with an enormous suitcase as she opened the door.

'Any news?'

'Ma!' Her mother's hug was as fierce as ever, and she smelled like the farm – line-dried linens, dogs and baking. She'd got the rosiness back in her cheeks, and she looked a little plumper. 'No news yet.' Tears sprang to Rosie's eyes. 'They saw the plane crash in the sea and a parachute, that's all I know. He's officially missing in action.'

'He's a strong young man. You need to have faith. And if he is gone, maid, you'll need to have even more faith.'

'I can't bear the idea...' There was no need to finish the thought – Ma was looking at her with such understanding. 'I'm just working, and saving for our future. Cas said he'd like to buy a house on Dartmoor, when we have enough money, to live near the farm.'

Marion walked up the stairs, Rosie helping to lift one end of the heavy case. 'This is a nice little place,' she said, looking around. Rosie was immediately aware of the worn armchairs, the utility blanket over the bed, the smell of the barber shop below.

'It's enough for now,' Rosie said, tidying her cup and saucer into the sink and filling the kettle. 'I know it's not much but, it's ours. For when he comes back.' *If.*

'Maybe you'll hear good news soon enough. Let's hope so. In the meantime, let's have a look at Grandma's old linens, and make the place more comfortable for him to come back to.'

Rosie choked down the frog in her throat. 'How's Dad?'

'He's well, as usual. Oh, my dear, you still look very peaky.'

'I don't get enough sunshine. But you look better than the last time I saw you. Let me make some tea.'

'Lovely,' Marion said trying one of the chairs, undoing her scarf and draping it over the arm. 'Where's your bathroom, lovey?'

Rosie deliberately clattered around while making the tea, over the sounds of her mother being sick. 'Is everything all right?' she asked, when her mother came back.

Rosie held out a glass of water. Marion drank a little. 'That was a long time on the train. Goodness, that's better. I have some biscuits in a tin in my bag, that will help.'

'Help what?' Rosie said, feeling her heart flutter at the thought that Ma – Ma of all people – might be really ill.

'You know about the change of life, don't you, maid? When old women like me stop having monthlies and get hot flushes.'

Rosie didn't. Marion had never really discussed her own health with her. 'I remember Grandma getting terribly hot and carrying a fan around like a duchess,' she recalled.

'And you know it was really hard for your dad and me to have children of our own, so we were going to adopt. But then you surprised us all by coming along.'

'I know,' Rosie said, the pieces starting to click into place.

'Well, sometimes, just before the monthlies stop, women can get extra fertile. They can get pregnant.'

Rosie could feel her mouth hanging open. 'Ma? You're – having a baby?'

'It would seem so,' Marion said, fumbling to unlatch the suitcase, which was crammed with fabrics and the biscuit tin from home, the old one with the old queen's jubilee on it. 'Have a shortbread.'

'Why didn't you tell me?'

'Well,' Marion mumbled around a biscuit, 'sometimes babies don't stick. I've miscarried before, many times. We waited to make sure the baby was growing before we told anyone.'

'When is it due?'

'Not for another five months or so. There's no way to be sure about these things but the doctor thinks the baby will come after Christmas. I could do with this blasted sickness stopping, though.'

'Oh, Ma,' Rosie said, hugging her mother.

Marion started pulling out bundles of material. 'Now, these I took from your grandma's house after she moved in with Auntie Ida. There's a couple of pairs of sheets – I've washed and ironed them – and a nice chequered tablecloth.' She looked at the table and smiled. 'Although you'll have to fold it in half, or even quarters if it's to go there.'

'How do you feel?'

Her mother looked into her eyes. 'Do you remember that old brooder cow we had for the calves – Marigold? She was well past having her own calves but she looked after the babies so well we kept her. But then Bart the bull got out and covered her.'

'I do!' Rosie said, although she was only eight or nine at the time. 'She had a heifer calf, she adored it.'

'Yes, but everything went wrong with her while she was pregnant. We had the vet out several times to her, we nearly put her down. She went off her feed, she had stomach problems, she nearly died having that blessed little thing. We barely managed to raise it. The vet said she was born a couple of weeks too early.'

'I remember you put one of my old jumpers on it, and she lived in the barn until she toughened up. I remember giving her a bottle, too.'

'Because Marigold only milked in two quarters. That's me, an old cow with half an udder and needs the vet all the time.'

'Oh, Ma!'

Her mother smiled and patted her hand. 'I'm forty-three, my girl, I'll be forty-four when the baby gets here. It's going to be much harder than having you. I need to rest in the afternoons already.'

'But we'll all be there to help. The war can't go on for ever.' Rosie sat at her mother's feet and lifted the linens. They smelled of the country air and for a moment she could see the moorland, the tor in the distance. The flower scent was from her mother's own laundry soap recipe. In the linens were two blocks of it, wrapped in paper, and beneath that a cushion and an embroidered bedspread. She could remember tracing the little swallows, in blue thread, running between the flowers on Grandma's bed. 'This is so lovely.'

'I know Grandma would want you to have it.'

Rosie frowned at the tone of voice. 'Doesn't she know?'

'She's gone downhill since you left. She was getting very forgetful before, but now she's just happy to sit in a chair and to hum along with the radio.'

'Oh.' Rosie missed the next thing her mother said. 'Sorry?'

'We're all changed by the last year. You and me, we've got our own journeys to travel, but for now, I want to eat biscuits and enjoy my little holiday. And wait for whatever happens with your man.'

With that, Rosie's tears came.

41

PRESENT DAY, MAY

The alarm crept into Zosia's dream, insistent, getting louder as sleep faded. She sat up abruptly, smelling something acrid.

'Zosia!' Hazel's shouts came over the blare of the alarm.

Krystof. Adrenaline rushed through her, making her feet shake as she staggered out of bed. 'Krys, Hazel!' she screamed, then coughed. A tendril of smoke crept into the flickering light of the candle she had put up high on the wardrobe. '*Fire!*' She had no idea whether she was speaking in Polish or English as she skidded past Krys's open door to look onto the landing, where the smoke was thicker. He raced into her arms.

'Mama, what's happening?'

'Hazel!' she bellowed. The smoke was coming from down-stairs, and she couldn't see the bottom, just a yellow glow where the candle had been left. *Did we do this? Did we catch the house on fire with our candles?* 'Where are you?'

Hazel appeared from the bathroom, in her dressing gown, with a towel over her face, handing two more to Zosia.

'Wet cloth,' she explained, holding one out. 'Breathe through it. Come into the back bedroom, we can shut the door and get onto the kitchen roof.' She took Krys's other hand.

'Go ahead. I'll call the fire brigade.' Zosia ducked into her room for her phone. There was little charge on it – she hadn't plugged it in before the electricity went off. There was no signal in the house, the internet must be down too.

She grabbed it anyway and followed Hazel into the back bedroom, cool and unused all spring. She shut the door against the billowing smoke filling up the hall, and laid the wet cloth around the threshold to keep the smoke out. Hazel struggled to open the window.

'It's stuck,' she said, coughing. 'What on earth happened? All the candles were safe, I swear it. I've done that a hundred times, one hasn't even fallen over inside the jar.'

'I thought I smelled—' Zosia helped Hazel force the window open. 'I'll have to go up the garden to get a signal.' She peered out, the first light of dawn giving a grey light to the back garden. The kitchen had a gently sloping slate roof about four feet below the windowsill. 'I'll call the fire brigade when we're all out.'

'No, you go out first, catch Krys and make the call.'

'What about you?'

'I'll be fine here. Maybe I won't need to climb down. I don't want to hurt my new hip,' she confessed. 'Look, I can breathe fresh air and I promise, if the smoke gets too bad, I'll risk it.'

Zosia clambered onto the windowsill, then lowered herself as far as she could, dropping onto the kitchen roof, skidding a little on the slope.

'It's not too bad,' she said, climbing back to right under the window. 'Krys, I'll catch you. Just sit on the windowsill.'

'I'm scared,' he wailed, but Hazel hugged him and lifted him up. 'Just go to Mama,' she said, and Zosia reached up to take him.

It wasn't easy to get down – the kitchen roof led to the glass roof of the conservatory, but Zosia knew the wooden corner of the frame by the back door had a sturdy water butt below, covered to stop birds falling in. She lowered herself down, feeling the lid's solidity. She reached back to Krys and the two of them balanced on the barrel.

'I can jump down, Mama,' he said, and as there was a large, soft bed of newly planted herbs she let him. He fell onto his bottom and scrambled up, reaching up as if he could help her.

'Thank you, baby, but you need to step back.'

She slid to sitting, then lowered herself into a patch of mint and rosemary that filled the air with aromatic scents. She turned to see Hazel waving, and grabbed Krys's hand to take him up the garden. She managed to get one bar of signal, enough to call the emergency number.

'Which service do you need?' a calm voice inquired.

'Fire, our house is on fire!' Zosia rattled off the address, twice because she couldn't remember the postcode. 'It's on the Dartmeet road, Foxglove Cottage. I think the fire is downstairs, maybe at the front. I can't see any flames at the back.'

'Is anyone still in the building?' the operator said, clacking at a keyboard. 'Stay on the line, we have help on its way. Is there anyone else in the house?'

'Hazel's still inside. She's leaning out of the back window, but she broke her hip a few months ago, she doesn't want to climb down.'

'That's Hazel Wojcik, the homeowner?'

'Yes. I'm her—' Words failed her. 'I live with her, I help her. I have a son, he got out with me.'

'If the fire or smoke become more intense let me know straight away.'

'Hazel!' Zosia bellowed. 'Is it getting worse?'

A distant voice floated over the smoke alarm and the distance of the long garden. 'No. And I'm fine!'

'She's all right at the moment.'

'How about you and your son? Are you feeling OK?'

Zosia coughed again before she answered. 'Just a bit of a tickly throat.'

'Sit down somewhere comfortable and stay on the line.' She said something else but it broke up.

'I'm sorry... what did you say?'

Nothing. The call had dropped out. Zosia walked closer to the house, looking through the conservatory. The kitchen door was open, and a haze of smoke obscured the hall. She could just see a red glow through the glass of the front door.

'It's at the front of the house, the porch,' she shouted up to Hazel. 'And I can hear a vehicle.'

A car screeched to a halt on the gravel at the front of the house and heavy footsteps rushed around the side. She ran round and was caught up in a bear hug that lifted her off her feet.

'Leon,' she managed to say before he kissed her.

'Where's Krys and Hazel?' he said, putting her down, leaving her stunned, pressing her fingers to her lips.

'Leon!' Krys said, before being caught up in a hug as she had been.

'Hazel!' Leon bellowed, looking up at the back of the house.

'I'm up here,' Hazel said. 'I'm fine. But I don't want to fall off the roof.'

'Have you called the fire brigade and ambulance?' When Zosia nodded, Leon handed Krys to Zosia. 'Stay away from the house,' he said with authority. He ran up to the summer house and pulled out the ladder Zosia had been using for decorating. Within a minute he was on the kitchen roof, helping Hazel down from the windowsill, then handing her down the ladder by the water butt.

'How bad is the fire?' Hazel asked, a little out of breath. Leon steered her to a bench and she opened her arms to hug Krys.

'It's the front porch, it's well ablaze,' he said, turning back to Zosia and looking at her as if assessing her for damage.

She touched her fingers to her lips again. 'You kissed me.' She touched her fingers to her lips again, her cheeks heating as she became aware of her flimsy nightdress.

'I did. In the heat of the moment,' he said, then his smile stretched across his face. 'I'd like to do it again, when the house isn't on fire.'

She couldn't help an answering smile. 'Is there anything we can do for the house? We have a garden hose.'

'It's too dangerous to go indoors, and I don't think it will help. Once the front door goes it will spread inside. The fire brigade will be here shortly, they are the experts.' He turned to Hazel. 'I'm so sorry about the house. There's going to be some damage.'

'My dad bought it as a burned-out wreck. We can rebuild again.' She hesitated for a moment. 'I hope we can save his papers, though. I feel like I was just reconnecting with him. They're in his study.'

Zosia sat beside Hazel, with Krys in between them. Leon turned to the conservatory and tried the door. It turned easily, and he peered into the study window at the end. 'If the fire spreads any further, we can ask the fire brigade to get to the study to rescue the papers.'

He reached up for the couple of gardening coats hanging by the back door.

Zosia pulled on her old fleece and, putting Krys on her lap, wrapped him up inside it too. Leon went back for their gardening boots and she realised she had bruised her bare feet on the gravel around the house.

Leon vanished around the house as the sound of a fire engine growled along the road and turned into the drive.

'Can I see?' Krys asked, and she slipped the boots on, carrying him just a little way down the side of the house.

Enough to see the front of a fire engine, lights flashing blue, contrasting with the pink sky of dawn. Men in heavy unforms and helmets ran to the front of the house.

'Let's go back to Auntie Hazel,' she said. 'While they try and save the house.'

He pulled back, looking into her eyes. 'Where will we live if it burns down?' he asked.

'Maybe it will need a bit of fixing,' she reassured him. 'But then we can come back. I expect we'll find somewhere nice for a few weeks. Maybe near Auntie Hazel.'

His bottom lips shook. 'I want to live *with* Auntie Hazel.'

'Me too, but we have to be brave.'

Leon reappeared, his face hard. 'Come away, they're getting on top of the fire but the smoke is bad. It's killed a lot of that plant Hazel likes—'

'—the wisteria,' Zosia added.

'But mostly the fire is in the porch, which is pretty well destroyed. Which is strange in itself. You wouldn't have thought there was much that was flammable in there. Did you smell anything odd when the smoke alarm went off?'

'We had candles lit, because the power went off,' she said. 'But there was something else. Like a chemical smell.'

He frowned but didn't explain. She bent her head to kiss Krys's forehead. 'Go and warm Auntie Hazel up,' she said, and he trotted off in his boots to Hazel. 'The fire is deliberate?' she said, not able to find the right word.

'Arson. It looks like it.'

Declan? She dismissed the thought. He would never endanger Krys. She wrapped her arms around herself. 'Was it one of our criminal neighbours?' she said, nodding towards the bungalow.

'Maybe. Or maybe their bosses.'

'Did they mean to scare us?'

Leon seemed to change what he was going to say. 'Maybe.'

She started shivering, she wondered if it was shock. He opened his arms and without hesitation she stepped into his hug. He was warm, his T-shirt was soft and smelled like him. She closed her eyes and let the moment stretch out, feeling safe for the first time – maybe in years.

'I was scared,' she confessed. 'How did you know the house was on fire?'

'Mags hardly sleeps any more, she was trying to get her cat back in because Puddles was yowling outside. She heard the sound of your smoke alarm, banged on her neighbour's door thinking it might be a car. They saw the smoke up the hill, called the fire brigade then woke me.' He looked down at her, eyes dark. 'I came straight up.'

'So, we owe your presence to Puddles, the cat?' She pulled away a little and stared into his face, the early morning stubble, the eyes looking back at her. 'Kiss me again,' she breathed, and he did. It was nothing like she expected, warm and safe... She lost herself in his arms for a moment, shutting her eyes and breathing in his scent. He smelled somewhere between toast and clean dog.

'Can we go on a date sometime?' he said, and kissed her again, this time more passionately.

'We'd better, since people now think we're a couple,' she said, and giggled. It had been a long time since she'd giggled.

'Hazel can't act surprised, she's been setting us up for weeks,' he said.

Her smile faded. She pulled away and he reluctantly let her go. 'I am worried about Declan. I mean, if someone tried to burn the house down—'

'—with you all in it.'

'Well, yes. But I don't want Declan to get any ammunition. If he thinks I'm homeless again, and if have a boyfriend he may say I'm not looking after Krys properly...'

He smiled down at her as a paramedic walked past to Krys

and Hazel. 'I'm an ex-policeman and vicar. That's pretty solidly respectable in a custody case. You're allowed to have a boyfriend.' He waved at Hazel. 'You won't be homeless, anyway – when I left, half the village were up, ready to take you all in. You'd better get checked out, and make sure Krys is OK after all that smoke.'

She took his hand. 'Don't go away, will you?'

He grinned. 'Not a chance.'

42

SEPTEMBER 1940

As I crawled over rocks slimy with seaweed, trying to conceal myself from the view of the patrol boat which was now retrieving my parachute, I was grateful for the deep shadow of the cliffs. I could see how far up the rocks the tide reached, and I had shed my brightly coloured life vest. Staring up at the cliff, I could almost see a way to climb up. If I was a mountain goat, perhaps. It would be hard in the dusk, impossible in the dark as the moon would be just a sliver in the sky. I curled up, shaking with the cold, rubbing my hands together to move some blood around them. They were as blue as when I had played for too long in the snow as a child.

The first time the words were hissed down to me I wondered if they were a bird, but the second time I heard clearly.

'Sind Sie verletzt, Herr?'

My heart galloped as I heard the German words. Many feet up, maybe fifty or sixty, the brown face of a child leaned over the ragged grass. I waved weakly. 'Bonjour. Je suis Anglais, ne me tire pas dessus.' *Do not shoot me.*

The boy disappeared to speak to someone else in rapid

French. Then a man with grey bushy hair and long whiskers leaned over to inspect me.

'Pilote?' He spoke again quickly, and I tried to remember my months' flying and training with the French. The shudders came again, making me shake and my teeth chatter as I remembered. I was in German-occupied France and there was a bounty on my head.

— *EXTRACT FROM THE MEMOIR OF*
CASIMIR WOJCIK

Time dragged while Rosie waited for news of Casimir. Work was a distraction. On her lunch breaks, she quickly penned notes to her mother. She told her she had a break coming up in November and would try to come home. If Cas was home she would bring him too. If he came home.

After lunch she sat down at her machine, ready to get back to work, when there was a blinding flash. For a moment she thought it was a lightning strike, like the bolt that had hit the tree in the four-acre field and killed two cows. The thunder rolled over her, the air was dark with dust and swept her off her stool onto the floor.

She couldn't hear anything except the ringing of alarms, whether in the building or in her head she wasn't sure, and when she put her hand up to her face she was bleeding, although there was no pain. She pulled herself up and looked around, straining to see through the smoke. Her stomach lurched at the sight of a blazing red glow a few yards away.

A woman mouthed something at her, but she couldn't hear. She grabbed Rosie's arm, pinching her skin, and dragged her towards the door. Another girl, who had lost her cap and whose hair was fanned out and white with powder, pulled her along towards the exit.

Women were stumbling past her to get out of the unit. Her

head was filled with the stink of chemicals. She heard the sound of people shouting, as if far away. 'Explosion! Fire!', and now distant high-pitched screaming.

'Audrey!' she screamed, although it sounded like a whimper inside her head.

Two of the women dragged her outside, and her vision was obscured as someone pressed a wet cloth to her eyes.

'Audrey!' she croaked, the smoke now in her throat, in her lungs, making her cough.

A doctor and nurse were assessing which workers were injured and which just shocked. Rosie was able to hear their questions distantly through the ringing.

'You need stitches,' one of the nurses shouted at her, and Rosie looked back in a panic at the shed, now besieged by men in protective suits, dragging fire hoses.

'Is it a cordite fire?' she asked, grabbing the nurse's arm. 'My friend is in there, Audrey Dreyfus. Did she get out?'

Blood had been dripping in her eyes along with grit.

'Never you mind about anyone else,' she said. 'Let me look at you.' With gentle efficiency, she rinsed the blood and grit from Rosie's eyes before directing her to a waiting ambulance.

There was a long bench seat in the back of the vehicle, and Rosie and two other girls were squashed in one side. Then a stretcher was loaded. Rosie couldn't recognise her but one of her companions did. 'That's Joan Carter.'

Joan's station had been next to Audrey's. She seemed to be unconscious, her face had been washed but was now swathed in dressings. The tip of her ear was burned black, the backs of her hands scarlet with scorches and the front of her hair was burned into a ginger crisp.

'Poor thing,' the girl said. 'At least she's out of it for the moment.'

Rosie started shaking, she felt cold down her back as if someone had dropped ice down it. She looked at her own hands, scorched as well, and wondered if her face was burned too. Tentatively touching her cheeks, she found they weren't too sore, although her hip and knee now ached from hitting the floor, and she realised little bits of glass were sparkling all over her work uniform. *Where is Audrey?*

By the end of the day, Rosie learned Audrey had survived, but was on the burns ward in critical condition. There was still no news of Casimir, and Rosie continued to pray that he was a prisoner of war, safe in some camp with his English papers.

Still with bandaged hands but on the mend, and not allowed to visit her friend, Rosie caught the early train home to the farm as soon as she could, two days later. She was desperate to see how her mother was doing, pregnant at the age of forty-three, as her letters had become less cheerful or frequent.

She walked down the track to the building she had known all her life. She noticed differences straight away. The ivy was overgrown and had spread onto the roof of the scullery. Dad's truck was more rusted and one tyre had gone down. Weeds were growing in the herb garden. Children's voices came from behind the house in the stableyard, so she walked around the side to see two little boys kicking a ball around.

Ma, sitting on a kitchen chair with her coat wrapped around her, looking pale and thin, watching the boys.

'Oh, maid, your dad wanted to pick you up! How are you?' She stood and hugged her almost painfully, her collarbone digging into Rosie's chin. She cupped her face in both hands, looking at the small burns on her forehead. 'Oh, my lovey, you've really been in the middle of it. Any news of Casimir?'

'No,' Rosie said, eyes filling with sudden tears. 'Not yet.'

Marion led the way back into the house and the boys followed.

'How are *you*?' Rosie asked.

'Oh, you know. Well, I suppose you don't. I am so tired!' She lifted the heavy kettle and put it in the sink, half filling it. 'I *am* much older.'

Rosie put her hand on the kettle. 'Let me do that!'

'I'm not an invalid,' Marion said, sitting by the stove. 'But if you must.' Her smile faded. 'How are you, really?'

'I'm on the mend. The explosion was a shock and I'm still waiting to hear if—' She couldn't say *if he's been killed.*

'And no baby?'

Rosie's face heated up, and she looked around but the boys had scampered upstairs. 'Well, you know, Cas does something.'

'That's for the best. Those boys did a great job, winning the Battle of Britain.'

'The Germans are just doing many more bombing raids now. That's what Cas was doing when... intercepting bombers heading for the south.'

'But the bombs aren't falling near you?'

Rosie hesitated before answering. 'They're falling everywhere. I think it's worse by the docks, but there are so many targets. They just want to terrorise the whole of London.'

Marion turned away to lift the teapot down. 'I hate the idea of you being in danger at work and at home. You could come here. Dairying is war work, too.'

'I don't want to be away when Cas is risking his life every time he takes off,' Rosie said, her voice small but steely. 'I want to be there if he comes back.'

'Not even if we need you?' Marion turned to look at her. 'I have a part-time land girl but she's not that good at milking, the cows don't let down for her. Our yield is dropping.'

'You just told me you aren't sick, you're pregnant.'

'I need to rest more; I can't carry so much.' Marion ran her hand over her belly, now pressing against her apron. She bit her lip. 'Maid, I think I'm going to need help with the birth, too. We both know old cows struggle to have their calves. Maybe it's the same with people.'

'But you've got Dr McLellan, and the midwife.'

Marion put cups and saucers onto the table. 'I'm not normally a fusser, but I have a bad feeling about this baby.'

'Oh, Ma!' Rosie could see how pale she was. 'Do you have any reason to be anxious?'

'I've had some bleeding,' Marion whispered. 'Not much, but some. I don't know why.'

Rosie clasped her hands between hers. 'Ma, we have to sort this out. We'll phone the doctor and find out what's going on.'

Rosie telephoned him from Mrs French's house. The doctor wanted her mother admitted to hospital, so Rosie walked back to the farm trying to work out how Dad could cope without Ma. Maybe another land girl, one who was better with the cows. Maybe a retired farmhand could be brought in, if they could find one.

Her father had spent the day at market, and by the grim look on his face it hadn't gone well. He reached out long arms, in his second-best suit, to hug her.

'Any news of your young man?'

'Not yet, Dad. He may be a prisoner of war.'

'Let's hope so.' He hung his jacket carefully on the back of the chair by the stove. 'It's mortal cold out there, maid. It'll be the first frost of the autumn, we'll be glad of a fire tonight.'

'I haven't been back long,' she said, loading more coal into the stove. 'I spoke to Ma when I got here. I called the doctor.'

He froze, his eyes wide. 'She's all right?'

'Not really. She needs to go to the hospital tomorrow. The doctors will decide if she needs to stay there until the baby comes or whether she can rest here.'

'How much rest?'

'Lying down,' she said, moving the stew pan onto the stove top. 'Bed rest.'

'She had a hard time with you,' he said slowly. 'That's why I thought we didn't have any more children.'

'The afterbirth is bleeding,' she explained. It really was too important to protect her father's sensitivity with euphemisms. 'If it comes away she'll need an operation immediately, or she'll die. That's the main reason they would want to keep her in.'

'Is she in labour?' he said, his face so pale she could see his freckles.

'No. The baby's too small to survive yet, but another two months would make a big difference.'

He sank onto the chair, put his face in his hands. For one horrible moment she thought he was crying.

'I need you to come home,' he said. 'I can't manage the children by myself. The milking and dairying takes up half a day and the land girl is useless with cows. You know I'm no good at dairy.'

'I can't right now,' she said, feeling pulled in half, torn between worrying about Casimir and wanting to help run the farm. He was right, she probably could do the dairying now and they could cope between them. 'I'll get the hens in,' she said automatically.

The chickens lived in a shed across the stableyard, but some had already settled to roost in the hay barn next door, open to foxes. She lifted their grumbling, feathery warmth and stacked them in the hen house in a row. The others clucked and ruffled their feathers before they squeezed up for the next one. She found two eggs, laid in the hay, too. No one was keeping an eye on them – they were getting into bad habits.

When she returned to the kitchen, Dad had changed into work clothes. 'I'll get the cows into the parlour for milking. The land girl will be here soon, she's been cutting hay over at the Yeo farm,' he said. 'Give the children their tea, will you? Bridget will be home, she's been playing with a friend over at the Cawseys'.'

'Of course. Once I've got them sorted, I'll come and help with the herd, I can manage hay even with my hands in bandages.'

An hour later, the children were all together, washed and fed. They looked anxious that Marion was resting upstairs, and she had to reassure them that she would get better. The oldest boy whispered to her that his eldest sister had been killed in the bombing of London, so she had to promise him that Marion would be well.

Rosie made herself a cup of tea and one for Peggy, the land girl, who wore a checked handkerchief over dark curls that bounced out in all directions. She poured the rest into a flask for her father, knowing he wouldn't get back to the kitchen for hours, and wrapped two slices of Ma's fruit cake in a napkin.

'Now,' she said, sternly to the three children. 'You be quiet, Auntie needs to rest. When I get back in I'll read you a story.'

'Aunt Marion's reading us *Treasure Island*,' Bridget said.

'Well, I'll read some of that, then. Fred, can you wash up for me? There's some warm water in the kettle but it's not too full.'

'They should be all right,' Peggy said. 'They know the routine. What's wrong with Marion?'

'She's got to rest. She could bleed. The afterbirth is low.'

'Oh.' Peggy pushed open the door to the back kitchen and lifted down a couple of scalded, sterilised churns. 'I saw a cow deliver the placenta first when I was in training.' Rosie knew how horrible that would be, as the cow would bleed to death and the calf die.

My mother is not a cow. Rosie lifted two more churns, checked they were clean. 'She needs a rest. Once the baby is grown they can do an operation to get it out.'

She stalled in her tracks. *It?* No, he or she – her baby brother or sister.

43

PRESENT DAY, MAY

Zosia stared at the blackened skeleton of the porch. The front door was almost burned through, the glass at the top cracked and dark. A fire officer with soot around his eyes stood next to her.

'I'm sorry to say this is unlikely to be an accident. I'm writing this up for further investigation as possible arson. It's lucky it didn't affect the house, except some mild smoke damage.'

'Arson.' It was a new word but the meaning was plain. Someone had tried to kill them.

'Your smoke alarm saved you – just remember that when you renew the battery. I tell people to do it every year on their birthday or on the first of January.'

'Message received,' Leon said over her shoulder. 'Why didn't it spread?'

'Look here,' the fire officer said, pushing at the smashed deadbolt with a gloved hand. 'They broke the outside lock, then sprayed an accelerant around the porch and through the letter box into the hall. Then they lit a match and *boom*.'

'Accelerant?' Zosia said, still stunned by the violence of setting fire to a house with a child in it. 'What does that mean?'

'This one smells like petrol. But this is what really concerns me. You can't go in yet, this is now a crime scene, but look here...'

He pushed the charred and blistered front door open, and pointed to the wooden floor inside.

It had a long stain, almost like water had got in under the door. 'Someone squirted petrol inside,' he explained.

The dark stain stretched towards the carpet at the bottom of the stairs. Zosia felt shaky, shivers running through her. That staircase carpet led to her bedroom, and Krys's beyond. The euphoria of the rescue, their safety, Leon... It evaporated.

'Now what do we do?' she whispered. 'Some tried to kill us.'

'*Tried* being the word,' the fire officer said. 'I don't know why the flames didn't spread under the door. It's a big house, you might still have got out if that had ignited, but the smoke would have been much more dangerous to you all. You might not have survived.'

'Can we go indoors? To at least get some clothes.' *And all our documents and money.* She shut her eyes and fought down the panic, the impulse to run.

'One of my officers will escort you upstairs from the back. We have an investigation to conduct, we don't want to lose any evidence.'

Leon's hands were on her shoulders, heavy and reassuring. 'You can pack a few things, I'll take you all back to my house.'

'We need to go somewhere away from here, somewhere they can't find us,' she said. Her voice came out high-pitched, like a child. She took a deep breath. 'No, we will not be chased away like frightened children. When can we move back here?' She could see the smoke damage to the walls in the hall, to the ugly face attached to the doorway that Krys and Hazel had recently hung there.

The fire officer nodded. 'We're going to neutralise the petrol in the boards. We're going to have to lift them to make sure there isn't a pool of accelerant under there, and we can let you in through the back after that. The place will stink of smoke for a while, though.'

Hazel joined them, looking exhausted, holding Krys's hand. 'I think I need to get some sleep, so I would love to go to your house, Leon.'

Zosia took her other hand. 'Why don't you two sit in Leon's car? I'll pack us the clothes. And the cookies you baked yesterday should be fine in the tin.'

Hazel nodded, and Leon led them to the car. There was a big blanket across the parcel shelf and Hazel pulled it over them.

Zosia pulled her fleece around her shoulders. 'Come upstairs with me, Leon. I need to talk to you.'

The fire officer escorted them upstairs to check the other rooms. He snuffed out a guttering candle in her room and another on Krys's wardrobe. 'Very dangerous,' he said. 'Use electric lamps for emergencies. My kids have got wind-up torches.'

She nodded in agreement as he went downstairs, then took out a few clothes from Krys's chest of drawers. 'My baby could have died,' she said to Leon, holding the small jumper in her hands. 'We all could have died. Someone tried to kill us.'

He put his arms around her from behind, warming her. She realised at that moment how badly she was shaking. 'Someone failed. You're going to be safe and the police will catch the... the people who did this.'

Despite her shaking she managed a weak smile. 'Were you going to say something inappropriate?'

'For a priest, definitely. Let's go with "criminals". But they have a lead on the gang now, they will hopefully catch the whole network and then you'll be left alone.'

'I'm just so afraid it might be Declan. He tried to kill me before, he was in such a rage... But I can't believe he would do this to *Krys*.'

'This wasn't in a rage. This was cold and calculated.'

'But who hates us so much?' she wailed, turning to bury her face in his shirt.

'Maybe someone wanted to hurt Hazel,' he mumbled against her hair. 'Maybe the drug dealers wanted to drive you away, stop you being witnesses, I don't know. But the police will take this seriously, they will look at everyone.'

She rested in his arms while her shudders eased. 'I feel safe with you here,' she said, looking up at him. 'Is that pathetic of me? I came all the way here to create a new life with Krys and now I'm begging you to look after us.'

'Not pathetic,' he said, smiling. 'It's time you had someone look after you.'

Leon had abandoned the vicarage in such haste that he had left the front door open, and half a dozen of his neighbours had wandered in and made the place warm and comfortable for his return, and were now sitting around chatting. There was a small cheer when he led Hazel, Zosia and Krys in the front door.

By the time Zosia had been led to a chair, given a cup of tea, offered toast and had been asked a dozen questions, she found herself smiling again.

'We are all fine,' she explained, watching Krys as he scampered off with Toby to explore Leon's house. 'We're just a bit shocked someone would try and burn down Foxglove Cottage.'

'You stay 'ere in the village, maid,' one of the older women said, patting her arm as she passed by to sit next to Mags. 'Move over, stop maundering, uz don't sleep much at our age.'

'Not at *your* age, Lilian,' Mags snapped back. 'I'se lively as the chillern.'

Zosia laughed, exhausted, as the two old ladies exchanged increasingly strange insults, which seemed to give them great pleasure.

'I could do with a bit of sleep,' she said to Leon as he passed her another mug of tea.

'I have a spare room,' he said. 'It's made up, I have friends over regularly. Help yourself, second door on the left, opposite the bathroom.'

She smiled, squeezed his wrist as she passed, and dragged her feet upstairs. She had half expected Hazel to follow – her face was pale and she had smudges under her eyes – but she seemed to be enjoying being in the centre of her community.

My community. As she lay on the double bed, the smell of freshly laundered sheets against her face, she heard Krys chattering to Toby. Before she fell asleep, she wondered casually what laundry soap Leon used, because it always smelled lovely on his T-shirts...

44

SEPTEMBER 1940

It took ten days before I was airlifted back to England by the maquis, working with the Special Operations Executive. As I landed in England, I contacted the barber's shop to be told Rosie had been in hospital and had gone home to the farm.

The news of her injury in an explosion broke something in me. I knew I couldn't pretend to myself that she was safe any more. And that distraction could get me killed, could lose us the battle. I needed her to go back to the farm, more than anything I have ever wanted. To keep her in London was just selfish. I wanted her surrounded by her family, on that beautiful, terrifying moor. One day we would have enough money to move there, have a home, children, build a life together. The dreams were good but the nightmares haunted us both, and they were creeping nearer.

— EXTRACT FROM THE MEMOIR OF
CASIMIR WOJCIK

Returning from the farm, Rosie received the official notification that Cas was neither dead nor captured, but had just landed back in England. A telegram from Cas announced that he would be home by evening. Rosie collapsed into grateful tears that left her more exhausted than the recovery from the explosion or working on the farm.

When she ran out into the street that evening to meet him from the taxi, they stood there for a moment embracing, oblivious to the world. He was shocked by her injuries, the bandages. When they went upstairs, Cas needed to examine and kiss every one. Very gently, through the bandages.

His wrist was sprained, and he would be on ground duties until it healed, and he didn't want to talk about the crash that had nearly killed him. They fell into bed, and Rosie slept better than she had for a week.

In the morning, they didn't want to waste much time talking about the explosion or his rescue by French fishermen. Instead, they talked about their dreams for after the war.

'I would love to run a little hotel,' she said, scraping off her charred toast. 'Just a bed and breakfast with a couple of nice rooms.'

'Better learn to cook toast, then,' he said, eating a quarter in one bite.

She batted him with a tea towel. 'At least we would have a working stove. I could bake scones and make beds.'

He hesitated before he spoke, as if holding back. 'What job will I do?' he asked, eating the rest of what was admittedly mahogany-coloured toast. 'I could be engineer. Fly planes for airline?'

She shuddered at the thought. 'I'd worry every time you took off. Maybe you could learn to cook and help me in the hotel.'

For a moment, his smile dropped. 'Uncle Bronisław is baker, back home. I worked for him, two-three years to pay for flying lessons.'

She poured a cup of tea for him, and he put his arm around her to sweep her onto his lap. 'Maybe we could run a bakery,' she said, kissing the top of his head. 'Or you could cook for the bed and breakfast.'

'Make *bubka, pierogi*.' For a little while there were just kisses, then she caught sight of the clock.

'Let me go, I have to visit Audrey at the hospital when I get my bandages changed. Will you be here when I get back?'

'Should be. Have medical appointment again. Base doctors.' He rolled his eyes and gulped half the tea before standing to kiss her, holding her for a long minute. He stroked the hair back from her dressings. 'You must go home. To farm. For good.'

Rosie remembered the long days of waiting, not knowing if he was alive or dead. 'I can't. I need to be here.'

'*I* need to know you are safe. Duke's Farm. Your family need you, too.'

'No, Cas,' she said, staring up into his eyes. She had never seen him like this, his blue eyes dark like a stormy sky, his wide mouth straight and set.

'I worry about you,' he said, finally. 'Can't think. Need to think up there,' he said, pointing at the ceiling. 'Want you to be safe.'

She couldn't argue with that, but couldn't agree either. She managed to persuade him she would think about it, and when he left to report to his medical officer, she caught a bus to the hospital.

After her own bandages were changed, she walked up to the burns unit, where Audrey had been transferred. She crept into the ward to see a figure swathed in bandages by the nurses' desk, in a bed marked Dreyfus. 'I know it's not visiting time, but we were in the same explosion.'

'Miss Dreyfus is very unwell,' a senior nurse with a starched, winged hat told her. 'We have prepared her family for the worst, but she is young and fighting hard. The danger is infection.' She led a shaking Rosie to the desk and put a chair out for her. 'I'm guessing you were injured too?'

Rosie looked down at her bandaged hands.

'I was, but I was further away. Can I see her?'

'She's been asleep for a while. She wakes up when the morphine wears off, poor dear. You must not touch her, or the bed, that's the most important thing. Her face is healing well. We have a curtain we use for visitors, please stay behind it.'

She walked over to the bed and pulled across a transparent curtain – some sort of clear plastic Rosie had never seen before – shielding Audrey and making her look obscured and softened, as if she wasn't quite real. The nurse set a chair at a safe distance.

Looking around, Rosie could see that many of the quiet patients were wrapped in gauze. The place stank of antiseptic and every locker was empty of personal items, spotless. Looking back at Audrey, she could see her chest moving the sheet up and down slowly. She sat still for several minutes before Audrey moved, a soft moan escaping her.

'Is that Nurse Snowden?' she mumbled. 'Holding off on the cocktails, nurse? I need my morphine.'

'It's me,' Rosie said.

A white-wrapped hand crept out from the covers. 'Rosie? Really?'

'I can't touch you. You mustn't get an infection,' Rosie said. 'Anyway, my hands are bandaged, too.'

'Joe told me you were all right,' she said, moving her body a few inches and making a little cry of pain. 'He sent a letter, I made them read it to me. Is Casimir still missing?'

'Casimir came back yesterday.' She waved to a passing nurse. 'Can you help, please?'

The nurse came over quickly. 'I'll get your pain relief,' she said.

'Don't rush,' Audrey said, in a little, thin voice. 'I want to talk to Rosie.'

'Don't tire yourself,' Rosie begged, almost hurting with the effort of not reaching over.

'I won't. I sleep most of the time. My mother came last night but she cried all the time. I won't be much good now at hunt balls and tea dances.'

'You'll be all right.' She couldn't see all of Audrey's face.

'That's what Joe said. He said we'll walk out hand in hand and scare all the children.' There was a tiny edge in her voice.

'How bad is it? Have they told you?'

'I don't know,' she said, 'and I don't remember what happened. It was so quick. There was a flare and I got caught in it.'

'It knocked me off my stool,' Rosie said softly. 'I was lucky, I just cut my head and burned my hands.'

'It might still kill me,' Audrey said softly. 'But I'm doing my best to lie still and let them torture me with dressing changes to kill any germs. I'm having some horrible medicine as well, it's supposed to increase your chances.'

'Well, take the morphine and rest, then,' Rosie said. 'That seems to be a good plan.'

'As long as Cas and Joe and you are all right, I can concentrate on getting better.' Her voice was higher now, strained. 'I need that blasted morphine. Is she coming?'

'She's right here,' Rosie said, standing to allow the nurse to murmur softly to Audrey while injecting the drug and turning down the sheet a little. She was wearing as many protective aprons and gloves as they used in the factory.

'She's asleep already,' the nurse said. 'Come back when you can. I think it's been a bit too much for her mother,' she said, as she followed Rosie down the ward. 'Audrey's brother was killed a few days ago. We haven't dared to tell her yet.'

Rosie stopped. 'Gerard?' She recalled so many chats about Audrey's two brothers. 'Or Malcolm?'

'Gerry, her mother called him.'

Oh, this terrible, horrible war. Rosie walked out into the sunshine, tears flooding down her face, tickling the scorched and blistered skin.

45

PRESENT DAY, MAY

Scrubbing the smoke stains off the hall wallpaper was bringing the old pattern off. Hazel returned from town with a hired wallpaper stripper and she and Zosia spent the day taking off lengths of floral paper. Underneath, someone – Casimir and Rosie – had written messages in pencil. Some were in Polish, which Zosia translated for Hazel.

'*Boże pobłogosław ten dom* – God bless this house,' she said, smiling. 'How lovely.'

'My mother wrote something here about me,' Hazel said, squinting at the scrawling text. 'With love to all our children. Well, that's just me.'

'Perhaps they hoped for many more,' Zosia said.

'My mother wasn't able to carry a baby to term. She had a disease she caught from the animals, brucellosis. She had a few miscarriages, then me. I think her mother was the same.'

Zosia's arm was aching and the steam was making her face hot and damp. She scraped a stubborn corner away. 'Your dad used a lot of glue at the top,' she grumbled.

'Well, it's lasted all this time,' Hazel answered. 'They must have done this soon after Dad finished the rebuild.'

Zosia had been translating the part of his memoir that covered his life on Dartmoor. 'The staircase had mostly survived the fire when they bought it. The roof collapsed on it, and put out the flames.'

'I suppose it was a stronger wood,' Hazel said running her hands over the banister. 'You can still see the pitting where it got burned.'

'We nearly got burned, too,' Zosia said, her smile gone.

Hazel scraped at the edge of the paper over the bottom stair. 'Leon said the police interviewed Declan.'

The name made Zosia's stomach clench. 'I know. Declan said Krys might be unsafe staying here.'

'Nonsense.' Hazel wiped her shiny face with the bottom of her apron. 'He's just trying to wind you up.'

Zosia translated the idiom in her head. 'Well, it's working,' she said.

'Who else do the police suspect?'

Zosia dried her hands on an old towel. 'Honestly, I think they are still looking at the gang our neighbours were working for. They've found the two women that we saw at the school, and taken their boys into care. One of the boys was living in Tavistock with a car dealer, working illegally when he should be in school.'

'Which leaves the mystery woman who watched Krys being hurt.' Hazel walked through to the kitchen and Zosia followed her.

'When he was interviewed, Declan told the police he didn't employ anyone, but Leon says there are payments to a firm that follow people via the internet, checking their movements and social media.'

'You don't have any social media,' Hazel said, switching on the kettle.

'No, but you do, people in the village do. There are pictures of me on the church website, holding baby

Rowan. Now there will be a newspaper article about the fire.'

'So he *was* stalking you.'

Zosia slumped into the rocking chair. 'Maybe. Just not in person.'

'As far as you know.'

'As far as we can *prove*. One of his agents might have come down here to investigate in person. Or maybe she's one of Declan's friends.' Zosia rubbed bits of sticky paper off her hands into the bin beside her. 'I got a letter from his mother this morning.'

'I thought so,' Hazel said, filling up mugs and putting a splash of milk in the teas. Zosia had finally started drinking tea during the day, and even herbal teas late in the evening. 'It had a return address in the corner. What did she say?'

'Just chatty things,' Zosia said, remembering the dread that had gone through her when she opened the letter. 'Oh! And she said she rehomed our puppy when we split up, I'm so relieved. She would love to see Krys, maybe at a soft play venue near her home. She's in the Midlands.'

'Hardly around the corner.'

'She's willing to come to Devon if needed, maybe for a holiday.' She couldn't imagine her mother-in-law being on her side, she had always made excuses for Declan. 'On her own.'

'Well, perhaps you could meet up with her first, to set some ground rules for meeting Krystof,' Hazel said. 'Even if *I* am Krys's actual grandma.'

Zosia laughed. She felt it was time to reconnect with her own parents too.

'Do you think my parents could visit Foxglove Cottage some day?' she suddenly asked, almost afraid of the answer. 'I think they would love it. And my dad's a big fan of elves and goblins. He used to read me stories when I was a child. Some of them gave me nightmares, though, but most of them are safe for Krys.'

'Of course! It's not as if we don't have the room.' Hazel hesitated for a moment. 'You know I have family on the moor too, at Duke's Farm.'

'You said.' Zosia sipped her tea and waited for Hazel to explain.

'Nothing bad happened, we just live such different lives. I ran away from the family business, I wanted to see the world, we lost contact a bit after Mum died twelve years ago… I should take you over to the farm, Krys would love the animals. They have sheep,' she explained. 'And cattle.'

'That's lovely.'

Hazel sat opposite her, then touched her hand briefly. 'I hope you will make your life here, I really do. I want you to think of this as home.'

'I do already,' Zosia said, her chest tight with the words she wanted to say, words of gratitude.

'But one day, when I'm old and need looking after, maybe you'll still be here. I hope you will take the place on after I've gone. If you want to.' She looked at her clenched hands. 'I think it would be wonderful if some version of my parents' Fairy Café lived on. Dad used to tell my mother and me stories, just like your dad did. I know we haven't known each other very long…'

Zosia didn't know what to say. A place to put down roots, a place to defend and develop and enjoy. 'I've never felt as home anywhere,' she said slowly.

'I don't really need the money, and I feel so close to you and Krys, like the child and grandchild I never had.' Hazel was looking away, as if awkward about something. 'I know Mum and Dad would have loved both of you. So, if you want to, you could start by making the bed and breakfast business work again, for some extra income for you along with the café. It would be good for the village, too – people would stop instead of just driving by.'

'That would be... amazing,' Zosia said, as Hazel looked up, her smile hopeful. 'We could make it really lovely.'

'Even if you and Leon...?' Hazel didn't finish the question Zosia had been asking herself.

'I've hardly seen him. He's been busy. I don't know if anything will come out of our friendship,' she said with a rush. 'If anything came of me and Leon, I'd rather live up here than right in the village anyway. I love them all but it's hard to have any privacy.'

'But you really like him? Obviously, I'm asking for Mags and everyone else because they are watching you both.'

Zosia's mouth felt like it was full of cotton. 'I do,' she mumbled, and sipped the rest of her tea. 'But I really liked Declan. I'm not sure I'm much of a judge of character.'

'Maybe you should pop over and talk to Leon,' Hazel said. 'You could go now, I know he's just doing stuff at the church all day. I'll pick Krys up, we'll go for ice cream after school.'

Zosia decided to walk down the footpath parallel to the road to the village, bounded on one side by a wall with a thorny hedge growing out the top. The moorland was scrubby grass filled with gorse in coconut-scented flower, and foxgloves in bud dipping from between the stones of the wall. The path would come out at the back of the church and through a gate, leading to the churchyard. The hum of a lawnmower drifted over from beyond the wall.

As she strolled through the long grasses she could see something flashing at the bottom of the path. A woman with short dark hair, a little older than herself, was holding a camera of some sort.

'Good morning,' Zosia said as she approached, but her smile faded as the woman turned to her with an unfriendly look on her face.

'You're Zosia Armitage,' she hissed. Something about the woman's attitude slowed Zosia down, stopped her getting too close. 'What are you doing here?'

'Well, I live just up the road,' she said, unable to think of anything else to say.

'You're a whore.'

'*What?*' Zosia's gaze was drawn to the woman's hands moving towards her shoulder bag. 'You don't know anything about me if you think that.'

'You're with Leon. I saw you, after the fire. Kissing.' She spat an accusation at Zosia, the same words as on one of the cards she had received.

'It was you? You wrote the notes telling me to leave "him" alone?' she said, almost wonderingly, shocked at the thought of this unknown woman hating her so much. 'Just because I met Leon? He's my friend, he's Hazel's friend. He's our priest.'

'Can you deny that you seduced him?' The woman's face was twisted into a parody of itself, like she was possessed by jealousy.

Zosia took a step back as the woman retrieved some sort of bottle from her bag. 'Of course I didn't seduce him. You're upset – you're ill,' she said, trying to understand what she was seeing. It was a large water bottle with a spout, but something about the way the woman held it made it seem more like a weapon. 'Leon is a kind man, he's nice to everyone.'

She could just see something moving through the gaps in the hedge, and she realised the sound of the lawnmower had stopped. 'He's the devil,' the woman said, tears streaming down her face. 'He broke my heart, so I'm going to break his.'

'Please,' Zosia said, stepping back a pace. 'Please, no one is trying to hurt you.'

Without warning, the woman sprang towards Zosia, spraying her with liquid from the bottle. Zosia put up her hand to protect herself, screamed and turned away. For one terrible moment she thought it might be acid – some of it had caught the side of her face as she turned and it stung. Her T-shirt was soaked, and as she choked on the stench she realised what it was. *Petrol*. She stumbled into the long grass, yelling, 'No!'

The woman followed, clicking something in her hand. She was playing with a lighter. 'Will he love you when you're scarred up?' she hissed, as Zosia tore off her wet T-shirt, wiped the liquid from her face. 'Or dead?'

'He didn't choose *you*,' Zosia shouted, standing in her bra and jeans. From the corner of her eye she saw Leon charge through the gate. 'Hurting me won't help you.' She could feel the rage building, at this woman, at all the times Declan had beaten her down with subtle threats and pressure. 'I'm not afraid of you,' she said, closing the distance between them, as the woman stared, her mouth open. Zosia snatched at the hand holding the lighter, but the woman wouldn't let go, and flicked the wheel again, a tiny flame erupting.

'Harriet!' Leon bellowed as the flame caught and travelled onto the T-shirt Zosia was still holding. 'Stop!'

Zosia flung the shirt away and ripped the lighter from Harriet's hand. She slapped the woman, her whole rage trans-ferring itself to her hand. 'You tried to kill my child,' she raged as Harriet collapsed to the ground. Leon swept the bottle up out of the woman's reach. 'My *son*. He's six years old!'

'That's enough,' Leon said quietly, his deep baritone reaching through her fury.

Zosia hadn't finished. 'And if I love this man, this kind, generous friend, that's *my* business.' Her anger faded away as she looked awkwardly at Leon.

'Let's not complicate things any more than we have to,' Leon said, stamping out the burning shirt and smouldering grass. 'I'm going to call the police and fire brigade, just in case.' He grabbed Harriet's arm and dragged her to her feet. 'I'm making a citizen's arrest,' he informed her with the same authority. He patted her down. 'Any more weapons? Knives, guns?'

'Don't be ridiculous, you know me!' she said.

'I thought I did. But I never thought you could try and burn someone to death, let alone a child, and now...' He shook his head in disbelief.

'I was just going to scare you!' she shouted into his face. 'And burn your precious church.' She looked at Zosia, her face flooded with tears. 'But she came... I never thought the boy would *die*.'

'You watched him get beaten up, though, didn't you?' Zosia said, feeling ice cold suddenly, without her shirt. She could have been killed, all of them could have burned in the house fire. But the idea of a woman watching her son beaten to the ground and kicked in the stomach repeatedly was unbearable. 'You are a monster. Leon is better off without you. You can never go near him again.'

'Zosia, she's not going to listen to reason. Let's get her into custody.' He looked over Harriet's sobbing and bowed head, and mouthed, 'I'm so sorry.'

46

SEPTEMBER 1940

Before the war ended and real life began, I used to dream about the farm. Rosie's childhood room, the quilt her grandmother had made for her own wedding, the books propping each other up on the shelf below the window. Even the wind whistling across the chimney, the fire only to be lit in times of illness, she had told me, as I shivered walking across her room. I loved the smell of the cut fields, the stacks of hay bales, even the sour grass on the cows' breath as they ambled to be milked. I had marvelled at how easily she worked with the large animals, nimbly avoiding being trodden on, aligning them in their space in the milking shed, talking to each by name. Compared to my own life in Poland, they seemed rich. I could not see how I would fit in after the war, but now, the Battle for Britain was almost won, but the serious bombing of London was beginning. The British were to be battered and subdued into surrender. All I can say is the Germans underestimated both the British and Polish people.

— EXTRACT FROM THE MEMOIR OF
CASIMIR WOJCIK

Rosie had sorted out an extra land girl by calling the Ministry of Agriculture from London. She had talked to two local famers while in Devon to help clean up the farmyard and fix the truck (over Dad's objections). She had also employed a girl called Lizzie to watch the children and clean. Lizzie couldn't cook well, but she was cheerful, good at cleaning the house and patient with chores. Lizzie's mother would come for a half day and help with laundry, while Marion was in hospital on enforced rest.

Back at work on the cordite line, after her afternoon shift she caught the bus to the hospital. Many roads were damaged, buses were diverted, but everyone appeared cheerful.

Audrey was sitting up, and some of her face was visible although horribly red and shiny. She was behind a glass screen, so thin and drawn. She lifted a swaddled hand in greeting and looked out from one unbandaged eye. 'Have you seen Cas since you got back?' she said, her voice hoarse.

'Just for a couple of days. He's back on duty already.'

'Why don't you go back to the farm?' Audrey asked. 'Rather than stay here in this hellhole. Bombs dropping everywhere, sirens going off all the time, Cas flying overhead every day until his luck runs out.'

'Don't say that!'

'You know he's been promoted,' Audrey said, 'to Flying Officer. All the surviving pilots have.'

Rosie looked down at her hands. She hated him talking about his work, just mentally celebrated every time she heard he had landed safely. 'I'm so tired of this war.'

'Go home, make cheese or milk cows or whatever you do. When I get out of here, I'll come and stay, you can fatten me up on real cream and home-made cakes.' She rolled her head to one side, wincing as she did so. 'Josef can't climb in and out of his cockpit fast enough to scramble for missions,' she said, as casually as if it wasn't unusual. 'He could retire injured if he wanted. But do you know what he's been doing for months?'

Rosie shrugged, she couldn't see what he *could* do.

'He starts his shift by getting helped into his plane, and reading by torch until the siren goes. Then he's first in line to take off.' She paused, drawing in a raspy breath. 'Idiot.'

Rosie's eyes prickled with tears. 'But if I go home, if Casimir dies...'

'You're not going to be there anyway. He's going to be blown to bits or crash in a fireball somewhere.'

'He might be taken to hospital! Joe was.'

'So, you come up from Devon.'

Rosie started pleating her handkerchief. 'But I won't be able to visit you.'

'I'm off to a nursing home near my parents,' Audrey said. 'Since you aren't allowed to bring me chocolates or wine, I'll manage without. Joe comes when he can. He scares the other burns patients in case they end up looking like him.' Her voice wobbled, her mouth turned down. 'Or me. I look like a candle that's been left by the fire.'

'None of that will matter when the war is over,' Rosie said, brushing her tears away with the hankie. 'We have to stay strong.'

'Your war is over. Do you think you'll forgive yourself if your mother loses that baby – or you lose your mother?' Audrey gestured towards her although they couldn't touch. 'You could get pregnant, when Cas is on leave. Have a little bit of him to keep, whatever happens.'

It was the same argument that Cas had made, that went around and around Rosie's head when she couldn't sleep.

As she left the hospital onto the street, the air raid warning went off, and she followed locals into the basement of a nearby church. The bombs were falling much closer than she was used to, she could hear explosions and masonry falling, shouts and screams outside.

'In daylight, too,' an older woman said, sitting on her shopping bag on the damp ground. Rosie glanced at her watch, barely six o'clock. The dusk had drawn in, helping the planes. She could hear the rattle and boom of cannons and machine guns overhead. She couldn't bear the thought that the hospital would be bombed. Audrey still couldn't be moved; they just drew curtains around all the beds and hoped for the best.

The all-clear sounded again, and Rosie was one of the first people to walk to the door and look out.

The landscape was completely different. The hospital seemed untouched and a line of ambulances was coming from the west. The east of the road was a pile of rubble, smoke and fire beyond, lighting up the ghastly scene. She found herself walking forward, unable to help, unable to stop.

A man clutching something shouted to her. ''Ere! You, hold this. I got to get the mother.'

She unconsciously grabbed the bundle as he shoved it at her. There was something heavy inside. She unwrapped it to find a sleeping baby. Or maybe dead, she couldn't tell – its face was black with soot and its eyes were closed. She shook it gently, like she would a lamb, to shock some breath into it. Its mouth opened, and a little cry carved through the racket.

'It's alive!' she shouted.

'Take it to the 'ospital,' he called back. 'Tell them, 11 Bentley Street. That's the address. We're digging the mother out.'

She walked back, carrying the now silent baby through a veil of black smoke starting to cover the rubble.

She walked into the hospital and stood helpless, shocked. 'Out of the way, casualty coming through!' a man shouted, and she squeezed against the door frame. It was a woman, and she wondered if it was the baby's mother.

A doctor grabbed her elbow. 'Are you hurt?'

'No. It's the baby. A man gave it to me but I think – I'm afraid it's...'

He took the baby and laid it on a table, unwrapping as he went. He dragged a stethoscope from his neck and listened to the baby's chest. She was wrapped in a little pink nightgown and Rosie wondered if maybe her mother had sewn it herself, the stiches large and untidy around the hem.

'Still alive.' He whistled and a nurse came over. 'Straight to the children's ward,' he said. 'Shock, maybe internal injuries.' He handed the baby back to Rosie. 'Go with her, give the name and address.'

By the time she had said 'I don't know the name...' he was gone, and she was following the nurse to a staircase.

The baby was whisked away when they reached the children's ward, where cots were pushed two deep along both walls. Someone gave her a pen and paper for the baby's address and she attached it to the cot they had hastily made up for her. Rosie found herself smoothing the sheet, folding the blanket back, ready for the baby. *Please be all right.*

There were no spare chairs, all of them occupied by red-eyed mothers waiting for their children to be treated and admitted or discharged.

The baby was carried back, screaming, and Rosie felt faint with relief. 'No serious injuries, just shock,' a nurse said, handing her the tiny girl. 'I'll get the ward clerk to give you a bottle, unless you're nursing her?'

'Oh, no, she's not mine,' Rosie said. 'I just brought her in.'

'Well, we don't have time to feed her, and it would calm her down,' the nurse said. Her cry had an edge of desperation and panic in it. Rosie couldn't bear it, the sound was like an animal in pain. 'You can look after her.'

Rosie sat on the floor and hugged the baby, adding the blanket from the cot to keep her warm. At first the tiny girl was too upset to take the bottle, but after a minute, her cries died down and finally, she started sucking. Her sooty face was drizzled with real tears, her hands clenched on the blanket.

Rosie burst into tears with relief, hugging the infant, wondering why this war was being fought by babies and mothers.

'I'm going home,' she whispered to the baby. 'Because I can't bear anything to happen to Ma's baby. But I'll make sure you're safe first, I promise.'

47

PRESENT DAY, JULY

It was proper summer now, bees humming in flowers, drunk on nectar. The weeks had rolled on towards the end of the summer term, with a summer fete at the church and a sports day. Zosia carefully painted around the ears of the grotesque little carving she had restored, found under a tree in the garden. Casimir had made dozens of them, and bought others decades ago. As she added garish blues and greens, their expressions seem to come to life. She decided this one needed gold eyes, and dabbed a drop of gold paint in each. Painting them was therapeutic, after the last few months.

'Where's that one going?' Leon asked, lazing in one of the new garden chairs, hand curved around one of the old cups Zosia and Hazel had liberated from the attic.

'Up at the front, right in front of the porch,' she said, concentrating to make each eye the same. 'Last time we just put one up inside the porch, we needed one outside as well, according to Krys.'

'You know I'm not supposed to believe in fairies. I have faith in bigger things,' he said, looking over at Krys, who was trying to do a handstand on the grass.

'Yes, but then you've never seen a fairy,' she said, putting it down on the newspaper to dry and washing her brush.

'And you have? Seen a fairy?' His smile was lazy, his lips slowly curving up, the skin around his eyes crinkling.

She took a deep breath. 'When I was a little girl, we would visit my grandfather's house in Poland. It was a farm cottage, he was a slaughterman and butcher.'

'You told me about him.' His smile faded. 'He died at work in an accident.'

'He was crushed by a bullock when I was older. But when I was little, I used to play in his garden until it got dark. Then he'd bring out his cigarettes, sit on a bench he'd made, and watch the sun go down. He told me to be quiet – and watch.'

'Did you see anything?' He leaned forward. 'Go on, I'm curious.'

'I... sort of did,' she said, feeling her accent deepen in her voice. 'Like I was falling asleep, seeing wisps of mist dance around the plants, seeing glints – is that the word? – glints of golden and red light.'

'Not little people?'

She could remember it clearly, even as her grandfather's face had faded in memory. 'More like the ghosts of plants. But under the hedge were what looked like earthy mounds, moving almost too fast to see. I saw faces for just a tiny time, I don't know the word.' She struggled to find the English, staring into Leon's eyes.

'Moments?' he asked.

'Yes, small moments. Like people, smaller than a cat. Like a brownie. But big noses, tiny eyes flashing like black – I don't know what. *Obsydian*.'

'It's the same in English,' he said. 'Is that what Krys calls the *domowik* that looks after the house?'

She smiled. 'You think I was a silly child, and that we are superstitious to put food down.'

'No. I think there are more things in nature than we can see, with our limited senses.' He stared back and for a moment the whole world was his gaze, her heart beating faster. 'I've been dealing with the mess I've made with Harriet,' he said, his voice low. 'That's why I haven't been around as much.'

'You've been here lots of times.' To see Hazel and Krys. Once to help prune the trees.

'Yes, but I haven't tried to get you alone,' he said. 'I haven't asked you for a date. I thought – you might be a bit traumatised. And I feel guilty about that.'

Zosia still had nightmares about the look on Harriet's face. At that moment of rage, she intended terrible harm, but somehow it had lit a flame inside Zosia that enabled her to fight back. 'You don't have to feel guilty. Any more than I would if Declan took a swing at you.'

'Declan is back in his box,' he reminded her gently. She was willing to meet his mother occasionally, but a judge had decided it was not in Krys's best interests to see his father at the moment.

'And Harriet is in care.' She had been placed in a psychiatric hospital for assessment.

'Can we just go to dinner?' he pleaded. 'Maybe somewhere on the other side of the moor.'

'Why don't we have a couple of days in Exeter?' she asked, laughing at the expression on his face. 'We could stay in different rooms, obviously. Hazel has offered to look after Krys and I have a little money saved now.' Hazel was more than generous, and since Zosia had almost finished translating Casimir's journal, she was talking about donating it to the museum. The only chapters that were left were sealed in an envelope, stuck in the middle of the papers, and Hazel wanted to read those last.

'I work Sundays,' he said, and grinned. 'But there's a band I thought sounded good playing next Friday. We could have dinner first, go to the gig, maybe spend Saturday together.'

She could imagine what it would be like to have a glass of wine, listen to good music, he would take her to her hotel – her room... she could feel her smile growing. 'Maybe just one room,' she said, as he leaned forward and the world disappeared in a kiss.

48

It was hard living apart for four years during the war. I did my duty, I drank with my fellows on our days off, I slept in barracks dreaming of Rosie and a better life. Sometimes nightmares haunted my sleep, seeing Josef's plane explode like a firework, or being at Rosie's side after she sat with Audrey in her last hours, hearing her weep for her lost friend. Rosie said Audrey died of a broken heart after Josef died, and I begged her, fiercely, not to lose her life over me. Our letters sustained me, sometimes just notes, her too tired to write after running the farm with her father and caring for everyone, me on mission after mission. I was in a dark place of rage after Josef died, hoping to gun down the enemy that killed him. Rosie begged me to follow my duty to my country – and to her – to survive the war.

So, one day in June 1945, I was given a lift to the gate of the farm and waited. As if drawn by my presence, she walked up from the farm, then ran into my arms. We were never separated for more than a few days again.

There are some things I find difficult to talk about that I would want my daughter and maybe grandchildren to know. One of the hardest days of my life was when my darling Rosie gave birth first to a stillborn baby, then miscarried another after our tenth anniversary. One of the best days of my life was when she gave birth, in our own home, Foxglove Cottage, to a baby girl. Hazel Audrey Marion Wojcik. We were so grateful we rarely grieved again about those lost sons, except perhaps on the days they were born or when we hung up stockings at Wigilia, Christmas Eve. Many times I longed to tell her of the blood on my soul, and sometimes wondered if this was my punishment. But why would God punish Rosie, too?

First we lived at Duke's Farm, and I helped my father-in-law, mending machinery and working with the animals. Rosie helped look after the dairy with her mother, and we all cared for her little brother Matthew, born small but hearty before the end of the war. Then we rented an empty shop in the village and we set up our own bakery, living in two rooms over the top but frequently visiting the farm.

I yearned for a bigger, better life, even as I tried to persuade the villagers that Polish bread is best and they made me learn how to bake rolls, cobs and sandwich loaves. We had enough room for a few tables and people used to visit for my authentic hot chocolate or one of their insipid teas. Eventually, we started talking about having our little bed and breakfast and a café, selling Devon cream teas and Polish cakes. A few months later, an abandoned house came up for sale at auction, and gathering all our savings together with a little loan from my father-in-law, we bought it. It was high above the road, looking over the tor, and I felt the garden was filled with nature spirits that reminded me of my gremlins that had whispered in the corners of my planes. At every spare day or evening, I worked on the house with Rosie until we became sure she would keep the child. She stayed in bed or in the rocking chair in the kitchen at the farm for the whole of her pregnancy and it worked. We moved into it four weeks before the birth, where she transferred her rest to a bedroom overlooking the tor and the very spot where we met. When Hazel was born alive and well, I took a bottle of vodka and some flowers from the hedgerow and left them as an offering on the mile marker where I had crashed into Rosie's arms.

All the time, I waited for news from Poland, where my heart turned to in dark times, in the middle of the night or when I had other worries. I could not travel back there, men who had tried had been arrested or shot and no matter how much I longed to rescue my Polish family, I knew they could not leave.

When Hazel was born, I told Rosie everything I had done, from leaving my family to killing the Nazi spy and all the dark moments I had during the war. So many years after the war, it poured out of me like blood, leaving me weak. She never judged, nor blamed, just held me. One day, it was lifted, my guilt, my fear, all of it. Rosie and I left the baby with her parents, and we travelled to the Catholic church in Exeter. I confessed, in broken Polish and English, in tears. But the priest understood my pain if not all my words, and I felt light again. Ready to take on the rest of my life.

Finally, I heard the news from my youngest sister, Angelika. Kasia had been dragged away by many soldiers in the war, they found her broken body days later, with other women who had been abused. If there was ever a time when I was mad with guilt and rage and the impulse to end my life, it was then. But Angelika did not blame me, she was glad that I had fled because I would have been shot, as my father was.

Sabina joined the resistance and made her way to Warsaw with forged papers. She settled after the war and had a child with a Ukrainian, a son called Aleksi Casimir. Angelika had not escaped the abuse of the soldiers, although for her it was the

Soviets who took her innocence. But she fought to regain her health and optimism and worked with my uncle in his bakery until she took it over with my mother. We are both bakers, that makes me very happy.

— *EXTRACT FROM THE MEMOIR OF CASIMIR WOJCIK*

EPILOGUE

PRESENT DAY, JULY

The night before the grand opening of the Fairy Café, Hazel and Zosia sat in the fading light surrounded by foxgloves in flower. Zosia translated the last letter Casimir had left for his daughter, and they had hugged and cried. Later, they sat outside, staring over the mile marker where Hazel's parents' story had begun. The light had stretched out past ten o'clock and the dark sky had sunk over the Combestone Tor before they came in to go to bed.

The following morning was all about baking, getting tables ready, watching the early cloud burn back to a blue sky. Hazel put out the board that they had repainted: *Fairy Café – Open.*

The whole village had turned out, and everyone had enjoyed Zosia's first attempts at scones and Hazel's Polish doughnuts. It had been a riotous day. Baby Rowan was passed from friend to friend. Parents wandered in and out of the house to help Zosia. Two local teenagers, Millie and Corey, carried trays in and out, and learned how to take orders and make up drinks. The villagers insisted on paying even though it was a free event, and halfway through, two strangers had turned up and were welcomed and served by everyone. One had been before as a child, and remembered Rosie and Casimir, which made it special for Hazel.

Hazel had found a new energy. She chatted to people and showed visitors the garden. Krys had started an informal game of football on the lawn, and the whole of his class were charging around playing.

Zosia went into the kitchen to wash some cups up. 'The summer holidays seem to have given them more energy,' Leon said, unexpectedly, into her ear.

'I thought we could take Krys and a couple of his friends to that information centre,' Zosia said, turning within the circle of his arms to look at him. She started to grin. 'Not as a *date*, obviously.'

'Definitely as a date,' he said, his smile crooked. 'But not a very romantic one if we have to dress up as Bronze Age farmers and dig up bones.'

She kissed him quickly, still a bit shy in front of the villagers, several of whom were smiling and nodding in the conservatory. 'That sounds like fun.' Their weekend away had been so different, so unexpected, she was still processing. 'I loved going to the museum.'

They had wandered around the museum hand in hand, Zosia no longer caring who saw them or who knew. He had also taken her around the cathedral, and to St James's chapel, rebuilt after the war. It had a memorial commemorating pilots from the Polish Airforce. She knew so much of Casimir's history, it was overwhelming to be allowed in, to look around and spend a few minutes in prayer. Now she found her faith was a warm hug when she needed it. Declan was gone, his influence over. Her future was full of possibilities with Leon.

'Can I get you anything? You've been so busy looking after your customers...' Leon said.

'No, I'm fine. Could you go and referee that game, though? It looks like there's some arguments brewing.'

A chorus of shouts from the children welcomed Leon, who soon sorted out the arguments by dribbling the ball across the uneven lawn and scoring a goal. Hazel walked over to her with two glasses of wine. 'Jennie brought a couple of bottles, and Mags contributed some champagne from her ninetieth birthday party.'

Zosia took the wine, looked into the bubbles. 'Should we drink it? I mean, we are supposed to be running the café.'

'Everyone has had cake,' Hazel said, sipping. 'Anyway, what would they charge us with? Drunk in charge of a scone?'

Zosia laughed, sipped the wine. 'Congratulations on the rebirth of your fairy café.'

'Of *our* café.' They clinked their glasses solemnly then laughed.

A shriek overhead made Zosia shade her eyes. 'Is that a kestrel?'

'Looking down on us all as if we were ants,' Hazel said. 'He can see the mile marker from up there, and all the tors for miles around.'

'I feel like I was meant to be here, like somehow Casimir drew me here all the way from Poland.'

Hazel smiled. 'He did,' she said softly. 'If he hadn't left all those pages I couldn't read, I wouldn't have asked you to come here.'

It was a thought, Rosie and Casimir reaching out from their past love to embrace Zosia, and Krys too. 'I want to stay,' she said, turning to Hazel, suddenly out of breath. 'Let me buy in or work my way into the business.'

Hazel put her arm around her, kissed her forehead. 'I'm transferring ownership of Foxglove Cottage to you and we'll share the business.' She looked around. 'I think I'm less rooted in this place than you are. Now I've got my leg working properly, I'm off on my adventures again.'

Zosia pressed both hands to her racing heart, her eyes prickling with tears. 'But you will be back?'

'All the time,' Hazel said. 'To see you and Leon and Krys, and to see what you've done with the house. I'll be a sleeping partner, spending my part of the profits on making new friends.'

'I'd like to build a couple of eco-pods at the back of the garden,' Zosia said. 'Maybe offer a bit of camping in the summer, and start the bed and breakfast properly.' She was almost shaking with excitement. 'And stay here forever.'

'Like Casimir,' Hazel said softly. 'Like Rosie. Don't forget to put flowers on the mile marker. And look after the fairies.'

'Always.' Zosia could see her future now, clearly. This was her place.

A LETTER FROM REBECCA

Dear Reader,

I'm so glad you found *Secrets of Foxglove Cottage*. I hope you enjoyed meeting Rosie and following her journey towards finding love in the middle of a war, and Zosia's story to find home and family. If you did, you can keep in touch with future moorland stories by following the link below. Your email will never be shared and you can unsubscribe at any time.

www.bookouture.com/rebecca-alexander

I'm very fortunate to live near Dartmoor. It's the most beautiful but also austere place. You can get lost easily, weather sweeps in dropping you into dense cloud, heavy rain and then sunshine in a few minutes. The many springs and streams follow into valleys. I love to walk up slopes towards the monumental and overwhelming tors. There are thousands of years of evidence of round houses, ancient walls and farms, old forests. Nature surrounds you – skylarks, kestrels, rabbits and deer are all around. I get the impression anything could happen there.

I'm looking forward to writing more stories based on Dartmoor. Living in a small community where everyone knows everyone means secrets come to the surface eventually.

If you want to support me and the books, it's always helpful to write a review. This also helps me develop and polish future stories! You can contact me directly via my website or on X.

Thank you and happy reading,

Rebecca

www.rebecca-alexander.co.uk

 x.com/RebAlexander1

ACKNOWLEDGEMENTS

This book wouldn't be in your hands without the hard work and patience of my editor, Rhianna Louise. I'm astonished at how I deliver a rambling tangle of stories into her hands to get an orderly book back. She teases out what the book should be, rather than how I left it.

Thank you also to the wonderful team at Bookouture, for continuing the process of shaping the novel and making the story shipshape and my characters consistent. They also design the lovely covers and organise all the business end, which is a mystery to me. They are wonderful.

Much gratitude goes to my two beta readers, Carey Bave and Isabella Cousins. Both are great writers, full of stories of their own, when they choose to put them down on paper. Carey has read all my books from the very beginning, and always has a lot to say!

As always, much love goes to my patient family, especially my eight-year-old granddaughter Lily. She has an opinion about how the story should go! And I'm grateful for the support and patience from my husband Russell, who knows when to drive me to a field by the sea, or to the middle of the moor, and leave me to write in my vintage caravan.

PUBLISHING TEAM

Turning a manuscript into a book requires the efforts of many people. The publishing team at Bookouture would like to acknowledge everyone who contributed to this publication.

Commercial
Lauren Morrissette
Hannah Richmond
Imogen Allport

Cover design
Debbie Clement

Data and analysis
Mark Alder
Mohamed Bussuri

Editorial
Rhianna Louise
Lizzie Brien

Copyeditor
Angela Snowden

Proofreader
Liz Hatherell

Marketing
Alex Crow
Melanie Price
Occy Carr
Cíara Rosney
Martyna Młynarska

Operations and distribution
Marina Valles
Stephanie Straub
Joe Morris

Production
Hannah Snetsinger
Mandy Kullar
Jen Shannon
Ria Clare

Publicity
Kim Nash
Noelle Holten
Jess Readett
Sarah Hardy

Rights and contracts
Peta Nightingale
Richard King
Saidah Graham

www.ingramcontent.com/pod-product-compliance
Ingram Content Group UK Ltd.
Pitfield, Milton Keynes, MK11 3LW, UK
UKHW040618170225
4623UKWH00017B/68